EVERY TIME IT RAINS

Nikita Singh is the bestselling author of nine novels, including *Like a Love Song*, *After All This Time* and *The Promise*. She is also a contributing writer to *The Backbenchers* series and the editor of the short-story collections *25 Strokes of Kindness* and *The Turning Point*.

Born in Patna and raised in Indore, she spent a few years working as an editor in the publishing world in New Delhi before moving to New York for her MFA in creative writing at The New School.

Nikita lives in Manhattan, where she works as a fashion stylist. You can find her on Twitter, Instagram and Snapchat (@singh_nikita) or on Facebook.

NIKITA SINGH

Every Time It Rains

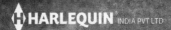
HARLEQUIN INDIA PVT LTD

First published in India in 2017 by Harlequin
An imprint of HarperCollins *Publishers* India

Copyright © Nikita Singh 2017

P-ISBN: 978-93-5264-373-8
E-ISBN: 978-93-5264-374-5

2 4 6 8 10 9 7 5 3 1

Nikita Singh asserts the moral right
to be identified as the author of this work.

HarperCollins *Publishers*
A-75, Sector 57, Noida, Uttar Pradesh 201301, India
1 London Bridge Street, London, SE1 9GF, United Kingdom
Hazelton Lanes, 55 Avenue Road, Suite 2900, Toronto, Ontario M5R 3L2
and 1995 Markham Road, Scarborough, Ontario M1B 5M8, Canada
25 Ryde Road, Pymble, Sydney, NSW 2073, Australia
195 Broadway, New York, NY 10007, USA

Typeset in 11/14.7 Minion
Saanvi Graphics Noida

Printed and bound at
Thomson Press (India) Ltd

To those who dare to love again.

Perhaps when we find ourselves wanting everything, it is because we are dangerously close to wanting nothing.

—Sylvia Plath

1

BLANK SPACE

It was dark and quiet at this time of the day. It was Laila's favourite time—she liked dark and quiet. Most bakers she knew woke early to bake, starting off their days on the right note, ensuring a draft of fragrant air escaping from every open door and window of their bakery to seduce customers in. She, on the other hand, liked to end her day baking. During the day, she was a businesswoman, the primary person in charge of the operation of two rapidly growing bakeries in New Delhi. She worked long days, putting out fires, ensuring that everything ran smoothly. However, after their shops closed every evening, she took the time to go through the day's sales herself, wrap everything up, prepare the shops for the next morning and do her favourite thing of all—bake.

While her best friend and business partner Maahi was at their Shahpur Jat shop, closing for the day, Laila was at their second, newer shop, the one in Hauz Khas Village. They had opened it only four months ago, and it still wasn't as smooth an operation as their first shop and needed more attention.

They referred to their Shahpur Jat shop as One and the one in Hauz Khas Village as Two in order to keep things simple. After their two employees at Two—Javed, who helped them bake and Aparna, who managed the counter—had left for the day, Laila sat under a warm lamp hanging from the ceiling, checking inventory.

'Whoa! You scared me—sitting there like a ghost!' came a voice from the door.

'What are you doing here?' Laila asked, looking up from her iPad and smiling at Maahi. 'All good at One?'

'All good at One. Clean and shiny and closed, thank God. It was such a long day! Did you know Ram's grandfather once fought a lion and came out alive to tell the story? I do now. I heard the story—a very long and very dull version of it.'

'Hard to imagine a story of a human battling a lion being dull.'

'It was and I had to hear all of it because I asked!' Maahi's lips twisted to the side. 'I feel bad for him though. At least here Javed and Aparna have each other. There at One, Ram has no one to talk to all day except me.'

'So basically Ram is your new best friend.'

'Basically.' Maahi snorted. 'I came over to ask my old best friend an opinion on something. Walking here was a bad idea though.' Maahi hopped in front of the air conditioner vent and fanned herself furiously with her hands. 'I couldn't find an auto, and then this one dude asked for forty bucks—like I'm an idiot!'

'You do kind of look like one.'

'Laila! So mean!'

'What—just stating facts. You're the one jumping in front of the AC, looking like an idiot.' Laila laughed at Maahi and went to join her by the window. The cold air from the AC did feel nice on her face. Her hands automatically went to massage the back of her neck. 'Really that hot outside?'

'Usual Delhi summer. It's actually not that hot—just humid. It's been dull and rainy all day.' Maahi pursed her lips. 'At least I'm done with college.'

'At least you're done with college,' Laila repeated. She had slowly begun to delegate more and more responsibility to Maahi recently. Even though they had equal partnership in Cookies + Cupcakes, Laila had mostly been in charge since Maahi, who was a few years younger, was still finishing her BBA. When she had finally graduated a couple of months ago, it had been a welcome change to have her around full-time, and now, Maahi had taken over charge of One while Laila managed Two.

'There was this customer that came in today, demanding coffee—at like seven in the morning. I had just got in and started baking. Ram hadn't even come in yet, so I went to the counter and told him we don't have any. He literally hurled abuses at me all the way down the street.' Maahi shook her head. She walked away from the window, finally feeling cool enough to step away from the AC, and went to inspect the counter. 'I told him we were a specialty bakery and dealt with cookies and cupcakes exclusively as, hello, the name clearly suggests but he wouldn't listen, crazy person!'

'Dude, just keep the door closed till Ram starts his shift. You don't have to let the crazies in when you're alone, especially at seven in the morning!'

'I know that *now*. But it got me thinking,' Maahi said, her voice lower. She watched Laila closely as she said slowly, 'Maybe … we could possibly do coffee. Just saying.'

'Maahi.'

'I know, I know.'

'I've smelled enough coffee for a lifetime and I really want our bakeries to smell like bakeries,' Laila said.

Before opening Cookies + Cupcakes, both Laila and Maahi worked for a coffee shop, where their employer would treat their baked goods as the least important things on his list of priorities, and the coffee was always his primary concern. After opening C+C, Laila had been determined on leaving coffee behind in her past.

'Coffee ruins everything,' she said as she walked back to her chair under the lamp and picked up the iPad again.

'That's subjective. For that crazy man in the morning, the *absence* of coffee ruined everything. It was most likely the very reason behind his crazed mental state,' Maahi said, dropping her backpack on the floor and bending over to open it.

Laila rolled her eyes.

'It's just something to think about. Maybe we could have just one coffeemaker in each shop, something basic. Maybe serve coffee only in the first few hours of the morning—'

'Maahi.'

'Fine.' Maahi shut up, but Laila could tell she was going to bring it up again, sooner or later.

'What're those for?' Laila asked, pointing to the huge pile of clothes Maahi pulled out of her bag and now dangled from her arm.

'Help me choose a dress for my date,' she said, dropping everything on the chair opposite Laila's and pulling a dress out of the mess.

'Right. Forgot you were doing that.'

'Yep.' Maahi's voice came from behind the half wall that partitioned the seating area from the bakery. She reappeared a moment later. 'So? What do you think?'

Laila looked up from her iPad screen just for a second, long enough for her brain to register the violently orange dress wrapped around Maahi.

'Pass,' she said, with an air of finality.

'Ugh. Why d'you gotta be like that?' Maahi groaned. 'I'm telling you—this is exactly what I need. White's too plain, red's *way* too intense, pastels are boring, black's just lazy. This is perfect.'

'I think the word you're looking for is *compromise*.'

'Mean.'

'Honest.'

'Ugh, what happened to make you like this?

'Make me like what?' Laila raised her eyebrow, challenging Maahi to finish what she started.

'Forget it.'

'No, tell me.'

'I mean, whatever. You know who slash how you are. I don't get why. Have you always been this dark, twisted cynic…? I don't know.' Maahi studied Laila's expression uncertainly. She seemed to become more and more hesitant. 'It's not my place to ask. I meant it as a joke, but then you asked, and now I'm talking and can't seem to be able to stop talking. And you're looking at me like that, which can't be good. You're making me uncomfortable and frankly, a little scared.'

Laila snorted. 'Relax, dude. I'm just messing with you.'

Maahi looked relieved. 'So? Tell me.'

'Oh, you're asking me an actual question? You're worried there's actually something wrong with me?'

'I don't know. Is there?'

Laila sighed, putting down her iPad. 'I'm perfectly okay. I just don't want your dress to impair his vision. Are you kidding me with that colour? What else do you have?' She got up and sorted through the pile. 'What's with all these fancy dresses? What is wrong with what you were wearing today?' Maahi had been wearing a sleeveless, collared, pale yellow T-shirt with light blue jeans and sneakers.

'Jeans and tee on a first date?' Maahi cringed.

'Why not? It's more you than these *pretty* dresses. Bet he'll be wearing something like that.'

'One, you somehow make *pretty* sound *ugly*. And two, he's a boy.'

'Which is why he's allowed to be comfortable and you're supposed to doll up? I mean, of course there's nothing wrong with wearing a dress, but I'm just saying—dress for yourself and no one else.' Laila pulled out a grey skater skirt.

'That one goes with ... Let me look.' Maahi rummaged through the pile and found a red ruffled top. 'Here.'

'Hard pass. I think this skirt would go well with the T-shirt you were wearing earlier. Understated. Classy.'

Maahi thought for a second before agreeing. 'And I could wear sneakers with this outfit.'

'There you go.' Satisfied, Laila began folding the rest of Maahi's clothes one by one and shoving them into her backpack, while Maahi changed behind the partition. 'Cute.' She nodded when Maahi re-emerged.

'Thank you. Can you help me with make-up?' Maahi took

out her bag of cosmetics and walked over to the decorative mirror on the wall.

Laila followed her. 'What do you want to do?'

'Just hide this pimple scar'—Maahi pointed to the side of her right cheek—'and maybe something with the eyes?'

'Got it.' They became quiet as Laila applied minimal make-up on Maahi's face. She honestly didn't think Maahi needed any, with her clear, almost flawless skin and beautiful brown eyes. Her slender, five-foot-three-inch frame and long hair matched her cheerful, warm personality. She liked to wear a lot of colour and had recently taken to painting her lips in bolder shades of reds and pinks.

Laila still remembered the first time they'd met—Maahi had entered the coffee shop Laila worked at in a long flowing dress with five different versions of purple flowers on it. Quite in contrast with Laila, who stuck to the various shades of black, white and grey. If she felt like colour, Laila would go as far as wearing dull, solid ones like deep burgundy, mustard or military green. She liked how their choice of colours reflected their personalities and highlighted their dissimilarities.

'Who's the dude?' Laila asked, finishing Maahi's lipstick.

'Amit. I told you about him? He's from Delhi—born and raised. Works as an analyst for ICICI,' Maahi said. She collected all her stuff and shoved it back into her backpack.

'A banker? How did you meet him?'

'I haven't—yet,' Maahi said softly.

'Tinder.' Laila raised her eyebrow at Maahi.

'There's nothing wrong with Tinder. It depends on your intentions and mine are pure.'

'What exactly are your intentions?'

'Meeting new people. Companionship,' Maahi said a little defensively. 'Where else will I meet people? I've graduated, so there's no college, and I spend all my time running back and forth between One and Two.'

'We get a steady flow of customers, all in the right demographic. You could meet someone organically?'

'I can't.'

Laila paused, examining Maahi in the soft lights of their bakery, while Maahi examined herself in the mirror. Maahi's last relationship had been with Siddhant, who she had met at work, back when they used to work at Cozy Coffee in Gurgaon. Laila didn't want to bring him up. Even though things with Siddhant had ended almost a year ago, Laila knew it was still painful for Maahi to think about. She spoke in a much lighter tone, 'Hey, do your thing, girl! Show me a photo?'

Maahi cheered up and pulled her phone out. Laila went to bring an assortment of cookies and cupcakes and they sat down at their usual table by the window. It was kind of a ritual for them—ending the day with sampling whatever remained of each other's baked goods.

'Your lemon meringue cupcakes were a big hit today,' Laila said, digging her fork into the last one. 'All sold out now.'

'Yeah? Didn't do as well at One. We still had almost a dozen left there.' Maahi broke a piece from a large ground-walnut cookie. 'I gave them to the kids on my way here.'

Laila smiled. 'Did they say thank you?'

'Damn right they did!'

Hauz Khas Village had no dearth of little kids roaming around, trying to sell cheap jewellery and accessories to passers-by. Every evening around closing time, these kids would assemble outside Two and wait for their share of sweets. In exchange, they would sing C+C's praises to everyone in the neighbourhood willing to listen. Although Laila and Maahi hadn't asked them to do so, it wasn't bad for business and it helped them stick to their policy of selling only fresh baked goods; everything they baked had to be sold within twenty-four hours.

Over the last few months, the two girls had come to form a relationship with these kids, who were less fortunate, and roamed around in tattered clothes and chappals, but somehow managed to have bright eyes and quick wits. They had developed a sense of humour, which helped them live even in the situation they existed in. Laila was hesitant giving them money to help out, not knowing where it would go or if the kids would even benefit from it. Their cookies and cupcakes didn't replace a healthy meal, but they were made from the best quality ingredients. Also, they were delicious as hell and went straight to the kids' stomachs!

'It's funny when you think about it,' Laila said. 'We're teaching these kids manners, when they should be in school getting an actual education. How much can learning to say *thank you* and *sorry* actually help?'

'Maybe that's not such a bad thing. They're learning life lessons by living them,' Maahi said.

'You're saying education is not important?'

'Of course it is important. I just think going to school wasn't the best part of my childhood. Most kids hate it. But I know what you mean. These kids don't even have the option to go to school and hate it.'

'Exactly. Some of them are in school, but they either don't go or the teacher doesn't show up. Even when the teachers are there, I don't know how seriously they take their jobs and how much they actually want to teach. They're very underpaid,' Laila said. She sighed and got up. 'I read this article today and … I just … Everywhere I look, there's something wrong with everything and there's no easy fix because the problem is way deeper in the root of things. It's exhausting just to think about it.'

Maahi followed Laila to the kitchen, watching her with evident anxiety. 'Are you—'

'Yeah, I'm fine,' Laila said shortly and flashed a smile she hoped would pass for a semi-real one. 'I'm just being overly sensitive today for some reason.'

Maahi looked unconvinced. 'We should be sensitive towards these issues. Everyone should. There's nothing wrong with that.'

Laila nodded, hoping to close the topic. She had been agitated all day and was yet to figure out why. She would continue to feel restless until she pinpointed the reason behind her strange state of mind. But she didn't want to pull Maahi into the mess inside her head, especially not right before her date with a stranger from the Internet.

'You're all set?' Laila asked, glancing at Maahi.

Maahi checked her partial reflection in one of the doors and ran her fingers through her hair. 'Yep. Keep your phone with you though—just in case.'

'Just in case he's a serial killer or something?'

'Exactly. Or something less extreme like if I'm nervous or bored and need to pretend to text for a second, I could actually text you.'

Laila laughed. 'Yes, ma'am.'

'I won't be out long. I have to go all the way back home.'
Maahi groaned. She lived with her parents in Vaishali, which
was on the outskirts of Delhi, over an hour away from their
bakeries. Maahi left some of her stuff at the shop and with a
final glance at her reflection in the mirror, and after blowing
Laila a kiss, walked out.

Laila smiled. It was a long, lingering smile. Not exactly sad,
but definitely not happy. It stayed restricted to her lips, frozen
for several seconds, before receding. She walked back to the
window and turned the AC off, feeling as if it were providing
a fake sense of protection in a way, shielding her from reality.
Outside, the sky had been cloudy all day, occasionally letting
a dull ray of sunshine pass through. It had been raining, on
and off, but not enough to soak through even the topmost
layer of land.

The light showers seemed to intensify. There was a loud
crack of thunder and the world was lit in a whitish glow for
a spilt second. Laila slipped to the floor, crouching down,
holding her knees close to her chest. She rested her cheek
against the cool window and stared outside. She sat there for
a long time, hidden in the dark, staring at the blurred mixture
of yellow and white lights in the street, bustling with the Friday
night crowd, her eyes filling up with tears and then drying up
before finding escape over and over again.

As she sat and watched the held hands and rushed steps, the
flurry of people covering their heads and seeking refuge from
the now heavy stream of rain, their laughter rang in her ears.
In the absence of air conditioning, the shop was becoming
humid and stifling. Laila found it hard to breathe.

Her phone buzzed and she picked it up.

Maahi: You're fine tho, right?

Laila's eyes suddenly filled up with tears. What was wrong with her? From the outside, it would appear that her life was perfect. All the pieces came together to create a beautiful Lego house. She had a wonderful friend in Maahi, she loved their bake shops and was thrilled with their success, she truly enjoyed spending her days running C+C and nights baking. She didn't have a boss and was very happy with her employees, her mother was no longer sick, she loved living in Delhi. On paper, her life had never been better.

But there was still something amiss. Something that was missing, which had been missing for so long that she hadn't even realized the void it left behind. But the void was very real. She carried it with herself every day—a blank space that weighed heavy in her heart and kept growing heavier and heavier.

Laila wiped her cheek with the back of her hand and sniffed. She texted Maahi back.

Laila: Yep. Have fun!

2

SHINY

By the time Laila was finished baking and cleaning up that night, it was late. She had been extra meticulous, measuring every ingredient deliberately, taking her time getting everything exactly right. She liked having every minute detail under control, and achieving the exact results that she wanted. She found it relaxing.

She drove back home, Bollywood remixes playing softly in the background on the radio. She left the car outside on the street, not wanting to make noise and wake up her mother and the neighbours by parking inside. After gathering her belongings, she walked to the gate and opened it, willing it not to screech. She had been putting off oiling the hinges for a long time. The only times she remembered, she would either be going out or coming back, generally tired, and it would slip her mind as soon as the gate closed behind her.

Even before she turned the key, she heard movements inside. 'Maa?' Laila called softly, pushing the door shut with her foot. She walked through the living room and to the dining area, where her mother was sitting at the dining table, her laptop in front of her, surrounded by notebooks and pens. Laila raised an eyebrow. 'You're still up? It's midnight!'

'I could say the same to you.' Maa looked at Laila from above her glasses, resting low on her nose.

'Fair enough. I got delayed at Two and then figured I would wait a little longer to let the worst of the traffic clear out.' She slumped in the chair next to Maa's. 'What are you up to?'

'Not nagging, but just reminding you that we live in Delhi and it isn't safe alone outside this late at night—'

'Maa, no—'

'Just stating facts.' Maa pursed her lips.

Laila sat up. 'Okay, yes. From news, statistics and personal experience, I know it's not very safe, but what can I do? What can anyone do? We must try and exist in our situations and make them work for us. I'm doing the best I can, taking every precaution I can to be safe, but that's not fair! I shouldn't have to. If I don't, and something happens to me, it still shouldn't be my fault. The person who does something wrong should be the only one responsible.'

'I agree. But it's not about placing blame. It's about your safety and security and if, God forbid, something happens, I don't need someone to blame. I need it ... to not happen. We can't turn back time and undo things; what's done is done. So we take precautions. Prevention is better than cure. Especially when there is no cure.'

'Why? By taking these precautions—making sure my car's tank is full, or I don't stop anywhere on the way, being alert, keeping my phone charged, carrying pepper spray and all sorts of apps and what not—aren't I just playing a part in enabling these potential rapists and assaulters? In a way, isn't that what I'm—'

'Laila. Is there an alternative you can suggest? We can't hunt down every person who could potentially pose a threat and what—kill them?' Mom snorted. 'All we can do is make sure we're not at the wrong place at the wrong time. And if we are, we're prepared to put up a fight—'

'Why is there a wrong place? Or a wrong time? We're living right in the middle of the capital of the country—'

'I don't want to argue with you about this right now!'

'You brought it up!' Laila cried, her face hot.

'I only said that it's not safe. I want you to be careful—that's all.'

'And you think I don't know this?'

'Of course you do, but I am your mother. That's all.' Maa raised her hand. 'We're not discussing this anymore.'

'Fine.' Laila gritted her teeth. Her heart was beating fast in her chest, all her agitation from the day coming back. It seemed as though she had strong feelings about everything today, and once again, she found herself seeing problems in the root of the matter. Where is the cure? Everyone seemed to be worried about eliminating the symptoms. Taking precautions doesn't cure the actual disease. The disease still exists, hidden, out of sight. Disease-free and shiny from the outside, but inside, it's all still there. Laila shook her head to clear it of the depressing thoughts that she'd had all day.

'Have you eaten?' Maa asked.

Laila looked up. 'Kind of.' It was as if her stomach woke up at the mention of food, so she walked to the fridge and pulled it open. Leaning down, she inspected the various neatly arranged vessels and boxes inside. They were a family of obsessive-compulsive people. Not a thing out of place—ever. She grabbed the round, steel container with leftover plain white rice and walked back to the dining table.

'There's sabzi in the fridge. And daal too.'

'I'm good,' Laila said, pulling a fork out from the stand on the table.

Maa shook her head and smiled, but didn't say anything.

Laila ate the cold rice out of the box. She had been a very health conscious teenager, but somewhere along the line, she'd realized that her body didn't retain weight, no matter what or how much she ate. At twenty-seven, she was still as slender as she'd been a decade ago. Subconsciously, she'd begun doing the opposite of what dieticians suggest—ate carbs late at night, had no portion control, had a random meal schedule, an unbalanced diet. She loved food and ate everything. Laila thought about how Maahi was constantly worried about gaining back the weight that she had lost in the past couple of years—mostly because of working hard for C+C, which required a lot of staying on your feet, but honestly, Laila wouldn't mind a few extra kilos on herself.

'So listen,' Maa said, breaking Laila's train of thought. 'Remember Girish Uncle? My friend from Patna?'

'Yeah...?' Laila had been born in Patna, where she had lived with her parents for the first few years of her life, before their divorce. That's when her mother decided to move to Delhi with Laila. Laila had been to Patna with Maa several times over the years to visit her maternal grandparents during summer vacations. Maa occasionally talked about her friends from college, people she hadn't seen for three decades now, old friends who'd resurfaced on Facebook.

'His wife is the principal at Notre Dame Academy in Patna. She called me earlier today … about a vacancy.' Maa observed Laila and spoke quickly, 'It's a temporary position. Their science teacher was diagnosed with breast cancer. It's in the early stages and they're positive that she will be back soon. But in the interim, they asked me if I'd like to take her place.'

Laila swallowed hard. This had come out of nowhere and she didn't know how to react. 'What did you say?' she asked evenly.

'I told her I would think about it.'

'How long do you have to decide?'

'A week perhaps. They need to bring someone in soon. The new academic year has already started and the students are losing time. I have to let them know one way or the other soon.' Maa's voice became quieter towards the end.

Laila could tell that Maa was treading lightly, as if apprehensive about Laila's reaction. Maa had been a teacher at the school Laila went to in Delhi for twenty-two years, up until a couple of years ago when she got sick and was unable to continue working. She had developed cardiac arrhythmia, which seemed to worsen with stress and overwork. Her temporary leave of absence had slowly converted into a long one before she eventually resigned.

'You're thinking about taking it?' Laila asked.

'Maybe.'

'I didn't know you wanted to go back to work.'

'I'm not that old!' Maa laughed, clearly trying to lighten the mood. 'I still have several good years of work left to do. Most teachers don't retire till they're sixty, or even sixty-five.'

'Gives you fifteen solid years,' Laila said. She wasn't proud of herself for being unhappy about the news and it didn't go unnoticed.

'You don't seem very excited at the prospect.'

'It's not that. I just didn't know you were thinking about going back to work and now this—so suddenly. Just one week's notice!'

'Laila! I'm not giving you notice—' Maa started, but Laila didn't let her finish.

'Certainly sounds like it. You have to decide within a week and then you'll what—move to Patna?'

'Not unless you don't want me to. And I'm not moving— it's only a temp position. And I think it can be good for me. It's only for a few months and it's in Patna, so Nana and Nani will be happy. I'll get to spend longer than a couple of weeks at a stretch with them, which I haven't done in ages. It'll be good for them.'

'Sounds like it'll be good for everyone except me.' Laila hated that she was saying these things. She had no idea where all the bitterness was coming from, but she couldn't help it.

Maa smiled. 'It could be good for you too—living alone for a while. Everyone needs that from time to time. You didn't move away for college or work—'

'And you resent that? The fact that I went to college here in Delhi?'

'Of course not! On the contrary, I appreciate it. You think I don't know that it was partly because you didn't want to leave me by myself. I'm only saying that you've always lived

with me, growing up, through college and then again after
Abhi—'

'MAA!'

'Laila…'

'NO!' Laila said forcefully. 'NO!' She repeated, breathing
heavily. She pushed her chair back and got up with a jerk. 'Do
whatever you want to do but don't … Just don't.'

Maa watched Laila, her expression fearful. 'I didn't—'

'Please, Maa,' Laila begged, suddenly tired to the bone. 'Not
this. Not right now. I can't right now.' She closed the lid on
the container of rice and shoved it back in the fridge. Tossing
her fork in the sink, she picked up her bag and stomped to her
room. Once inside, she closed the door and leaned against it,
taking deliberate, deep breaths. She tried to contain the tears,
but they flowed freely down her cheeks. It was as if the pressure
had been mounting all day, one after the other, before finally,
it was too much. She couldn't take it anymore.

Laila felt weak. Her knees barely supported her weight. She
stumbled to her bed and lay down quietly on her side. She bit
down on her lower lip, her jaw tight, her eyes staring fixedly
at the wooden bedpost. Every time a sob escaped, she clamped
down hard on her lip.

It came in waves. It had been years, but still, every now and
then, she found herself caught in one of the waves. It built up,
became thicker, multi-layered and gained momentum before
washing over her and pulling her back with it. If she was lucky,
she would be left lying at the shore, coughing, sputtering,
gasping for breath. When she wasn't, she would come very,
very close to drowning.

She fought it actively, constantly. There were times when she could almost forget all about it and be somewhat normal. But just when she'd successfully fool herself into believing that it was finally behind her, another wave would hit, bringing her crashing down. She hated feeling weak. After all this time, she hated that she still let herself be affected by something that should've been long forgotten by now. It was a part of her past that she shouldn't allow to play a part in her present.

Laila wanted to be delusional. She wished she were one of those people who could deny their realities and keep living a normal life. Why couldn't she forget all about it? Why did she have to be transported to that night seven years ago every time she let her guard slip slightly? Why was she reminded so cruelly of that night every single night?

She had given herself time. Weeks to recover. Months to grieve. Years to find closure. Yet, she certainly hadn't recovered or found closure. And in moments like this, she came to the realization that she was still grieving. Perhaps she would grieve for the rest of her life.

Laila barely got any sleep that night. Instead of tossing and turning, trying to put up a fight, she lay quietly in one place, allowing the wave to consume her and eventually pull back. By the time there was light outside, her half-shut eyes were dry and dark. She sat up, causing her head to swim for a brief moment. She allowed it. When she felt slightly better, she got up and pulled open her cupboard. Assembling her outfit for the day, Laila padded barefoot across the cool marble floor to the bathroom.

When she emerged, an hour later, her hair was freshly washed and blow-dried, her make-up perfectly covering every sign of distress, her eyebrows expertly arched, her bruised lips hidden underneath lipstick. She was all bright and shiny from the outside. She wore grey ripped jeans with a plain black tee and black sneakers. She moved swiftly around her room and gathered everything she needed for the day and began shoving them into her bag. When she was done, she made her bed, put everything she had moved back in its place and left the room.

Maa wasn't in the dining room or the kitchen. Laila set down her bag on the table and went outside to bring in the newspaper. She poured herself some cereal and opened up the politics section. A few minutes later, perhaps alerted by her movements, Maa appeared in the dining room. Laila felt a pang of guilt when she looked up. Unlike Laila, her mother's face was clearly anguished.

'Good morning,' Maa said softly.

'Morning.' Laila cleared her throat. It felt raw.

They sat quietly, sharing sections of the newspaper between them. After a little while, unable to handle the silence any longer, Laila got up and brought her bowl to the sink. 'You want some orange juice?' she asked. 'I'm squeezing some.'

'Okay,' Maa said briefly. The dryness in her voice pulled at Laila's heart. It was all her fault. She had been selfish and she had overreacted. She'd known it while she was doing it, unable to control herself. In the light of the day, she felt even more ashamed of her behaviour.

Laila brought two short glasses of orange juice back to the table and sat back down. 'You should go,' she said quietly, pushing one glass towards her mother.

Maa looked up.

'You should absolutely go. There's no question about it,' Laila said, shaking her head. 'I'm sorry.'

'I won't go if you don't want me to.'

'Maa, you should go. It's only temporary. It'll be great for you, spending time with Nana and Nani in Patna for a while. You probably need a little change anyway, and if you're not ready to go back to work here full-time, this is the perfect alternative.'

'I thought so too.' Maa studied Laila closely. 'But I don't mind staying back at all, if you need me here—'

Laila reached for Maa's hand and held it lightly. 'Go. I'm fine.' She paused, unable to look into her mother's eyes. 'And I really am sorry about last night. I was … in a strange mood and I took it out on you.'

Maa squeezed her hand and nodded. They spent the next few minutes in a more comfortable and yet emotionally charged silence, hiding behind their newspapers till they were okay to speak again. Laila's throat felt tight. She forced big gulps of juice down it and got up. She brought both their empty glasses to the sink and took longer rinsing them to avoid looking at Maa.

'You should let the principal know today,' she said.

'I will.'

'I'll look at flights once I reach work and call you. If you were to join next Monday, perhaps it'd be best if you left early this weekend—you'll get some time to settle down before you start. And wait for me to get back home tonight so I can pack for you. I know you've been feeling better, but you don't need to strain yourself unnecessarily … especially when I'm here. Save your energy to teach teenagers science.' Laila forced a chuckle. 'I'm sure they've become more rebellious since you were last a school teacher. You'll need all of your energy. And oh, do make a list of things you need to take from here and if you need to buy anything. I can come shopping with you. We should get something for Nana and Nani too. Maahi was telling me about these beautiful saris she saw in Chandni Chowk last week. We should go there sometime—maybe tomorrow?'

Laila stopped speaking and turned off the faucet. She continued to keep her back turned. There was a pause.

'It's only a two-hour flight away,' Maa said.

Laila nodded.

'You can visit anytime you want.'

Laila nodded again.

'I'm sure Nana and Nani would love that.'

Laila walked back to the dining table to get her bag. She stretched her lips in the semblance of a smile and said, 'See you tonight,' before walking away.

3

CHANGE

They say change is constant. They go as far as saying that it is good and necessary even. It doesn't change the fact that change is also scary. Laila tapped her fingernails on the steering wheel repeatedly. Her back was taut with tension. Behind her sunglasses, her eyes were unfocused. She needed another minute before she could go out in the world. Till then, she preferred to remain hidden in the parking lot.

Her phone rang. She collected it from the dashboard and muted the call without checking who it was from. Just one more minute.

After that minute passed, Laila picked up her bag and her phone and got out of the car. She walked determinedly to Two, leaving the poor, sad Laila behind in the car.

Aparna, the girl who worked the counter at Two looked up as Laila walked in. Her face split into a wide smile as she sang, 'Good morning, Laila ma'am!'

'A very good morning to you too, girl,' Laila sang back. 'By the way, any update on when you're going to stop calling me ma'am?'

'But you're almost ten years older than me!'

'Wow. Always nice to be reminded that I'm getting old first thing in the morning!'

'NO!' Aparna looked mortified. 'I mean, no, of course you're not old or anything. Damn, I wish I was your age. You're so beautiful and confident and ... perfect ... I wish I could be more like you.' Aparna's soft voice became even softer towards the end of her fangirl episode, which she clearly felt embarrassed about, judging by the flush in her cheeks.

Laila tried not to laugh or hurt her feelings. So she nodded shortly and said, 'I feel honoured,' as seriously as she could. Aparna was a sweet kid, fresh out of school, about to start college, full of hopes and dreams—everything an eighteen-year-old should be. *No, she shouldn't want to be like me*, Laila thought with a grimace.

After leaving her bag in the miniscule office, Laila walked across the bakery to the kitchen. 'Yo! All good?'

Javed, their assistant baker, was on the floor, on all fours, clearly looking for something. He abruptly turned to look up at Laila and bumped his head on the counter in the process. 'Ouch! No, all is *not* good.' He massaged his head with his fingers and bent back down, resuming his hunt for the mysterious lost item.

'Really?' Laila leaned against the door frame lazily and continued to watch Javed. From that angle, she got a prominent view of his butt. 'You look pretty good from here.'

Javed snorted. 'That's sexual harassment.'

'Sue me.' Laila crossed the kitchen and peeked through the oven door. 'What's cooking?'

'I'm baking some red velvet cupcake bases for Maahi. She said she wanted about two dozen sent over to One before noon,' Javed said, appearing from under the counter with a measuring cup victoriously clutched in his hand.

'She hasn't sent over the cupcakes yet?'

'She did—coconut with sour cream frosting or something strange like that. She wasn't very happy with them, so we're redoing Cupcake of the Day.'

'We have enough of the Classics and Crowd Pleasers though?' Laila asked, checking the display unit. 'How are we doing with Creatives today?'

'There's the coconut thing, the red velvet thing—whatever Maahi's planning to do with them—and there's banana cupcakes with rainbow nuts from yesterday.'

'We're selling stale food now?'

'Well, technically, we baked them in the evening, so we're still well within the twenty-four-hour window,' Javed said. 'Do you have any ideas for today? I can start as soon as I know what I'm baking.'

'What's up with the attitude, man?' Laila frowned. 'Isn't the menu on the calendar?'

'Oh, yes. We have the timetable, all right. But it's blank.'

'Get started on the Classics and Crowd Pleasers then. Use your judgment on the numbers—go back to the books and estimate according to the quantities we sold last week. I'll talk to Maahi and come up with something for the Creatives,' Laila said, texting Maahi as she spoke. 'Meanwhile, I'll ask Ram to prepare the bases and frostings for Bake Your Own and have them sent over here when he's done.'

'Got it.'

'You good on inventory here?'

'Shit, I forgot—we're running low on sugars. We'll last today, maybe tomorrow, but all we've got is cane sugar, corn syrup and molasses. Seriously low on honey and other brown sugars,' Javed said, counting off the list on his fingers.

'We've ordered dark brown, so it should be here today. I'll check if we have any light brown in One and have it brought over. Hold on,' Laila noted all of it quickly on her phone. 'I think we're fine on flours, fats and flavours? I'm asking Maahi to check spices, dry fruits and toppings.'

'We could do with some fresh fruit.'

'Noted. If you think of more things, email me whenever. But make sure it's in the same thread and please, please, please email. I'd like my WhatsApp to not be bombarded with one word texts throughout the day.'

Javed sniffed. 'That was only the one time! And we were in a serious crisis.'

'All I'm asking is for you to please gather your thoughts and form one message with all the information. If you can't wait for your thoughts to collect, send me whatever pops into your head by email so that I'll at least have all pieces in one place.' Laila laughed.

'Whatever, dude.'

Laila laughed harder. 'Seriously, though, you have to tell me what's up. Why are you in such a bad mood?'

Javed began pulling out utensils and slamming them on the counter one by one. 'It's my life. My whole life,' he said, measuring flour and transferring it into a huge mixing bowl.

'Sure. That really narrows it down.'

'This isn't funny. Not everything is funny.'

'I'm aware,' Laila said, setting up the KitchenAid stand mixer for him. 'What happened to your whole life?'

'Vedika's family. We finally got her parents to agree to meet mine, but now there's this whole drama about where to meet. Vedika's sisters and cousins were all "shown" for marriage or whatever in temples and my Ammi and Abbu don't want to go to a temple to "see" Vedika.'

'Where do they want to meet?'

'Anywhere but a temple.' Javed shook his head. 'I swear to God—all the gods—this is the twenty-first century but nothing's changed. This Hindu-Muslim conflict is still very real. I don't know why we can't just follow our own religious beliefs without undermining others', you know? It's so frustrating.'

'It is.' Laila nodded. 'But I guess you'd be better off concentrating on smaller problems at the moment—one small solution at a time. Decide on a neutral ground to meet. Maybe a restaurant?'

'That would be giving in and accepting their terms, when my parents are clearly wrong by refusing to go to a temple. Allah doesn't have a problem with Krishna!'

'You've got to pick your battles if you want to win the war, man. The point is—let this one go. Meet them in the middle, compromise, get it over with. There might well be bigger, more important battles you'll need to save your energy for.'

Javed thought for a moment before shrugging. 'I guess that makes sense. It's just so narrow-minded and annoying. Anyway, how come you have so much gyaan?'

Laila snorted. 'It's easier to have perspective on things when you're not the one dealing with them. I'm not in it, so I have all this gyaan for you.'

'For a second there, I was concerned about you. I thought you were turning all philosophical and deep.'

'Well, I'm not, but I am still your boss, so get to work!'

'Yes, boss,' Javed said, tipping his invisible hat.

Laila checked on a few more things at Two before going to One, leaving Javed and Aparna in charge. When she got there, things barely seemed under control.

'Whoa! What's all this?' she asked, walking into the disaster zone.

'Don't ask. Been putting out one fire after another all morning. First, the new coconut recipe turned out to be a disaster. Then Ram called and said he'll be coming in late today. I've been alone here and now the oven's exploded.'

'*Exploded*?' Laila inspected the oven, which was splattered with semi-cooked dough mixed with burnt crumbs. 'What the fuck happened here?'

Maahi was shaking her head furiously. 'My cupcakes exploded. I did everything right—I've done it a million times. But I put this batch in and started working on the Creatives over there and heard some sort of electrical noise … there were suddenly sparks and fumes. I couldn't turn the oven off right away because of the sparks coming out of the sockets, so I tried the digital buttons at the front. Didn't work. Eventually, it got worse and finally the oven gave up and died!' Maahi was out of breath. 'The cupcakes exploded. Can you believe it? I spent hours on the recipe. Literally all morning!'

'Cupcakes exploding isn't the same as the oven exploding. This is a bigger mess to clean but less dangerous.'

'Trust me—it was plenty scary! What do we do now? I'm still running behind on the Creatives for today—the first one sucked and we lost this one. And now the oven died! Dammit, not today. I don't have time for this!'

'I'll take care of it,' Laila said mildly, sinking down to the floor to look at the damage to the wires, which looked fried.

'No, I'll take care of it! You already have your hands full with Two.'

'Well, I did my baking last night, so I can be a businesswoman now. You go be a baker.'

'Are you sure? I mean, you're already so overworked. Don't worry, if it's really inconvenient for you, I can totally do it,' Maahi said, but her face betrayed how terrified she was.

Laila laughed. The oven was switched off, but as a precaution, she held a part of the burned wire carefully and pulled it out of the socket. 'Dude, you need to chill. Cookies + Cupcakes is all about fun and rainbows, remember? I've got this.'

'You have this?'

'I've got this!'

Maahi exhaled in relief. 'Oh, thank God,' she said.

'Which one?' Laila asked, her mind going back to her conversation with Javed.

'Whichever one sent you here today.'

'That'd be Krishna and Allah.'

'Is that supposed to mean something?' Maahi asked, starting a fresh batch of cupcakes.

'Javed's having problems with both his and Vedika's families. The whole Hindu-Muslim thing.'

'Oh, right. He told me about it. It's so sad. They're so in love and so good together. They should be excited about having found each other but instead, they have to go through this family drama.'

'It's definitely not going to be an easy road. Because these aren't everyday issues for us, we think that they don't really exist anymore,' Laila said. She thought about when she was a kid, she would go to school and make friends without the question of religion or caste ever occurring to her. Because her mother was a progressive woman, a teacher, she never allowed these discriminations to grow in Laila's mind. And they were taught equality and unity in school, given moral science classes. Such stories of religious tension seemed like something they only read about in history books but never noticed in real life. It was only as she grew up that she slowly started seeing how much of a reality the tension was. The unfair stereotypes and animosity towards people from different religions still very much existed, and many people lived with it every day.

'But it exists for Javed and Vedika,' Maahi said, shrugging.

'I have a question,' Laila asked, as a thought occurred to her. 'When we were scanning résumés for the assistant baker positions, did you notice Javed was Muslim?'

'Looking at his résumé? No. I didn't really pay attention to the names as much as to qualifications. I figured when he came in for the interview though.'

'Did that affect your opinion at all?'

Maahi looked up. 'The fact that he's Muslim? You think I wouldn't want to hire someone because of his religion?'

'I'm not saying that I think so. I'm trying to …' Laila paused for a moment, collecting her thoughts. 'Okay, so you and I? We are from middle-class Indian families. We weren't taught discrimination. Our parents are reasonably progressive and encouraged us to be the same way, right? But just because that's how it's been in our homes clearly doesn't mean it's the same for the whole country.'

'I guess. There are definitely people who care about other people's religion and stuff. Some of my friends in school were always talking shit about people from other castes. Their festivals and clothes and foods and all that,' Maahi said thoughtfully.

'Exactly! People make light of those things. Religion wasn't a factor or even a thought for us when we were considering Javed for the job. But I was wondering whether, while waiting to hear from us, he thought it would weigh in on our decision.'

'Maybe … now that I think about it.'

'I hope not. I'd hate to think that we said or did something to make him feel that way.' Laila pushed back hair from her face and got up from the floor. 'I better get started. I'm going to find someone to come take a look at the oven and also check inventory. You do your baking at Two.'

'Got it. I really am sorry about this. I have no idea what happened!'

'I don't know if I can forgive you for this,' Laila said in all seriousness. 'How do I know that you didn't blow up your cupcakes because your second Creative was also sucky?'

'That's not true! I mean, I don't know if they were sucky— they could be. I'm a sucky baker today. But I definitely didn't blow them up on purpose!'

'Can you prove it?'

'How?' Maahi's eyes grew wide as she searched around the kitchen, clearly looking for a way to make Laila believe her. 'I don't even…'

'God, Maahi! Of course you didn't blow up the oven on purpose! How would you even know how to? I'm just playing with you!'

Maahi went quiet for a moment, exhaled and shook her head.

Laila laughed. 'You're awfully tense today. I'm noticing a pattern—all the people I work with seem to have issues today. Aparna, Javed and now you.'

'I don't know about them, but look around you—my stress is justified.'

'Be that as it may, there's definitely more going on with you than a morning of disasters at C+C.' Laila squinted her eyes. 'How was your date last night?'

'Oh, this is not about *that*. The date was fine,' Maahi said. 'He seemed good enough and we had an okay time.'

'He was shorter in person, wasn't he?'

'Come on!'

'Admit it,' Laila pressed, enjoying watching Maahi squirm.

'Fine. He was a couple of inches shorter than he appeared in his picture. He was, like, five eightish.'

'Technically though, did he say he was five ten or did you assume that from his pictures? Because if you assumed it, it's on you.'

'He didn't say it but, hold on, let me show you his pictures. They're very strategically taken, you know—sitting down, with short friends and girls and animals or alone on a cliff. Definitely a lie by omission.' Maahi scrolled through his pictures and shoved them in Laila's face.

'I believe you,' Laila said. 'I don't need proof. Also, I don't need to see this stranger's picture again, especially if he's not going to be a part of our lives. Is he going to be a part of our lives?'

'Maybe … He was nice and seemed like the kind of person that's great once you get to know them. There was some awkwardness, but that's just a first-date thing, right?'

'Dude, I've never met him. You have to trust your own gut.'

'Yeah, I know, I know. I'm just wondering …' Maahi bit her lip. Her eyes were unfocused, clearly remembering last night and trying to form an opinion.

'You don't have to decide the future course of action *right now*. Take your time,' Laila said.

Maahi nodded and focused on her batter, but Laila couldn't help feel that her friend felt lost and maybe a little afraid. She gave Maahi some space and went out to track down an electrician. When she got back, Maahi had already left for Two. All day, at the back of her mind, she had a nagging feeling that Maahi wasn't being completely honest with her. She was hiding the truth, and Laila tried to understand why that could be.

At the end of the rather long day of putting out all the fires and restoring the shops, Laila went over to Two, where Maahi had packed up and was ready to leave.

'I've decided,' she said when Laila walked in, 'I'm going to give it another shot. I'm going to see him again and see how it goes.'

'No, you're not,' Laila said firmly.

'What?'

'You're doing no such thing. I'm sure he's a good guy and maybe if you guys try again, it might become something good. But do you want good, or do you want great? I've been thinking about this all day. You said the date was okay and he was good enough. That's so dumb! Do you want *okay*? Do you want *good enough*? You deserve so much more. You're a wonderful, kind, compassionate person and you deserve more than good enough. I never say this to you because it's cheesy and disgusting, but I hope you know that any man would be very, very lucky to be with you!'

Maahi was frozen to the spot, standing by the counter, staring at Laila unblinkingly. Her eyes were shining with unshed tears.

'Dammit, don't cry! How am I supposed to have a real conversation with you if you—' Laila began to joke but stopped suddenly, noticing Maahi's head drop to her chest, her body shivering. 'Hey, come on,' Laila said softly and went to her.

Maahi swiped the back of her hand over her face and sniffed. 'I *had* great.' Her voice was barely a whisper and Laila knew exactly who she was talking about.

'It wasn't great at the time. The timing sucked.'

'I lost it. I lost great.'

'Maahi, listen to me. You did what needed to be done, what was right at the time for you and for Sid. You guys were great, but … in a vacuum. You worked only in an isolated box, away from all outside factors like the time you had for each other, your baggage with your ex and his baggage with his family. It wasn't practical,' Laila said. She was grasping at straws now, trying to find a way to placate her. Maahi and Sid had been very much in love with each other when they had decided to break up. Laila believed that it was the right decision at the time—neither of them was prepared to take care of something so special and rare. It didn't mean that a year later Maahi couldn't still miss him.

Maahi nodded, sniffing quietly. 'It's all … in the past.' Exhaling loudly, she rubbed her face. 'Anyway, you're right about this guy. I don't want to settle and it's unfair to him too. He shouldn't have to settle for someone who's settling for him. He deserves better too.'

That brought a smile to Laila's face. This was why she loved Maahi so much. Even in a situation like this, where she wasn't responsible for a stranger's happiness or owed him anything, she still thought about his feelings. 'Exactly!'

'But I'm not giving up. I won't settle for good enough. And I won't give up on great either.'

'You'll keep dating?'

Maahi nodded. 'I want to keep trying. I can't be that bitter, once heartbroken, twice terrified person—I'm too young for that. I have to keep trying. I can't give up hope.'

'Aw, relax, you drama queen!' Laila said, wrapping an arm around Maahi and squeezing her. They laughed, but Laila sobered up and said in a whisper, 'You'll be fine.'

'How do you know?'

'Because I still see the twinkle thing in your eyes,' Laila said. And sure enough, it was right there. Maahi hadn't lost it; her eyes still shone with a twinkle of hope.

After a moment of quietly standing side by side at the counter, under the soft light from the lamp, holding each other, Maahi stretched her arm and asked, 'You want to taste my third attempt at Creative cupcake today?'

'Most definitely!' Laila said, forcefully cheerful. 'How sucky is that one?'

'Not even a little bit.'

'Also, you still haven't told me why you were in a bad mood in the morning. If not the dude, what was it?'

'Ugh, it's my parents. They're driving me crazy. I really can't date if I have to also be here at Cookies + Cupcakes every day—you know, living my dreams—and then go back home to Vaishali. The commute is long enough as it is without trying to squeeze in a date after work,' Maahi said. She extracted cupcakes from the display and placed them carefully on a plate. 'Are there forks at the table?'

'Yeah,' Laila said. 'Are Uncle and Aunty worried about you getting home late?'

'Understatement of the year. I wish I was like other kids who either move away for college—which, by the way, I did before I was dumb enough to come back—or move away for work. But again, I decided to work here too! I have no escape.'

'Technically, your home's in UP and your work's in New Delhi.'

'Not far enough to move out!' Maahi cried, flopping down on a chair and pulling out a fork from the stand in the centre of the table. 'Three hours of commute to and from work every day is a lot though. I wish I lived closer to work.'

Laila sat down next to Maahi and pulled a fork as well. She dug into the curiously blue cupcake, which turned out to be much better than the coconut one from the morning. 'That one's easy to solve. Move in with me,' she said, digging her fork back in the cupcake just as Maahi yelped in excitement, 'Oh my God, really?'

4

THE HOVERER

Over the weekend, Maahi brought her stuff over to Laila's place in instalments, which Laila stored in a corner of the living room. On Sunday morning, Maahi arrived with the last few boxes and her parents. Laila was happy to see them. Irrespective of the conflicts Maahi intermittently had with her parents, Laila had always liked them. They were warm, caring people who had been especially sweet to Laila right from the beginning. They might not understand Maahi's perspective on things sometimes or support her plans, but they always wanted the best for her. Laila thought of them as two of the very few people who didn't have a single mean bone in their bodies and were genuinely good. Now that she thought of it, she realized that that's where Maahi got her kindness and compassion from.

'Namaste Aunty,' Laila said, pulling the door open. She moved back to allow them to enter with their boxes and closed the door behind them. 'Namaste Uncle.'

'Namaste beta,' Maahi's parents said at the same time.

38

'Kaisi ho?' Maahi's mother asked.

'I'm great! No longer alone now that Maahi's moving in,' Laila said, winking at Maahi, who followed her parents inside, dragging an oversized suitcase behind her. They had decided that the best way to convince Maahi's parents to let her move in with Laila would be to pretend that it was for Laila, not Maahi. 'My mom left just a few days ago and the house feels so empty without her. I'm already getting lonely.'

'Don't worry, beta. Now Maahi will be here to keep you company, no?' Aunty said, her forehead wrinkling as she added, 'She told us about your mom. It's good for her that she's working again, but I do hope she takes care of her health.'

'Me too,' Laila agreed.

'How long is she going to be in Patna for? Maahi said she's only joining the school temporarily?' Uncle asked.

'For a few months, maybe longer, depending how soon the teacher she's covering for gets better.'

'Cancer,' Aunty said, shaking her head.

There was a pause before Maahi said, 'Let's get everything in the room, shall we?'

'Which one is it?' Aunty asked.

'It's the one on your right,' Laila said, pointing to it. She took one of the bags from Aunty and led the way. 'It's a guest room, but it's always empty. We rarely have any overnight guests. It has two huge windows and gets a lot of sunlight in the morning, so Maahi won't be able to sleep in till late, which is good for business.'

Everyone laughed.

'She turns her alarm off and doesn't wake up even when it rings twenty times,' Aunty said, complaining fondly. 'You will have to wake her up every morning—'

'Ma! I can wake myself up,' Maahi interjected.

'Then why don't you? Why does Aunty have to wake you up *every morning*?' Laila asked, tongue-in-cheek.

'The truth is always bitter,' Aunty said wisely.

'Whatever,' Maahi said and set down the suitcase she was slugging next to the ancient bed. She looked around the room, taking in the white and gold curtains, the desk shoved in a corner against the wall, the rather large wooden cupboard opposite the bed, and nodded approvingly. 'I'm feeling it.'

'Feeling what?' Uncle asked.

'The place. I feel it.'

'What do you mean by that … ?'

'Just that I like it!' Maahi said.

'Then why didn't you just say that?' Aunty asked.

Maahi opened her mouth to speak, thought better of it and let it go.

Laila chuckled and said, 'Weird girl, this one. Says the stupidest things.'

'You only teach her something now,' Aunty pleaded with Laila, as if sick and tired of her unruly child. 'She never listens to us. Very stubborn she is.'

'I know.' Laila shook her head in disproval.

'Laila! You traitor!' Maahi cried, her eyes wide with horror.

'Don't talk to Laila like that!' Aunty came to Laila's defence. 'She's older than you and knows better. Listen to her. Learn something from her.'

'Why don't you just disown me and adopt Laila?' Maahi said heatedly.

'We—'

'For now, let me adopt you,' Laila said, patting Maahi lightly on the back. 'Don't worry, Aunty, I'll take good care of her.'

'I know, beta,' Aunty said fondly.

'How much should we … ?' Uncle said. He paused, cleared his throat and spoke again, 'How much do you suppose we should pay you … as rent?'

'Oh, don't worry about that, Uncle. I'm not taking money from Maahi for living here—' Laila said, slightly embarrassed to be discussing money with her friend's parents.

'You're not taking money from Maahi. We'll pay—'

'I can't take money from you either!'

'No, no. We can't allow that!' Aunty said.

'Seriously, Aunty, it's okay. This room was empty anyway. And Maahi is coming to live here to help me out, keep me company—'

'Are you joking?' Maahi said, pausing in the middle of opening up a carton. 'Of course I'm paying rent! I can't just live here for free.'

'You can—' Laila began, but was cut off by Maahi's loud protest.

'No, I can't. If I pay my share, like I would if I lived anywhere else, we'll be roommates. If I don't, it's just charity and I don't want charity.'

'It's not charity! It's friendship.'

'Which is why money shouldn't come between it. Just let me pay,' Maahi said, in a very end-of-conversation sort of way. Laila had rarely seen Maahi so determined.

'Yes, beta. Maahi is right. We'll pay the rent—'

'Papa! I don't want your charity either!'

'Taking money from your parents isn't charity,' Aunty said, looking horrified at the thought. 'We raised you—'

'And you did a good job at it. Now I'm all grown up. Not taking money from my parents any more should be a good indication of it,' Maahi said. 'You should be proud.'

Nobody spoke about the matter after that. She didn't know about Aunty, but Laila did feel proud of Maahi and how much she had grown in the few years they'd known each other. From the unsure, easily overwhelmed girl she had been three years ago when she first came to the coffee shop Laila worked at looking for a job, she'd now become a spirited, headstrong young woman. A lot of it was the result of finding her passion in baking and working so hard to pursue it building Cookies + Cupcakes. She was now a businesswoman and an artist who'd been hurt many times but still hadn't lost hope, who had dreams and made plans and followed them through.

Maahi was presently bent over her open suitcase on the floor, seething. Laila went over to help her put her clothes away in the cupboard, but Aunty intervened, muttering about how unorganized Maahi was. Everyone got out of her way and watched as Aunty unpacked all of Maahi's stuff and organized the room. Laila made tea while Aunty asked Uncle to throw away the boxes and cartons and told Maahi to sweep the floor. She herself went about stacking Maahi's books on the desk. Once they were done, they had tea in the now-ready room and Maahi's parents left immediately after. They had a lunch to get to at their friends' home and Maahi could not look more relieved even though Laila could tell she was trying.

As soon as Laila closed the door behind them, Maahi let out an exaggerated sigh of relief. 'God, that was torture!'

'Oh, shut up. You know you're glad they came to help you out,' Laila said, making her way back to Maahi's new room.

'Glad? She compared me to you twenty million times. I don't get how despite doing the exact same thing with our lives, you are in better graces with her.'

'Look at it this way—if she approves of what I'm doing, and you and I are doing the same thing, it means she approves of what you're doing. Hence proved.'

Maahi rolled her eyes. 'It's just double standards. Anything you do is great, everything I do is stupid—even when we both do the exact same thing.'

'We don't actually do the exact same thing.'

'What does that mean? We both bake, own the same bake shops, go there every day and do the same thing—'

'Not precisely the same thing. We have different sets of responsibilities.' Laila leaned against the doorframe and studied Maahi's room. She could picture Maahi living there. It could even be fun. It had been a long time since Laila had lived with another person apart from her mother. 'This will make the commute more convenient for both of us—we could go together and take turns driving. It would also give us extra time in the car to discuss work. We can plan things in the morning on our way to work and then go over the day in the evening on our way back.'

'That's what you're excited about?' Maahi asked, looking a little hurt. 'Work stuff? You're not excited that I, your bestest friend in the whole world, am going to be living with you?'

'Meh.'

'Laila!'

'Maahi!' Laila said, mimicking her tone. 'Of course I'm excited, you idiot! I'm just saying that there are other positive things about this. One downside may be that I basically never get rid of you. You'll be there when I wake up, there when I have breakfast, there when I go to work, there when I get to work, still there when I leave work, and *still* there when I get home—I don't think I thought this through.'

'We're basically married now,' Maahi said, very pleased with herself.

'Except that this is not a marriage between equals. I'm your landlady. And you haven't paid your rent yet, so technically, you're in my debt.'

'Technically, you're a mean person.'

Laila laughed. She joined Maahi on the bed, lay down next to her and looked at the ceiling. 'How bad do you think things are at the shops right now?' she mused.

'Javed and Aparna are probably fine at Two.'

'Ram, on the other hand …' Laila didn't need to finish that thought. Not only was Ram new, he was also kind of hopeless without supervision. They had hired Javed when they'd opened the first shop. They moved him to Two because he was seasoned and capable of setting up a new shop, and left One, a well-oiled machine by then, in the new hire's hand. Two was only four months old and from time to time, Ram still had problems holding the fort down by himself. 'He's a good kid. But we should probably hire someone to help him.'

'Probably. Can we afford it?'

'Not really. Not yet. But maybe someone part-time to

come in for the first four hours or something, help with the customers perhaps? I'm sure Ram would appreciate it.'

'We could post an ad on job sites. I'm sure there are plenty of college students who have afternoon classes and can come in from 8 a.m. to noon or something. They won't mind the extra money,' Maahi said. 'And not that we are in a position to pay them much at this point.'

'Yeah, but as soon as we get more stable, we will. I'd like to keep our people close.'

'Human resources—I hear you,' Maahi said. 'They taught us all about it in college.'

'See? The value of education. You know all about the value of humans now.'

'Sure.' Maahi sat up on the bed and looked around. 'Moving into a new place is so much fun when you have a little money. Last time I moved, I was going to college in Bangalore, living in a hostel, and it was awful not just because I didn't want to be in Bangalore or study engineering, but also because I was broke. I couldn't make that place home.'

'And you're going to make this place home?' Laila asked, turning on her side and supporting her weight on her arm.

'Damn right. I could get some nice bedsheets and cushions. Maybe an area rug here—something to match those pretty curtains. A mirror, maybe in that corner, with a dresser—oh, there are so many possibilities. Photo frames, lamps, flowers, string lights—I could do so much with this place!'

Laila watched the glee on Maahi's face, which seeped under her skin too as if through osmosis. 'Maybe one of those magazine holders that we can bolt to the wall? Those are cute. Or a bookshelf? Never really thought about decorating before, especially not this room. Not even my own room for that matter. I grew up here in the same house, same room, and it just, sort of, changed over the years. It grew up with me. But I guess it isn't until you move in somewhere new that you actually look around and see the place and plan.'

'We can decorate your room too!' Maahi said excitedly. 'We'll make it all new and beautiful. Leave it to me.'

'If I leave it to you, it'll be all pink and purple!'

'First, what is wrong with pink and purple? And second, I know your style and I can customize my services based on your needs.'

'Can you?' Laila raised her eyebrow, but she knew that Maahi could. She was responsible for designing everything at Cookies + Cupcakes from the décor to the logo, website, napkins, cutlery—everything. So they went to her room and explored the possibilities briefly before rushing to C+C.

As Sundays at bakeshops go, the day wasn't half bad. Ram was holding fort alone and managing to keep his head above the water. They had a steady flow of customers all day and no crisis situations. The kitchens were stocked with baking supplies, the displays were stocked with baked goods and Laila and Maahi had a fun but productive day baking together while Ram handled the counter.

At closing time, after everyone else had left for the day, Laila and Maahi went to Two to check on things. Considering that they had to plan for the menu for the whole week ahead and order ingredients accordingly, they were pleased to find that there was still light outside when they walked to the car afterwards.

'So, what now?' Maahi asked.

'Now, we're done for the day,' Laila said, frowning.

'That I know. But like, what are we doing now?'

Laila grinned thinking about how Maahi was trying to follow her routine now that they were living together. She said, 'Well, when I'm lucky enough to leave work at a decent hour, I usually go to the gym. I've anyway gone only three days this week and I make it a point to go at least four times.'

'Gym? Are you serious?' Maahi said, looking appalled at the thought.

'Yes. You know, it's what some people do to stay fit.'

'I would love to get a lecture on fitness and health from you right now, but this is my first night of freedom! How can you do this to me?'

'I'm not doing anything—'

'The gym,' Maahi repeated gravely. 'Fine. If that's what you want. Who knows—maybe I'll lose some weight and be skinny like you in a month or so.'

'I'm not making you come and you don't need to lose weight.'

'Have you seen my butt?'

'I try not to but occasionally, yes,' Laila chuckled.

'It's big. And my thighs and my boobs. I'm curvy—'

'Which is awesome. Stop feeling sorry for yourself. You've got what most women want. You're curvy *and* slim. Do you know how rare that is?'

'I'm not feeling sorry for myself. I'm just saying that I could do with a bit of toning. Especially now that I'm out in the dating market,' Maahi said. 'I know what you're going to say—no, I'm not doing anything for guys. I'm doing it to be awesome and irresistible.'

Laila snorted. 'Yeah, okay.'

Once at the gym, Laila proceeded to the treadmill while Maahi signed up for a trial. She had got into the habit of running several years ago when she'd realized she needed physical strength. Since then, running had become an indispensable part of her life. It cleared her head when she needed to tune out the world, be with herself and just sweat it out. Baking also helped her clear her head, but now that it was also her full-time occupation, it was hard to see it as a way to relax. Now when she baked, there were a thousand thoughts about Cookies + Cupcakes going through her head. Also, as much as she loved Maahi, she couldn't exactly be with herself and clear her head with Maahi chattering in her ears. It was fun, of course, but it wasn't head-clearing space.

'You're doing it again,' Laila said.

'What am I doing?' Maahi asked. She had joined Laila at the cardio stations, getting onto the elliptical machine next to her.

'Hovering.'

'I don't know what you're talking about.'

Laila looked sideways at her and narrowed her eyes. 'You've been doing it all week—ever since I told you Maa's leaving. You've tailed me all day, hovering.'

'I haven't tailed you or hovered or whatever. We work together, remember?'

'Yeah? When was the last time you set foot inside a gym?'

'That's not the point,' Maahi said dismissively. 'But fine. I was looking out for you because I know this was sudden and even though you don't tell me anything, I know Aunty leaving can't be easy on you.'

'I'm fine.'

'Of course you are. That's why I didn't say anything.'

'But you hovered.'

'Stop it! I'm just trying to be your friend if you'd let me.'

'Be my friend by backing off,' Laila said, now out of breath. She wiped her forehead with the back of her wrist and slowed the treadmill down a little.

'You know what you need?'

'Yes. But I'm guessing you have other ideas?'

'You need love. A man in your life, someone to talk to, go out with, have fun and chill with,' Maahi said, her eyes bright as if a light bulb had turned on inside her head.

'Turn up the speed. You're barely moving,' Laila said.

'No, seriously! I'm telling you. Love makes everything better.'

'Spare me the Tumblr quotes, please.'

'Just listen to me now and you'll thank me later,' Maahi said in a tone that implied that she knew what she was talking about. Laila doubted it—highly. 'What about that man? He's got nice abs. I'm sure he'd be into you, with your flat stomach and toned arms and all. He looks like a male version of you. You guys will have a lot to talk about.'

'Who, Ronny? I know him and neither of us is interested. Also, stop looking at my stomach.'

'How do you know neither of you is interested?'

'Because we aren't,' Laila asserted.

Just then, Ronny saw them looking in his direction and waved. Laila nodded at him while Maahi waved back excitedly. She got off her elliptical machine and said, 'I'm going over there to work out with him. He seems way friendlier than you. And I'm sure *he'd* let me look at his stomach.'

5
THE GAME

❦

Laila and Maahi weren't speaking to each other. They didn't speak to each other on Monday, barely looked in the other's direction on Tuesday and made their employees relay their messages to the other rather than speaking directly on Wednesday. By Thursday evening, Laila was ready to leave Maahi behind when she still hadn't come out after Laila had honked three times outside One.

Just as Laila honked the fourth time, Maahi appeared, juggling boxes and files, rushing towards the car. Laila glanced her way briefly before resuming staring right ahead of her at the street. They sat next to each other in the car, letting the radio fill the strained silence between them. When they reached home, they dropped their stuff on the dining table and proceeded to their separate rooms wordlessly. Laila slammed her door first, and sure enough, heard Maahi's door slam a second later.

Laila spent the next couple of hours locked in her room, reading. When her stomach growled with hunger, she reappeared in the dining area to find Maahi in the kitchen already. Laila had always liked the layout of her house—the open dining and kitchen setup allowed her to work at the dining table while her mother was in the kitchen, or vice versa, so they could spend time together—but right now, she resented it. Noticing that Maahi was making paneer paranthas, Laila got started with raita. When they were done, they sat at opposite ends of the table and ate their dinner quietly, retiring to their rooms immediately after taking the dishes to the sink.

Laila woke up in an even worse mood on Friday morning, something she hadn't thought possible. In the car, Maahi seemed more anxious than she had been the rest of the week, which put Laila in a slightly better mood. Of course Maahi should be anxious. She should have thought about what she was doing before she did it—or at least after—and even though she refused to accept that she'd crossed a line, her anxiousness proved that she did feel guilty about it.

They spent another day not talking to each other, and it wasn't until they were back in the car, heading home, that Maahi broke the silence.

'It'll be fine,' she said, turning towards Laila.

'Shut up,' Laila said, without looking at her.

Maahi sucked in a breath, and for a moment it seemed as if she was going to launch into an argument, but she didn't. Once again, they slammed their room doors as soon as they reached home.

Laila immediately took a quick shower and pulled open her cupboard. She hadn't been on a date since college and here she was, a decade later, picking out an outfit to please a man. All thanks to Maahi, who had figured out exactly what Laila needed in life and arranged it for her—a stupid date with

Ronny from the gym. Laila could think of twenty different things she would prefer doing on a Friday night. But this was what she had to do instead.

She ended up choosing a pair of blue denim shorts and a white wrap top. She paired her outfit with pointed black pumps and red lipstick to make it more date appropriate. She didn't even know where they were going. Ronny had insisted on picking her up from her house, which was very old-fashioned-charming of him, but it eliminated the option of an early escape. Not that she intended on ditching him midway through the date—she was too polite to hurt another person's feelings like that—but it still made her feel a little cornered. Although she had already decided that this would be their first and last date, she tried to look at the best-case scenario. They could have a good time, a conversation, good food, some wine and part on good terms so that they could still say hi to each other at the gym without any awkwardness.

Promptly at 8 p.m., there was a knock on her bedroom door. 'Ronny just texted. He's outside,' Maahi said when Laila opened it. Without acknowledging her, Laila grabbed her handbag from the dining table as she stomped out. Ronny, who was sitting in his car outside, rushed out when he saw Laila approaching.

'You look ho—' he said, stopping himself. His face flushed and he finished, 'Nice.'

'Thanks,' Laila said. Ronny held the passenger door open for her, somehow getting in her way, which resulted in them doing an awkward dance around each other before she could finally get in. 'Thank you,' she said again.

Ronny got in and drove rather rashly in the bad traffic, honking over the Punjabi hits blaring from his music system, rendering conversation impossible. Laila preferred the music over awkward conversation, but with every minute they spent not talking to each other, the awkwardness only seemed to escalate. Finally, after a good forty-five minutes, Ronny pulled over outside a loud-looking club in south Delhi. There was a line of men with gelled hair and in tight jeans and women with straightened hair and winged eyeliner outside.

'Are we going dancing?' Laila asked once Ronny had turned off the ignition and the music stopped.

'Yep. Super fun, no? Delhi clubbing scene is fire!' Ronny said, his face lit up at the thought of the 'fire' clubbing scene.

'Mmm.' Laila really wanted to not make this unpleasant, and even though she had no interest in going to a club that night, she let Ronny lead her to one.

Laila followed Ronny to the door, walking behind him as he made his way determinedly to the bouncer. She had to struggle to keep up with him in her heels as she walked on the uneven street, but tried not to be annoyed with him for it. Maybe he was just nervous and he walked really fast without thinking about someone else trying to walk with him when he was nervous. Laila caught up with him just as he shook hands with the second bouncer and half-hugged him. They were allowed to go right in.

'My friend owns this place,' Ronny yelled in her ear as they stepped into the club, Kendrick Lamar booming in their ears.

'Awesome,' Laila yelled back.

Ronny said something to the hostess at the entrance and she led them to a table up the stairs, overlooking the dance floor.

It was sort of a closed, private balcony, with their table pushed against the glass railing. There were only four tables there, with an electric candle flickering softly in the centre of each. The hostess removed the 'Reserved' sign from their table as Laila sat down, looking to her right at the excited crowd dancing downstairs—whatever she could see of it in the blinking neon pink and blue lights.

The hostess left after pouring them full glasses of champagne, which apparently came with the table, and Ronny yelled, 'Great place, hai na?'

Laila widened her eyes and nodded.

'Friday nights here are bomb, I'm telling you. Awesome crowd and all.'

'Yeah.'

'You go out clubbing a lot?'

Laila cleared her throat and prepared to yell. 'Not a lot. Maybe once a month. Usually on friends' birthdays and stuff.'

'Where do you go?'

'There are some cool spots in south Delhi with great music. Sometimes we go to Gurgaon.'

'Cool!' Ronny nodded approvingly. 'You have a lot of friends?'

'Sort of. I went to college in Delhi and I work here now too, so I know a lot of people.' Laila was about to tell him that even though she couldn't hang out with her old friends as much, she tried not to miss birthdays and therefore saw the group quite often, when the song changed to an even louder one, and she swallowed the rest of her sentence.

They smiled politely at each other across the table and sipped their drinks, waiting for Rihanna to finish singing. A waiter carried a large platter of appetizers to their table and placed it between them.

'We didn't …' Laila started to say, when Ronny leaned back to make way. The waiter placed the platter between them, smiled and disappeared into the darkness again.

'You *have to* try the chicken tikka masala. So yum!' Ronny said, poking a toothpick into one and shoving it in front of Laila's mouth. She tried to take the toothpick from him, but he insisted on feeding her. *That's kind of sweet*, Laila thought. Sweet in an intrusive, overbearing sort of way, but she could let it go. They ate their appetizers without speaking, communicating only through smiles and nods. Ronny's eyes were wide with excitement as he looked here and there, bobbing his head to the music. He was fidgeting in his seat, as if unable to sit in place, out of excitement. Laila was glad that she'd let him bring her to this place since he was so clearly thrilled about being there.

Laila looked down to see a couple grinding in the middle of the dance floor. She shifted her gaze to a group of five girls in a loose circle, dancing with their hands in the air, some holding their phones and clutches, some spilling their drinks on their own or other people's heads accidentally.

'So, what do you do?' Laila asked over the music.

That was all the prompting he needed. Ronny screamed through the next five songs, telling her about everything he did *all day*. At first, Laila thought that his energy and excitement for his work was sweet but midway through the third song, she had to accept that he was self-absorbed and even a little shallow. Turned out, he didn't just go to the gym, he was a trainer there. Laila wondered how she'd missed it, going to the same gym every day. It was probably because she kept to herself at the gym and he'd only been working there for a few months. He had been born and raised in Gurgaon and lived for fitness. He gave her a lot of fitness and diet tips, which he apparently charged a lot of money for at the gym. Laila laughed dryly and politely thanked him for the favour. Ronny seemed to be having a great time, moving with the beat, mouthing Drake's lyrics and scanning the dance floor intermittently, chatting happily whenever the music allowed. He had a goofy sort of a voice, and something about his body language made Laila feel as if he were a child trapped inside a grown man's body.

'What are your hobbies?' Ronny asked suddenly.

'Umm, I like to read.'

'What is your favourite storybook?'

Laila bit her lip at 'storybook' and said evenly, 'I don't have one favourite book. I can never compare them because all my favourite ones are brilliant yet so different. I have a lot of favourite writers though.'

'My favourite is Chetan Bhagat.' Ronny nodded intelligently.

'Yeah? What else do you like to do?' Laila asked, trying to steer the conversation in a different direction.

'Music is my passion. I'm very passionate about it, from school time only, ever since I was like sixteen.'

'Oh, do you play an instrument?'

'No, no. Not play. I love listening to music.'

They fell quiet for a moment after that, Ronny pumping his fists and bouncing to a Fetty Wap song and Laila sipping her champagne.

'You're not drinking?' Laila asked, noticing that while her glass was half-empty, Ronny had stopped after the first sip.

'Yeah, I don't drink. Just a sip. But you like the champagne, no?'

'Why did you order it if you don't drink?'

'Champagne is good on dates and stuff,' Ronny said, winking at her. 'I toh don't even eat anything after 7 p.m. Just some chicken … protein is very good.'

Laila dug her toothpick into a seekh kebab, trying to shake off the discomfort she felt. She took another sip of champagne, almost in defiance of the stupid dietary regulations her date was telling her about over dinner.

A little over an hour into their date, three men in shiny shirts appeared. As soon as Ronny saw them, his face split into a huge smile and he got up to receive hard thumps on his back. Laila heard a flurry of 'What's up' and 'Bro' and fixed a smile on her face for when it was her turn to greet this group of men.

'Guys, this is Laila,' Ronny said, turning to her.

'Laila, like Laila-Majnu Laila?' The dude in the sparkly magenta shirt chuckled at his own joke.

'You should change your name to Majnu right now!' the one with three gold chains of varying thickness suggested.

Even though he laughed with them, Ronny seemed slightly embarrassed as he glanced sideways at Laila.

'Hi,' Laila said, exposing just the right amount of teeth for the semblance of a smile.

'Let's go dance, bro!'

'Yea, bro, the club is rocking tonight!'

'You go, we'll join later—' Ronny started to say, when the dude in the magenta shirt wrapped his arm around Ronny and pulled him towards the stairs. As he was being dragged away, Ronny turned back to look at Laila with a helpless expression on his face.

If she was going to do this, she'd need liquid courage to dull her senses. Laila turned to the table, chugged down Ronny's glass of champagne as well, picked up her purse and followed the men downstairs to the dance floor. She found relief in the fact that at least they wouldn't have to talk. Trying to make the best of the night, she danced with the group. The music boomed loudly in her ears, vibrating through her entire body and for the first time that night, Laila began to have fun. However, after the first song ended, Ronny decided to hold her hands, twirl her around and groove with her awkwardly instead of dancing together but apart, individually, being responsible exclusively for their own bodies.

Laila let him have a couple of more songs, before shouting into his ear that she should probably head home. Ronny's friends wouldn't have it. They kept a protesting Laila on the dance floor for another half hour before Ronny finally listened to her and walked out to the reception with her, away from the music.

'Come on, yaar! It's not even eleven!' Ronny said, wiping the sweat from his forehead with his shirtsleeve; he had spent the last five songs attempting to set the dance floor on fire with his buddies.

'Really, I would stay if I could, but I need to go,' Laila said, politely but firmly.

Ronny threw his hands up in the air dramatically and said, 'Fine, as you like. I'll drop you.'

'Nah, it's all right. I can call an Uber or something. Can we first go settle the bill?'

'You're not going home alone, and the bill is settled,' Ronny declared, in an end-of-discussion tone.

Laila breathed deeply to calm herself and said, 'What do you mean the bill is settled?'

'I'll take care of it. Let's go.'

'Wait. Let's split it.'

'Arrey, it's fine—don't worry about it.' Ronny's voice betrayed annoyance, as if *she* were being unreasonable.

'Listen, you didn't even eat or drink much. I'd really feel much more comfortable if you let me pay or at least split the bill. Please,' Laila added as an afterthought.

But Ronny wouldn't listen to reason. He seemed to take offense that the girl was offering to pay for their date. After arguing for a minute or so, Laila thought it best to let it go. His ego was hurt and he became more and more unreasonable by the second. To avoid another argument, Laila let him drive her home as well. He seemed much happier once they were back in the car and the music was back on.

'Usher-Vusher is great and all but nothing comes close to Honey Singh, yaar. No comparison only,' he announced, having a good old time singing along. 'I'll take you clubbing to this place in Gurgaon next time—faad music. Full desi.'

Laila loved the clubs in Gurgaon that played Hindi music, but somehow, no matter how hard she tried, she couldn't imagine herself being sucked into a second date with Ronny. Ronny, on the other hand, seemed very happy. The night was probably a grand success to his mind, but outside the small world inside his head—not so much.

When they reached Laila's house, he hit the brakes rather harshly, causing them both to jerk forward. After steadying herself, Laila turned to him and said awkwardly, 'Umm, good night then.' She pulled on the door handle, not wanting to prolong the disaster date any more.

'Wait!' Ronny said, leaning in. Laila had barely turned back towards him when she realized he was aiming straight for her lips. She moved away and Ronny ended up planting a kiss on her cheek. He laughed. 'Why such a hurry? Stay with me, baby.'

'Ronny,' Laila said in a firm voice, one hand on the door and the other one clutching her purse securely. 'I think you got the wrong idea. This ... isn't happening.'

'What do you mean? You didn't have fun with me tonight?'

'Yes, but ...'

'Then let's have more fun!' Ronny said. He held her elbow and tried to pull her to him.

'Ronny, stop!' Laila looked at him, holding his eyes with hers. 'No.'

The smile on Ronny's face faded slowly, and Laila could see the realization slowly seep in and make its way from the real world into the little world inside his head.

'We're very different people,' Laila said evenly. 'I'm sorry, but this isn't going to work. Good night.'

With that, Laila stepped out of the car and to the gate, which creaked when she pulled it open. She made a mental note to oil it the next day as the car behind her accelerated angrily as Ronny drove away. She paused to catch her breath, her heart beating wildly in her chest. Even before she'd reached the door, Maahi pulled it open from inside and peeked at her anxiously.

'So?' she asked, following Laila inside. 'How was it?'

Laila pursed her mouth and walked wordlessly to her room, ignoring Maahi, but she persisted.

'How was it?'

'It was whatever.'

'What did you guys do?'

Struggling to control her emotions, Laila muttered, 'Let it go,' and slammed the door shut.

Maahi pulled the door open and entered. 'What happened?' she asked, sounding scared.

Laila paused near her bed and spun around to face Maahi. She had had enough. First Ronny and now Maahi. Why did people think they could or should dictate what she should do even when she didn't want to do it? All she wanted was to be left alone, but Maahi had had to come marching in, asking questions that Laila made clear she didn't want to answer. All her anger at Maahi, pent up from the week and that horrible night, came rushing out of her. 'What happened is that he is a child who decided to take over the evening and made decisions for me *all night*. He fed me, *literally* fed me chicken tikka masala, which he ordered, by the way, without even asking me if I ate meat. What if I were a vegetarian? And what if I didn't like champagne or didn't drink at all? He made me dance like a couple and wouldn't let me go, or just be, for *one* fucking second. He did all of the things he probably thought were sweet in his own little world and instead of it being Laila and Ronny, we spent the night trying to be his perfect, imaginary couple, probably from some bad rom com. It was like he was following a script—checking off a list of things he was supposed to do. He wouldn't even let me pay for my meal—even when I told him it would make me way more comfortable.'

Maahi was staring at Laila horror-struck, worried that her friend might burst into flames. The way Laila was feeling, internal combustion didn't seem entirely unlikely. As she inhaled huge gulps of air, Maahi left the room and reappeared a short moment later with a bottle of tequila, which she raised as a peace offering.

After glaring at Maahi for another few seconds, Laila finally sighed and nodded.

'Come with me,' Maahi said and left the room.

Laila followed her to the kitchen, where Maahi was setting up glasses. Out on the counter were two flavours of ice cream, garam masala and the bottle of tequila. Laila watched as Maahi scooped ice cream in tall glasses and sprinkled garam masala over them followed by tequila. As she began to stir the weird mixture, Laila looked at her as if she'd gone mad. 'What the fuck are you even doing?'

'Just trust me.'

'Are you joking? You're the last person I trust right now. I prefer this,' Laila said, taking a swig of tequila straight from the bottle. 'This stupid dating game—it's not my scene, man,' she said, sliding down against the counter to the floor.

Maahi joined her a minute later, once she was done stirring or whipping or whatever on earth she was doing, with two glasses full of dirty brown liquid. 'That bad?' Maahi asked softly, slipping next to her and handing her a glass.

'Dude.' Laila turned to Maahi and looked at her. 'He. Asked. Me. My. Hobbies,' she muttered slowly.

They sat in silence for a moment, frozen like statutes, before bursting into laughter. Once they began laughing, they couldn't stop. Tears escaped from the corners of Laila's eyes and her entire body relaxed, as she finally let go of her anger and annoyance and let herself laugh at the humour of the situation.

'And somehow,' Laila said between chuckles, holding the stitch in her stomach, 'not once in the entire evening did he ask me what I did for a living!'

'Seriously?' Maahi exclaimed, looking less anxious now that they were laughing. She contained her giggles long enough to take a sip of her drink. 'Try it. Might help.'

'That looks disgusting.' Laila screwed up her nose.

'Yep—disgusting and delicious.'

Laila relented. She took a hesitant sip as Maahi watched her. Laila gulped, waited a moment, and looked up at Maahi approvingly. She was surprised to find that the disgusting brown liquid wasn't half as bad as she'd expected. It was warm in her throat in a way that ice cream should never be, but cooler than tequila should feel. It wasn't good but still way better than the rest of her night had been.

'I told you!' Maahi declared victoriously.

'Well, you also told me to go on a date with Ronny from the gym. So forgive me if I don't trust your judgement immediately!' Laila laughed at the worried expression that immediately reappeared on Maahi's face. 'But fine, I trust you on this,' she added, taking another swig of the cocktail as proof.

Maahi relaxed again and began asking Laila for more details of her date. They talked for hours, sitting with their legs stretched out before them, on the cool kitchen floor. Three brown cocktails later, they agreed that Maahi would never ever try to set Laila up for a date again.

6
COFFEE

Maahi kept her drunken word, and Laila spent the next few weeks in peace. Apart from having to find a new gym, she'd come out of that disastrous date pretty much unscathed and they put it behind them. But just because that matter was put to rest didn't mean that Maahi hadn't come up with other ways to give Laila a headache.

Since Laila and Maahi had divided their roles from the very beginning, they weren't as good at some operations of Cookies + Cupcakes as others. Maahi knew nothing about inventory and ordering and Laila didn't know much about their digital marketing plans and brand design. While they didn't necessarily need to have complete knowledge of what the other person did and how, they agreed that it was a good idea to at least show each other the basics.

The plan seemed both reasonable and easily executable in theory, but as soon as they began, Maahi got distracted. She became obsessed with the idea of expanding Cookies + Cupcakes further. They opened their first shop one year ago, and the second five months ago and quite honestly, they weren't in a position to expand the operation just yet. And even if they were, Laila wasn't sure that was necessarily what she wanted for their brand.

'For the last time, Maahi—not now. Not yet,' Laila said.

'I hear you. But would you listen to me for just one second, please? We've done so much better than we'd imagined. People want more—I'm telling you. There was this group of kids that came in this morning? They love our cupcakes so much, they want us to make a cake out of cupcakes for their friend's birthday!'

'We don't do cakes.'

'Dude, but we can. It's—'

'We're a specialty bakeshop. We do cookies and cupcakes—exclusively. That's our selling point—we concentrate on the things we do best and do them better each time, and that is what sets us apart. We're only two people, Maahi, and if we take on too much, we'll be less than extraordinary. Is that what you want?' Laila said.

Maahi went silent and then muttered, 'When you put it like that...'

'Because you refuse to listen! We can't become arrogant or pretend to know everything because we haven't been doing this very long—and we've got so much more to learn.'

'Yeah. Yeah, okay, but can we please just do this one?' Maahi spoke quickly just as Laila was about to interrupt, 'For the kid. It's his birthday and I already said yes. And I *am* sorry, but I already said yes. I promise you it's not a cake in the shape of a cupcake or anything. It's going to be actual cupcakes placed on a base of a huge-ass cookie, arranged in the shape of a pig.'

'A pig.'

'A silly, fat, pink pig with a snout and a swirly tail and everything. I have designs, see?' Maahi pushed a notepad with a pencil sketch towards Laila. 'That's the cookie base at the bottom and the cupcakes on top. I'll need to make sure I get the colour of the frosting right, and we could use smaller cookies in different shapes for the snout and the eyes.'

Laila took a moment to think it through. 'I'll allow it,' she finally said. 'As long as we're sticking with cookies and cupcakes. Maybe add some green mini cupcakes on the bottom corners for a shrub or something?'

'Good idea!' Maahi said, grinning widely. 'And it would be so great for our social. Just imagine how much love this post will get on Instagram! People love cute stuff, and our pig is going to be so damn cute.'

Laila laughed. 'I'm sure. By the way, I was thinking—should we invest in a good camera? I mean you're pretty good with your iPhone, no offense, but a professional camera could be a game changer for our social. Check this out.' Laila led Maahi to their minuscule office, not much bigger than a cupboard. There was a door on one end, opening into the bakery and a long desk shoved against the opposite wall with two chairs placed next to each other. The only slightly redeeming feature of this cupboard-office was the window in front of the desk, from where they could see the street outside. So even though they were basically sitting in a cupboard, it was a cupboard with a view. Laila pulled out her laptop and opened a few Instagram accounts. 'Look at how clean these images are. Sharp, minimal and very chic. Also, not hard to achieve. We make new, cool desserts every day—all we have to do is take beautiful pictures.'

'Totally agreed. A good camera and also, we should get Photoshop. A little contrast and exposure adjustment is the difference between a good and a great picture,' Maahi said sagely.

Laila rolled her eyes. 'What else can we do? We could get some cute crockery. Not entire sets, but individual plates and bowls in different designs and colours. Perhaps some place mats to mix up the background?'

'Dude, *I* handle the design!'

'Yes, and I should help. And *you* should help me with my stuff too.'

'But you do all the boring operations stuff,' Maahi moaned.

'You mean the stuff that runs this place?'

'Yeah—and I make it pretty so people come to this well-run establishment.'

'Stop being a child. We're doing this role-reversal thing at least for a few weeks. Fresh set of eyes means new ideas. I'm taking over your departments and you go do my job and apply your fresh set of eyes to find new, more efficient solutions,' Laila said firmly. 'What else did you have scheduled for today?'

Maahi seemed reluctant to speak. 'A meeting.'

'With?'

'Forget it—I'll call and cancel. You're never going to entertain the idea anyway so what's the point?'

'What? Tell me!' Laila asked, closing her laptop. 'I'll go to the meeting. Is it for design? Advertising?'

'Advertising, sort of,' Maahi said. Hesitantly, she said, 'It's with this guy I met through Instagram. He wants to collab with us.'

'Collab on Instagram? You mean we give him a shout out and he returns the favour or something like that? What's his product?'

'Coffee.'

Maahi's voice was so low, Laila barely heard her.

'Don't bother.' Maahi put her palm up before Laila could speak. 'I know—we're a specialty bakery, we don't want to dilute our brand, we don't do coffee. I'll call and cancel.'

'We don't call and cancel so late either. Where and when?'

'Roast House's coffee shop in South Ex at three. I've been talking to JD, their head of marketing. Cool guy. I could let him know that I have to cancel. I mean, if you're only planning to go and turn him down, there's no point wasting his time,' Maahi said, not trying to hide her disappointment. 'I was waiting to tell you till we had spoken—and maybe had something that would benefit both C+C and RH.'

'I'll hear him out.'

'You will?' Maahi's eyes widened.

'Don't get too excited. I'm not promising anything.'

Laila barely escaped Maahi's excited hug as she walked out of One. Meeting this JD guy was the least she could do to support Maahi at this point, who seemed insistent on changing things. They weren't ready to open another new shop, or to branch out into custom cakes or even to collaborate with coffee chains, but Roast House was a big fish with shops all over the country. Laila could give them half an hour of her time and find out what they were thinking.

So she drove out to South Ex. The middle-of-the-day traffic was light and she got there early. She shoved the parking slip in her bag and checked the time on her phone. She had a good twenty-five minutes. She figured she'd do some research on Roast House before the meeting.

Roast House coffee shops were all over Delhi. Laila recalled at least five branches she had seen around South Delhi. This one was the big, swanky one, with two floors that had floor-to-ceiling tinted glass walls that allowed her a view of the entire coffee shop. There were high counters with stools against the walls, where people sat with their laptops in front of them, facing the street. Impressive, Laila had to admit.

As she pulled open the door and the cool air blew her hair back from her face, she heard a consistent murmur of conversation over the music. They seemed to be playing old Hindi film songs. While she waited in line to place her order, the song changed from 'O Mere Dil Ke Chain' to 'Bahon Mein Chale Aao'. She got her coffee and found a table for two upstairs. She had been to several RH cafes before, but this one seemed to have a completely different energy. It buzzed with the chatter of millennials, scattered around in bunches, huddled in groups, heads leaning together over laptops, pushing around notes across tables, or simply chatting. The vintage Indian wooden furniture, the embroidered tapestries and carvings on the walls and ceilings teamed with glass walls, polished floors and modern architecture gave the place a fresh look—an exciting fusion of India with the West.

Laila could have spent hours just sitting there watching people, and their reaction to what the place offered. She overheard comments about the music every time a new song played. People were showing each other their unique vintage cups and plates, taking pictures. RH seemed to be doing everything right—the smell of freshly brewed coffee, the wonderful music, the interiors that gave a very Mughal-palace-like feel to the shop.

After she sipped her coffee, she found it even harder to hate the place. She had worked in a coffee shop for a few years before setting up Cookies + Cupcakes with Maahi, and remembered those days as being frustrating, sometimes even suffocating. The coffee, or even the coffee shop, wasn't to blame for it. It was her who wasn't happy there, but it was easy to shift the blame. Perhaps she could get over it and they could collaborate with Roast House after all. She wanted to hear what they had in mind first, but she promised herself she'd keep an open mind.

Reading through the emails Maahi had exchanged with this JD guy, Laila found out that this wasn't just about shout-outs on Instagram, although that would give C+C a good boost since RH had a gigantic social media following. They probably wouldn't gain anything by C+C stocking their coffee anyway. The 15,000 Instagram followers Laila had felt proud of now seemed meagre compared to the 1.2 million that followed Roast House. There was something in the emails about some people in RH liking C+C products. Maybe this wasn't an advertising thing, after all. Did they want their products—

'This seat taken?' Laila's thoughts were interrupted by a tall, lanky, goofy-looking man with curly hair pointing at the seat in front of her.

'Actually, I'm meeting someone soon—'

'I'll be super quick.' The dude had already dumped his food on the table and was pulling the chair. 'You can always kick me out if your friend arrives before I'm done shoving this down my throat.'

Laila opened her mouth to protest but let it go. Even though he looked to be in his mid-twenties, he was skinny like a nineteen-year-old. Or maybe it was just because he was so tall. But in any case, he needed to eat, and as long as he did it quietly, Laila didn't have a problem. The real problem was that he wasn't quiet.

'Ah, love this song!' he exclaimed as '*Ek Ajnabee Haseena Se*' started playing.

'Mmm.' Laila nodded politely and returned to her iPad.

'You know what—that was real romance. Brave. Fearless. Boy likes girl and just goes for it. No *talking*. No weighing options, calculating, trying to fit people into this mathematical equation you've made up in your head. They let people be and loved them for who they were.'

'Yes, Kishore Kumar was very romantic and wise.'

'You don't talk much, do you?' the dude asked, forcing huge forkfuls of green leaves into his mouth. He cut up a piece of chicken and looked up at Laila. 'This stupid diet. My friend is making me do the greens and protein thing. He's trying to bulk me up for the ladies.' He snorted.

Despite her better judgment, Laila asked, 'What's so funny?'

'I'm never going to bulk up! I have the best metabolism you'll ever see. I work a lot now so don't get time to eat that much, but even when I had nothing else to do in life and ate professionally—nah. I never gain weight.'

Not wanting to comment on this stranger's body, or talk about her own to extend the conversation, Laila smiled and turned to her iPad once again.

'You're very pretty.' He said it as an observation, as if it just occurred to him. It was so unexpected that all Laila could do was look up at him and stare. He chuckled and said, 'Not trying to hit on you or anything. Although … why not? I'm single and you're stunning and clearly smart I can tell. Are you single?'

'That doesn't concern you.'

'It does, actually. I just told you—I think you're really—'

'Dude, stop,' Laila said, not trying to be polite anymore. 'Not interested.'

She checked the time, JD would be arriving any moment now. As if reading her mind, the man said, 'Hoping for your friend to rescue you?'

'He'll be here any second. If you're done eating, would you mind giving me the chair back?'

'Sure,' he said. He looked a little upset by her blunt rejection. His face looked like that of a small child denied candy. For his boisterous, uninhibited behaviour, he seemed to be a decent person inside. 'Didn't mean to bother you or make you uncomfortable or anything. I should really put a filter on and stop saying everything I think.'

Laila watched as he picked up his empty box of salad and downed the cold-pressed juice. She felt bad about her behaviour and said, 'It's okay. You didn't make me uncomfortable, I guess.'

A slow smile spread across his face followed by a wink. 'Works every time.'

Laila narrowed her eyes.

'Here. Take my orange.'

'What?' Laila asked, staring at the fresh, whole orange inches from her face, wondering if this was some kind of a joke.

'I like you. I'm giving you my orange.'

Laila kept staring.

'It's not poisoned or anything! Come on, take it. Think of it … as a rose. Only, it's less like a rose and more like an orange. You can eat it and get nourishment instead of going to the trouble of finding a vase, filling it with water and then throwing away the depressing, dead flower a week later.'

Laila burst out laughing and he joined her. She held on to the orange but didn't take it, 'Only if you promise to leave right after.'

'I do.'

Laila took the stupid orange from him, shaking her head at his 'I do' wordplay.

He winked again, his curly hair bouncing happily as he got up. After giving Laila a goodbye salute, he walked a few steps away and looked around as if searching for something or someone. He pulled out his phone and dialled someone. 'Hello! Maahi? I'm here. Are you on your way?'

7

ORANGE

Laila gaped at the man in front of her, wondering how she hadn't seen it coming. But it had been her fault for making stereotypical assumptions. She had expected the head of marketing of a giant coffee shop chain named JD to be a middle-aged, suit-wearing, potentially bald or balding man with glasses. His name would mostly likely have been Jaideep Singhania or something. She'd clearly watched too many movies.

She cleared her throat, prepared to call out to the tall, lean man who was unable to put on weight no matter how hard his friend tried to mess with his diet. Before she could, however, he turned towards her, a rebellious curl falling over his forehead.

'Are you …' he began unsurely, taking a step towards her, 'from Cookies + Cupcakes?'

Laila got up and breathed, 'Yes.'

'You're not Maahi.'

'Astute of you to notice.'

The dude, now revealed as JD, laughed. 'Sorry—I was expecting Maahi.'

'And I was expecting…'

'Go ahead, finish that sentence. I dare you!'

Laila's eyes widened. The last thing she wanted was to offend him. She searched her head for an appropriate response, taking in the mustard and black plaid shirt he wore over a grey T-shirt. Maybe she could comment on his clothes? Or say that he looked so young—people always seemed to like being called young. In the end, hot with embarrassment, she said, 'You're not wearing a suit.'

'Astute of you to notice,' JD said, using her line from before. 'You aren't either.'

'I was stereotyping. Sorry!'

'It's all right.' JD looked down at the chair he had been occupying moments ago. 'I guess that's my chair after all.'

Laila sat down and JD followed. They both looked at each other, as if revaluating their positions and calibrating their behaviour for a business meeting, not a fateful boy-girl meet-cute at a coffee shop. He was no longer the annoying, exuberant stranger who had borrowed a seat from her for fifteen minutes and had insisted on giving her his orange. Her eyes went to the orange.

JD's eyes followed hers, and he broke down into helpless laughter. After studying him uncertainly for a brief moment, Laila joined him. People were starting to turn and stare. They must have looked like idiots, laughing uncontrollably for no apparent reason. After they managed to get their behaviour under control, Laila offered JD her hand.

'Hi, I'm Laila Kapoor.'

'Hello, Laila. I'm JD.' He shook her hand. His was firm and warm and for some reason, Laila felt that warmth travel all the way up to her cheeks.

'JD?' Laila raised her eyebrow.

'Jayesh Diwakar.'

Laila tried not to laugh, but Jayesh Diwakar noticed her struggle.

'My friends used to call me Jay, which sounded exactly like the letter J. So then, they thought it was too short and indistinctive, and decided to use my initials instead.'

'Jayesh Diwakar wasn't distinctive enough?'

'It's a bit long,' he said sourly. 'So you're a bully then? Not just to strange men who hijack seats, but also to people you're meeting for possible business liaisons?'

'Every chance I get basically.'

JD nodded intelligently. 'You must've been a terror in school.'

'Nah, I didn't bully teenagers. Just grown men.'

'Got it.'

'Grown men who give me their oranges,' Laila said. 'And have names like Jayesh Diwakar but call themselves JD to sound cool.'

'Says the girl named Laila! Are you serious?'

'Are you going to make a Laila-Majnu joke, because, you know, can you not?'

'How many of those do you get on an average?' JD grinned, which made his face look much younger.

'Two out of every three new people I meet. "Laila, as in Laila-Majnu?" and "Where's Majnu?" are staples. I also get "I could be your Majnu" occasionally.'

'Your name does provide a great pick-up line opportunity. I don't blame the guys,' JD said. He looked down for a second, and looked back up with what he probably thought was a flirtatious smile. 'Let me be your Majnu, Laila.' He finished with a wink and a click of his tongue.

'Ew.'

'Aw, come on! Don't tell me that didn't work!'

'Not even a little bit,' Laila said firmly, but a small smile managed to escape her lips.

'Aha! See. You're totally in love with me now,' JD announced victoriously, clearly pleased with himself.

'Yeah, *totally*. The "hasi toh phasi" logic?'

'Bollywood has taught me right.'

Laila rolled her eyes. She unlocked her iPad again and placed it on the table between them. 'Shall we?'

'We shall,' JD said. He pulled his laptop out of the backpack he'd dropped on the floor. He repositioned his chair so that they were now sitting at ninety degrees from each other instead of 180, and Laila bit back a personal space joke. JD's demeanour had changed from cheerful and flirtatious to strictly professional and all-business. He adjusted his laptop screen so Laila could see.

'I have a presentation for you. I would've called the meeting at our office, with the projector and everything, but I really wanted you to see this outlet.'

'That's all right. I thought this shop was very nicely done. Great concept.' Laila nodded, looking around again. 'Very connected to the root.'

'That's exactly our intention. My marketing team and I are working with the advertising and sales departments to change the way people look at Roast House. In India, modern has become synonymous with American. While that's all fine, we're also not focussing on a lot of the beautiful things we have in our country. Every single outlet of the big, international coffee chains has the exact same design. They're basically recreating the same shop everywhere. It could be literally anywhere in the world; you can't distinguish from the inside. Our intention is to make RH Indian. Our mood board is very medieval India, everything inspired by mahals—carvings, tapestries, fabrics, embroideries, crockery, furniture, lighting. While on the other hand, the products we offer are world class, so it's a fun fusion. Which is what sets—'

'—you apart from your competition.'

'Exactly.'

'And you're planning to incorporate this model across the country?' Laila asked.

'That's the plan. We tested it at three major locations and so far …' JD looked around, waving both his hands to point out the bustling crowd surrounding them. 'It'll take us about a year to fully renovate—we're doing it a few stores at a time so that we don't shut down completely at any point.'

'Yeah, that's not a good idea.'

'No kidding. I can't even imagine what would happen if we were to shut down all twenty-three stores at once. We definitely wouldn't be having this meeting.'

'What do you mean?' Laila said.

'A part of this rebranding is enhancing what we have to offer—the whole experience. This includes adding new items on the menu. We're primarily a coffee shop, so that remains our first priority. So even though we're very interested in including baked goods, we're looking to outsource it.'

'Which is why you reached out to Maahi?'

'Yes. We've been looking at bakeries in Delhi, Mumbai, Kolkata and Chennai. Ideally, we'd select a few in each of these cities, and we'd sell their products in their respective regions.'

'And how far along are you in that search?' Laila asked. She'd come to this meeting thinking Roast House wanted Cookies + Cupcakes to sell their coffee in their bakeshops, which was something Maahi had mentioned recently. But this was a completely different ball game. She wasn't sure C+C was ready for production at such a large scale yet, but if they could pull it off, it'd be huge for them—bigger than anything they had ever consciously planned, even though they usually dreamed big.

'We have a long list. For the northern region, we've shortlisted twenty-seven bakeries in the Delhi-NCR region, taking multiple aspects into consideration.'

'Including trying out their products?'

'Of course! That's the first thing we did!' JD said, the boyish grin back. 'I spent a month on a diet of cupcakes, croissants, cookies, pound cakes—every fattening baked food you can think of! Still no weight gain though,' he added as an afterthought.

Laila laughed. 'Our products are less fattening than cookies and cupcakes are expected to be. We use all organic ingredients, substitute with non-fat options wherever we can, and ... provide moderation advice.'

'Does the last one ever work?'

'Not if we do our job right!' Laila said smugly. 'Moderation goes out of the window as soon as you bite into one of my cookies.'

'I wish I could make fun of that somehow, but speaking from personal experience, you're actually very right.'

'Ha!'

'I'm easily impressed when it comes to food though. What we need now is for you, by which I mean Cookies + Cupcakes, to impress my team,' JD said more seriously. 'We're organizing a party at the CEO's bungalow in Golf Links.'

'Ooh, fancy.'

'Overlooking India Gate—*very* fancy. The point is, we're inviting everyone on the longlist to set up a table on his front lawn, showcasing their best stuff. All RH employees will be attending, along with a long list of VIP guests of the CEO and we're having each of them pick the three tables they like the best. I don't know what exact parameters everyone will be judging you on, but I'll take a wild guess and say taste and quality. In fact, to ensure that we get unbiased opinions, we're giving you numbers and keeping the names of your bakeries a secret.'

Laila nodded thoughtfully. 'So it's like a swayamwar.'

'Not exactly …' JD looked at Laila uncertainly.

'I'm just kidding! But yeah, this sounds exciting! Count us in. When is this fancy party?'

'This Friday.'

Laila's jaw dropped. 'You're saying … *this* Friday. As in three days from now? Is this a joke?'

'Look, I know it's short notice, but we also need to see if you can deliver enough goods on short notice. If we end up signing with you, you'd need to increase your production several times over without increasing the production time too much.'

Laila thought for a moment. It was near impossible, but there was no other response. 'Yes,' she said. 'We're in.'

'Excellent. I'll send over details—venue, head count, dietary restrictions and all that. Folks from RH stores will be helping you set up your counter and we're assigning two per bakery. I'll connect you with them on email and you can sort out the plan amongst yourselves?'

'Sounds good.'

'I guess that's all then,' JD said, packing up his laptop. He got up and turned to Laila, who also got up, shoving her iPad back into her bag. He stuck out his hand, 'Pleasure meeting you.'

'Same.' Laila shook his hand. He wouldn't let go.

'I have to admit—I won't be an impartial judge at the party.'

'Maybe you shouldn't come then.'

'Oh, you're not getting rid of me that easily,' JD said, his grin back. 'Besides, my vote will help you.'

'Meh. It's one vote. It'll get lost in the many, many others we get.'

'Ouch. To think that after everything we've been through together, my vote is just that for you ... one vote, like any other...'

'Stop pouting,' Laila said. 'God, you're dramatic.'

'Don't call me dramatic—these are my feelings and you're hurting them. I even gave you my orange.'

Laila looked back at the table, where the sad little orange sat next to her empty coffee cup. She picked it up, trying and failing to stop the smile spreading across her face.

When she reached home, Laila lay down on the living room couch for a while, going over the game plan for the next few days. Collaborating with Roast House would be huge for them. She planned to call their investors and mentor first thing the next morning to discuss this opportunity. They were doing very well on their own locally, but when a national chain as big as RH added your products to their menu, things tended to blow up overnight. Their customer base would go from the few thousand who frequented Shahpur Jat and Hauz Khas Village to the lakhs of people who patronised RH outlets in northern India.

Of course, it was a very long shot. They were competing with twenty-six other bakeries and the competition was only three days away. She sat up, held her bag upside-down over the centre table and shook it. Finding a pen, a notepad and Post-its, she began writing down her ideas. The first thing they'd have to do was set a timeline. Once that was done, they could take each task at a time.

'You're here!' came a voice from the door that flung open.

'I'm aware. I live here.'

'I'm aware,' Maahi repeated. 'But you never returned to the shop. I had to take the metro back.'

'Oh.' Laila looked up. 'Right. Sorry—I forgot to tell you I was heading straight home.'

'What's all this?' Maahi came closer and angled her head to try and see what Laila was writing.

'Plans for the fancy party the Roast House CEO is throwing this Friday.'

Maahi looked exasperated. 'Now you're interested in Roast House? Why are all ideas bad when I suggest them, but one meeting with those guys and you're suddenly in?'

'He gave me his orange,' Laila said quietly.

'So what—? Wait. What?' Maahi paused. 'Who gave you his orange?'

'JD.'

'Is that some kind of new slang for virginity? Are we not calling it *flower* anymore?'

'Ew, no! I didn't take the dude's virginity. He *literally* gave me his orange.' Laila pointed towards it, lying on the table between the junk from her bag.

'What's so special about that orange? And why did he—' Maahi stopped suddenly and sat down on the other side of the table, facing Laila. 'Do you like him? He's cute, isn't he? I've never met him, but we follow each other on Instagram.'

'He looks like someone who'd be secretly famous on Instagram.'

'With the hair and all? Plus he's *so* tall! Looks a little like Kunal Kapoor to be honest.'

'I guess …' Laila said, thinking. 'No, not really. I don't see it.'

'What's this orange thing though?'

'He said "I like you. Take my orange" and so I took it.'

'So you like him back?' Maahi asked excitedly. 'You guys should date. You'd be so cute toge—'

'Okay, stop,' Laila said. The sudden seriousness in her voice made Maahi pause and stare at her nervously. 'Never again. We decided you won't bring up dating again. I don't do that. I … can't. I'm only telling you this to make you stop with this nonsense. You have to promise to keep it a secret—never bring it up with anyone including me.'

'What … ?' Maahi asked slowly.

Laila took a breath and prepared herself. She'd say it once and she'd say it quickly and clearly. And when she was done, they would bury the topic forever and never talk about it again. 'I used to be married,' she began, and spoke in bullet points for Maahi's benefit. 'His name was Abhishek—he was my best friend in college—we fell in love—got married right after college—he died in an accident eight months and three days after our wedding—he was hit by a Mercedes driven by a seventeen-year-old kid under the Moolchand flyover—I was twenty-two—it's been six years—I'm over it—but I don't play the dating game—I don't like oranges anymore—so stop.'

There was a deep, confounded silence.

Maahi's mouth was half-open, her eyes fixed on Laila's. She breathed, 'You're *joking*.'

Laila didn't say a word, but just held Maahi's eyes.

'Oh God …' Maahi said, her eyes suddenly filling up with tears. 'Oh my God … I'm so sorry … Oh God…'

'Maahi—stop. Please. Just … can we not?'

'Okay … okay.' Laila could see Maahi physically control herself.

'Anyway, listen,' Laila said. She spoke quickly, her voice breaking. 'Roast House is very into keeping Indian culture front and centre. We're setting up a counter at this fancy party this weekend, and it's a formal event. People will be wearing suits and gowns. I was thinking we could wear Indian formal wear. I have a trunk full of fancy saris, lehengas, suits—you know, from when I was married. Let's have a look.' Laila closed her notebook and got up. 'Come on,' she said to Maahi, who was still frozen on the spot.

Maahi hadn't moved since Laila had told her about Abhishek, her eyes wide, tears flowing uninhibited down her cheeks. 'Let's go,' Laila repeated and made her way to her mother's room, aware of Maahi's stunned gaze at her back. The faster Maahi got over it, the sooner they could move on and get back to business.

8

THE BRINK

Laila's back hurt worse than her neck, and her neck hurt a lot. She had been on her feet for eight hours straight, and yet they were nowhere close to being done. She had four trays full of cookie batter waiting to be baked, but no free ovens. She was baking at Two with Javed to help her, while Maahi was at One, working with Ram. Even though they worked quickly and efficiently, they simply weren't equipped enough to produce such a large amount of goods in such a short amount of time. They had two industrial-sized ovens, one in each shop, but according to the guest list JD had sent over, there were going to be roughly five hundred people at the party. Laila was interested in seeing how big this bungalow and its lawn were to contain these many people.

Since there were twenty-seven bakeries offering their products, in all certainty, not all five hundred guests would come to their counter, or if they did, they couldn't possibly eat from every single counter. However, they had to make sure that if every single person showed up to their counter, they had enough for everyone. Selling out was a good thing, but not if potential voters wouldn't get samples. Laila wanted to do 500 of cookies and cupcakes each. Maahi thought it made more sense to do 250 cookies and 250 cupcakes. After many arguments, they finally reached a compromise they could both live with—350. It was already Thursday evening, and the only way they'd be able to reach their target was if they pulled an all-nighter.

After loading all the remaining trays they had with cookie dough, Laila took a step back and re-evaluated the situation. The kitchen at Two was filled with all sorts of cookies. There were no empty surfaces. It looked as if the cookies were building an army to overthrow the government and take the iron throne.

'Thoda zyada nahin ho gaya?' Javed commented, following her gaze.

'Kya karein?' Laila said. 'It's the demand. This kitchen definitely wasn't built do handle this scale of production.'

'How many more do we have to make?'

'About a hundred. The main issue at hand is storage though. Let me call up Maahi and see how it's going at One.' She sat down on a stool by the kitchen counter and dialled Maahi.

'Don't even ask!' Maahi cried as soon as she answered.

'*That* bad?'

'It's impossible. I still have, like, 200 more cupcakes to do and we don't have enough trays and oh God, there's. NO. Space. I can bake more, but I'll have to put them on my head!'

'Well, that's one way to accessorize!' Laila laughed.

'Not funny, Laila! I'm dying here—for real.'

'I know. It's getting pretty bad here too. Want to go out for a couple of hours—take a break? We could check out the venue, figure out storage and transportation? Javed, can you stay here a couple of extra hours and finish baking these?' Laila asked. When he gave her a thumbs up, she said into the phone, 'It's cool with Javed. Ask Ram if he can handle One.'

'Yeah, I have enough batter in moulds to keep him occupied for a while. Ram, will you be ...' Maahi's voice faded away for a second, before she returned and spoke more loudly, 'Yeah, cool with Ram too.'

Ten minutes later, Laila honked in front of One, and Maahi came rushing out, looking like an escaped prisoner.

'It's intense in there,' Maahi exhaled loudly, getting into the car. 'Where are we going?'

'To the fancy CEO's fancy bungalow in Golf Links.'

'Right. We should've done this yesterday—or the day before. Setting up is going to take all day tomorrow. What time is the party? 6 p.m., right? We'll have to set up the table, bring everything over without breaking or crushing or squashing, and we have to find a way to decorate to make sure it looks pretty—presentation is key—and stash the rest of the goods somewhere they won't go bad. It's still really hot, especially for August, and this thing is outdoors.'

'Whoa. It's a good thing that you're not freaking out or anything.' Laila chuckled.

'How is this funny?' Maahi almost looked hurt at Laila's behaviour.

'Dude, we can do our best and that's all we have. The primary concern is the product and, well, it isn't exactly under control at the moment—but it will be. For everything else, we have the whole day to figure it out. The two people from RH are going to help us with transportation and storage at the venue. We only have to worry about storing everything at C+C.'

'Yeah, everywhere I look, I see cupcakes. I mean, of course, we're a bakery, but I've never seen so many cupcakes at the same time in real life.'

'Oh, let's buy that camera!'

'What? Now?' Maahi asked, looking at Laila as if she'd gone mad.

'Why not? We're going to pay the exact same amount whether we buy it today or next week, so why wait? We can do behind-the-scenes pictures at both shops before we pack everything away.'

'We *are* doing all of this for the first time ... Okay, yes. I think it's a good idea. I could post hourly updates on Instagram.'

'Then you'll be posting a lot because we'll be baking all night long, girl.' Laila grinned. Even with all the pressure and last-minute panic, this was exciting. To think that a year ago, they had barely been able to pool everything they had and start the first shop. This felt surreal. Even if they didn't end up collaborating with Roast House, just doing the party was a big deal. If they ended up signing ... Laila couldn't even begin to imagine how quickly the scope of their business would change. It felt as if they were right on the brink of something big, and it very well could be this.

'Do they know we're coming?' Maahi asked.

'Yes, I called the RH guys. They'll show us our spot and go over the transportation and all that. JD's email said they've apparently set up a walk-in freezer in the fancy CEO's fancy backyard.'

'I'll be a fancy CEO one day.'

'Be a fancy social media manager right now! Have you decided which camera we should get? We could look up some stores on the way.'

They ended up making a short detour to buy the camera Maahi had chosen online. Pleased with how productive they were being, Laila drove straight towards Golf Links. As she reached the address Google Maps brought her too, Laila's mouth gaped. She had expected it to be fancy, considering it was the fancy CEO's fancy bungalow, but this was another level of wealth.

'How is this a real thing?' Maahi muttered next to her.

'This is no bungalow. This is a fucking palace.'

'Un. Real.'

Laila shook her head in disbelief. 'How does one person afford this kind of real estate right in the middle of the national capital?'

They were right in front of a gigantic black metal gate, where they waited for someone to let them in. Laila pulled closer to the gate and heard a voice over the intercom ask who she was.

'We're from Cookies + Cupcakes. We're here to check out the venue for tomorrow's fan—' Laila stopped herself just in time. 'Party. Tomorrow's party.'

'One minute.'

Laila looked at Maahi, who giggled.

'Welcome,' said the voice a moment later, and the gate opened in the middle, slowly parting to let them in. Laila drove on the gravel path, which was surrounded on both sides by vast lawns. The bungalow had its own driveway, leading up to the five storied building, which looked nothing less than a mansion. The walls were made of red brick and smooth clear glass and were surrounded by beautiful, exotic-looking shrubbery. Laila could see an infinity pool on the right, with tall Ashok trees on one side and lounge chairs on the other. When she'd reached the front of the bungalow, she slowed down, and a valet rushed forward to greet her.

'Welcome, ma'am!' He looked not a day older than twenty-one. 'I'll take your car from here. Just call for Jasmeet when you're ready to go.'

'O … kay.' Laila got out of the car and exchanged a look with Maahi over the hood. Maahi had also got out and was looking around. Jasmeet drove away swiftly, leaving Laila and Maahi with their mouths hanging open. 'Talk about fancy!'

'You've got to stop saying fancy,' Maahi said. 'You almost said it to the intercom lady or robot or whoever.'

'This is beyond fancy. This guy must be so insanely loaded.'

'Clearly.'

They looked at the lawns, divided right in the middle by a gravel path leading up to the bungalow. There were many people on the right side of the lawn, motioning with their arms as if drawing a sketch in the air. There were no tents, canopies, tables or anything in sight, just a bunch of people looking around, measuring lengths. Laila guessed the CEO was the kind of person who could pay to ensure the event planners were quick and efficient. Not knowing where to go, Laila called one of the RH guys to let them know they were there.

A middle-aged man wearing a magenta shirt and square glasses left the group on the lawn and walked swiftly towards them.

'Hi, you're Laila?' he asked.

'Yes. Hi Praveen, this is my partner Maahi.'

'Nice to meet you both,' he said, sounding preoccupied and rushed. 'Come with me. Your table will be six feet by four, covered in a white tablecloth with a silver pattern on it, in case you wish to coordinate your food stuff accordingly to go with the colours. We also have large bowls, platters, trays and all that at the back, which you can pick and reserve now.'

'Sounds good,' Laila said crisply, walking next to him on the soft lawn.

'You also mentioned something about a freezer?' Maahi asked.

'Yes—that's also at the back. I'll show you. Okay, here. This is your spot.'

Laila and Maahi looked around. It was the corner-most space, facing the bungalow. Laila nodded. 'Great.'

'Good. Let me show you the freezer now.'

It took them ten minutes to do a full circle of the bungalow, stopping by the freezer, the door to the restrooms, an actual locker room for their personal belongings while they worked out front, and a kitchen where refreshments for the staff would be available. Once they were done, they thanked Praveen for his time, which was clearly very valuable, and asked if he could have Jasmeet bring their car around.

'I feel like a servant,' Maahi said, once Praveen had left.

'We practically are servants. Staff,' Laila said.

'We're CEOs too though. Not too far from having all of this.'

They were very extremely far from it, but Laila didn't have the heart to point it out to Maahi. *Let the kid dream.* 'I think tomorrow we should get here noon-ish, store the food in the freezer and start setting up the table. I'm re-thinking the pig cupcake-cake now,' Laila said, waving her arms around to point at their surroundings, just in case Maahi missed where they were standing.

'No, come on. I'm sure everyone else is doing classy and sophisticated. We'll do the bright and quirky. Trust me, the kids loved that cake.'

'Not many kids on the guest list to this fancy party.'

'Just trust me,' Maahi said, just as Jasmeet pulled up next to them with the car. 'Do we tip him?' she muttered softly.

Laila shrugged. They looked at each other for a second before giving up and getting into the car. 'Thank you, Jasmeet,' Laila said to him as he closed the door for her. She said to Maahi as she drove away, 'I've never thought about that before—do you tip a valet at a house you're visiting? It's not a hotel, so I'm guessing not. But then what do I know? Never known anyone who hired full-time valets for their house.' Laila made a mental note to ask JD if he ever tipped the valet.

'Also, technically, we're staff too. And staff don't tip other staff.'

'Especially unpaid staff don't tip the paid staff.'

'I know, right?' Maahi's face twisted with worry. 'How broke are we now? Buying all of these ingredients and everything…'

'Quite broke, but if they like us, it'll all be worth it … and more. And they're going to pay us for this afterwards regardless of the outcome, so we'll be all right.'

'It's insane, isn't it? I didn't know what JD wanted to talk about when he asked for that meeting, but I definitely didn't imagine *this*. This could be so huge.'

Laila was quiet for a moment, remembering her instinct from before. She spoke evenly, looking straight ahead, 'You know, I've had this feeling for some time now, that we're on the brink of something big. Something that's right in front of us but we're missing. We can't see it yet, but years from now, we'll look back and realize it was right there all along.'

'And this could be it?'

Laila nodded slowly. 'Who knows? I thought really hard about the idea of making Cookies + Cupcakes a nationwide chain, but it just didn't seem right. It would become too commercial, and not be personal at all. Also, how are we going to manage multiple stores in multiple cities just yet? We'd become businesswomen exclusively, the actual baking will go right out of the window. And then there's your custom cakes idea, which is too small. But this? This could be it. We'll be producing everything in one place, it'll all originate from here, right from us, so we'll control everything from one central location as we do right now. Except, it'll be distributed much more widely, validated under the influential and trusted name of Roast House.'

Maahi looked at her, eyes wide in excitement. 'Do you think we'll get in?'

'We're at the brink of … *something*.'

'This is something!'

Laila shrugged. 'Maybe,' she said, trying hard not to count C + C's chickens before they hatched, but at the same time, she felt hopeful.

9

FANCY

Laila woke up to find her right cheek covered in frosting, the cupcake underneath the frosting was completely crushed, which suggested that she'd been using a cupcake as a pillow. When she attempted to sit up, her bones and muscles screamed with stiffness. She also realized that she was freezing, having slept on the bakery floor, with the AC on and without a blanket. She sniffed and reached for the remote, which turned out to be a remote for the TV screen. Unable and unwilling to stand or even sit up fully, she dragged her half-asleep body to the air conditioner like a snail. As she got closer to the AC, a cool burst of air made her sneeze twice in quick succession, shaking her entire body.

'Maahi,' she groaned, pressing the power button to stop the chilly torture. She saw a colourful lump that could only be Maahi's clothes on the floor next to the counter. The last thing she remembered before they both passed out from exhaustion was sitting down on the floor at around six in the morning, after having put the second last batch of cupcakes in the oven.

Laila had finished with her cookies at Two around midnight and had come to One to help Maahi out with her cupcakes, which required more time because of the additional step after baking: icing. They'd baked all night, up until dawn, but a moment of weakness, sitting down for a few minutes, just to close their eyes had ended up in this. Laila let out another exaggerated moan, louder this time, 'Maahiiiii!'

'What? What? Oh shit!' Maahi suddenly sat up, her eyes wide open. 'Time kya hain?'

'Phone,' Laila said, speaking through gritted teeth, pointing at her phone lying on the floor next to Maahi.

'10.47 a.m.'

'Fuck, fuck, fuck!' Laila looked around, slightly panicky, assessing the situation.

'How did this happen? Dammit, I still have those last trays of cupcakes left to bake and oh God, I need to frost the ones in the oven!' Maahi said, getting up quickly and plugging both their phones in to charge. 'Dude, get up!'

'I'm dying.'

'Die tomorrow. Today's the fancy party, the big account, the cute guy with the curly hair—'

'Stop,' Laila said. She rubbed her face to wake herself up. 'Fuck. All right, let's see what we have. Fuck the last batch of cupcakes, let's do the frosting on the batch in the oven, and let's leave.'

'Why isn't anyone here yet? Where's Javed? Wait, no, we're at One,' Maahi said, looking around, clearly still a little disoriented. 'Ram. Ram kahan hain?'

'I told everyone to get here at noon. I thought that's when we'd all leave for the fancy bungalow together.'

'Should I call one of them and ask them to come in right now? Like, if Ram comes now, he could probably do the last batch of—'

'Okay, do it. I'm getting started on the frosting.' Laila got up and dashed towards the kitchen, almost tripping. 'Ugh, head rush.' She paused at the counter for a second to regain her balance and dashed to the kitchen again, successfully this time.

A second later, Maahi appeared. 'Javed's coming. I called Ram first, but he still hasn't decided his outfit for the fancy party. Seemed excited though.'

'We could've been excited too if we had our shit together. That's the difference between working for someone else and working for yourself. There's always more we could be doing,' Laila said, her hands moving in a swift, certain manner.

'We've got this,' Maahi said.

'We've got this.'

'We have it,' Maahi said.

'Yes, we have it,' Laila said. 'Now let's stop panicking and do what you do best!'

They got to work. Without wasting any more time, they worked efficiently with each other in perfect synchronicity. It took them forty-five minutes to finish icing the entire batch of cupcakes, by which time Javed had arrived. He took over the last batch, letting Laila and Maahi rush home to shower and change.

'Where's the stupid blouse?' Laila yelled in the direction of Maahi's room.

'Where's the food? I'm starving.' Maahi appeared from the bathroom, wrapped in a pink towel with ugly blue and green flowers on it.

'Where's my blouse?'

'Oh, drying outside with the rest of the clothes.'

'I thought we were getting everything dry-cleaned?' Laila asked.

'There was no time. I had to hand-wash your fancy sari and the fancy suit you've so kindly agreed to lend me.'

Laila rushed to the backyard and gathered everything from the clothesline, pinning the clips back on the now empty rope. 'These are completely crumpled. We'll have to get them ironed. You know what, let's just skip the Indian thing and wear western formal.'

'NO!' Maahi spun around quickly, holding a half-buttered slice of bread. 'Your sari is beautiful and so is the suit. I'll get them ironed. We can wear normal clothes for now and after we're done setting up the table at the venue, we can change into these.'

'Fine. Whatever. But wear something nice, just in case we don't get a chance to change.'

'We will. I'll make sure we will,' Maahi said, her mouth full of food. She pointed to the bread in the toaster. 'Want one?'

They ate quickly and got dressed. Laila suspected Maahi wore her dirtiest jeans and baggiest T-shirt deliberately so that there would be no way they could bypass changing. Her T-shirt literally said "MEH!" in all caps, but Laila didn't have time to get into it. They went to One first, where Ram and Aparna had joined Javed and they were packing the last of the cupcakes into clear, clamshell containers, ready to travel.

'All right, Ram, could you stay here with the cupcakes till the guys from RH come to pick them up?'

'Akele?' Ram asked, childishly.

'Dude, trust me, you're not missing any fun. Close the shop and come to Two once the RH people have loaded everything. We'll go pack the cookies now,' Laila said.

Once at Two, everyone worked swiftly. They were done in no time, and while they waited for Ram to get there with the RH people, Maahi quickly ran out to drop their outfits off for ironing.

'So, everyone's coming?' Laila asked, sitting down on one of the couches.

'Obviously,' Javed said.

'Yes!' cried Aparna, who apparently hadn't thought she was invited.

'Cool. So, we'll shut down both shops for today. Aparna, could you make a sign for the window saying we'll open late tomorrow? Probably noon-ish,' Laila said. 'We're all out of everything.'

'Sab ho jaaega,' Javed said, 'if everyone comes at eight a.m, tomorrow morning.'

'Except you, Aparna. You can come a little later, since we're not opening the counter till noon.'

'I can come early to help too. I'm sure there will be lots to do after the party and everything.'

'Great, thanks!' Laila said, smiling at Aparna's enthusiasm. 'There's Ram. Let's get started, kids!'

After they'd loaded everything in the van and double-checked to make sure all seemed right, Laila turned to her people. Lowering her cap to shield her eyes from the brutal afternoon sun, she asked, 'One person needs to go with them in the van. The rest can come in the car. Volunteers?' She looked from Maahi to Javed to Aparna to Ram, none of whom moved a muscle. She tossed her car keys to Maahi. 'Fine. I'll do it. You're all spoiled.'

Laila climbed the back of the van and crouched next to the cartons of cookies and cupcakes stacked on top of each other. She removed her cap and wiped her forehead.

'All okay?' Maahi asked, peeking in through the door.

'Yep. Got to make sure none of these fall.' She pointed to the mountain of baked goods they'd worked tirelessly on making over the last few days, and the last few years.

'See you soon,' Maahi said and slammed the door shut, leaving Laila in the darkness.

'Chalein?' came a voice from the front.

'Chalo!' Laila said.

Half an hour later, when the door reopened, Laila squinted against the sunlight and put her cap and sunglasses back on before getting off. Her team was waiting right outside with a trolley.

'How did you beat us here?' Laila asked in surprise.

'She drives like a maniac!' Aparna said, her face pink in the sun.

Maahi grinned. 'There was no traffic.'

'Because everyone was scared of the crazy lady driving like a maniac!' Ram said.

'God, I work with such children!' Laila exclaimed. 'Javed, a little help here? Let's load everything on the trolley and take it to the freezer at the back of the fancy bungalow. We can pick whatever we need for the initial setup from there and come back out front.'

'I'll go show Aparna our spot and begin setting up the table,' Maahi said. 'So, were you any good at art and craft in school?' she asked Aparna as they walked away.

After a few minor hiccups, which involved the accidental dropping of a dozen cupcakes on the lawn, the tearing of their tablecloth and the hot Delhi sun, which were rectified with the whole team dropping to their knees to clean up the mess on the grass, Aparna using expert safety-pin hacks on the tablecloth and Ram running to a nearby store to get three large umbrellas, they were all set.

'Stay close to the table so the food remains under the shade too,' Maahi said.

'Actually, I don't think this will work. The party officially begins at 6 p.m.—it's only 4.38 p.m. now. I'm sure nobody's coming for another two hours,' Laila said. She thought for a second. 'Who needs to change?'

'Me,' Maahi and Aparna said together.

'I just need to put my coat on over this,' Ram said. He was wearing a pink shirt with formal navy trousers. 'It's in the locker in the back.'

'I'm ready,' Javed said, pointing to his maroon and black pathani kurta pyjama.

'Let's take everything back into the freezer for now. The guys can bring it all back out in an hour.'

'Are you joking? What about the pig?!' Maahi cried. 'It took me an hour to assemble!'

'We won't break any arrangements. But we can't leave these out in the sun either!'

'You're just trying to find an excuse to stay back so you don't have to change!' Maahi glared at Laila. 'Javed and Ram will make sure everything remains under the umbrellas till we get back, won't you, guys?'

'We will,' Ram said.

'Easier than the back and forth,' Javed agreed.

'Fine,' Laila reluctantly gave in. She was the one who had suggested wearing ethnic clothes to begin with, but now that it was time to actually wear them, she really wasn't in the mood to get back into the clothes that reminded her of her marriage, of Abhishek. She fought the knot in her chest, looking out of the window, as Maahi drove like a maniac and Aparna sat at the back muttering prayers.

They picked up the freshly ironed clothes on the way to Two, where Aparna had left her outfit. Maahi went into the tiny office, Aparna went behind the counter to change and Laila took her sari to the kitchen.

As Laila spread out the sari, she felt a constriction in her throat. Her face suddenly felt hot, and she quietly walked to a corner and placed her head against the wall. She closed her eyes and let the feelings wash over her. She didn't have the time to breakdown; it couldn't have been worse timing. She clutched her chest with her hand, feeling it rise and fall rapidly, still holding the sari. She took measured, deliberate breaths to calm herself down. Once her breathing returned to normal, she wiped her face and pulled back from the wall.

Careful not to get anything on the fabric, in swift, sure movements, she draped the sari around herself. Even though she was wearing one after several years, it took her under five minutes to put it on. She folded the pallu and pinched it together between her fingers.

Laila cleared her throat and called out, 'Safety pin, anyone?'

'Yep,' Maahi said, appearing a moment later, rifling through her handbag, wearing Laila's suit. The kurta hugged her body like a second skin. It was white with a deep neck and back, paired with a multi-coloured bandhej salwar and chunni with mirror work on it. Laila remembered that the fabric was silk, extremely soft and smooth. She also remembered that it was Abhishek's favourite. She swallowed hard and looked away.

'Here, I have a big one and a tiny—' Maahi began, but paused suddenly, her hand stretched towards Laila.

'Thanks.' Laila took the safety pins from her and began securing the pleats.

'*Dude!*' Maahi said. 'You look hot. Full Bollywood heroine types! Aparna, come and look at Laila!'

'Oh my God, I love that sari!' Aparna shrieked in excitement. 'Where did you get it? I think I've seen Kareena wear something like that somewhere. So pretty!'

'It's old,' Laila said shortly. It was a plain black georgette sari with a thin, bright coral border. The blouse was a sleeveless black number covered completely in matte black sequins, cut low and held together with a knot at the back. 'You look beautiful too, Aparna.'

To avoid any further questions, Laila busied herself with make-up. The little restroom was overcrowded with three women fighting for the mirror. When they were done, Maahi took pictures for C + C's s social media and they set off to the venue. They had to make one stop on the way to buy shoes for Maahi and Aparna, who had both brought pencil heels with them. Laila was annoyed about the additional delay, but didn't want anyone to fall and hurt their ankles, so she drove them to the store. They bought wedges and block heels to navigate the lawn easily. By the time they arrived at the imposing black gates, which were left open this time, the staff was lined up on both sides, armed with guest lists and smiles, Laila was worried they were late.

However, it was only a little past six and they were relieved to see that the lawn was practically empty, except for all the tables lining the wall. They walked across the lawn to their table, admiring the other counters covered with all sorts of baked goods. The environment had a very reality-show, bake-off sort of vibe. The professional photographers scurrying about only added to that atmosphere. This party was definitely going to be covered by the local tabloids and with all participating bakeries posting about it, the bake-off was likely to trend on social media. There was a lot of buzz around it, and the excitement was rising. As Laila looked around, she felt that the place was basically a baker's heaven. There were tables laden with different kinds of breads, pastries, tarts, ganache, cupcakes, cookies, cheesecakes, croissants, pies, muffins, doughnuts, mousses, puffs, rolls and everything else imaginable. While they were extremely pleasant to look at and smell, they also gave Laila pangs of nervousness. Before guests arrived, everyone was busy taking pictures, proud of their respective displays.

Some of her anxiety was eased once they reached their table and looked at their own beautiful counter. Laila had to agree, the pig, although stupid, was also very quirky and fun and livened up their display. The sun had lowered, leaving them in the shade of the trees behind them, and the air was much cooler. Laila sat down on one of the three chairs behind their table and admired the surroundings as a smile crept on to her face.

'This is perfect,' she said. 'We're all set.'

'Loving the music,' Maahi said, looking around.

'Yeah, it's their bring-the-classics-back thing—a part of their re-branding plan, which is also why we're wearing these.' Laila pointed at their outfits.

'You look beautiful,' Ram said and as if realizing that he'd actually spoken the words aloud, he turned red and looked away.

'Thank you.' Laila laughed, catching Maahi's eye.

'You do,' Javed added. 'All of you.'

'Thanks. You gentlemen look quite dapper as well,' Laila said. 'All right—game plan. Three people behind the counter, one person needs to carry a tray around—not yet though— and one person checking what others are doing, gathering information.'

'Ooh, I'll be the spy!' Aparna said, walking away muttering something about the freezer.

'Javed and I could go around with the tray,' Ram offered.

'It'd be more effective if the girls did it, to be honest,' Javed countered.

'One girl is the spy and the other two are the owners who need to be at the counter at all times to represent the brand they worked very hard to build,' Maahi said, a little heatedly.

'Hey, I'm just saying you're all very pretty!'

'But that's not the only thing we are—'

'I didn't—'

'Simmer down, people!' Laila interjected before things escalated. 'We don't need pretty faces to sell our stuff. Just make sure to carry Cookies + Cupcakes napkins and serve every single piece on one so that people remember what they ate and where it came from.'

'Also, my cupcakes are *really* pretty too,' Maahi said.

'Fine!' Javed threw his hands up in surrender. He left, saying something about looking for a tray.

'You need to chill, girl,' Laila said, turning to Maahi, who slumped on the chair next to her. 'You're pretty, your cupcakes are pretty, this pig is pretty, this entire lawn is pretty. Look, even the sky's all pretty now. Everything's prett—'

'Not more than you though,' came a goofy voice from behind them. Laila turned to see JD standing in front of their counter, his eyes fixed on her. He was wearing a bright purple suit, which actually shone in the dull sunlight. He had a white silk shirt underneath, and a black bowtie to match the lapels on his coat.

Laila smirked. 'What do you think of our table? You know, the thing we're actually here to showcase?'

'I'm quite happy with what I see,' he said, his eyes not leaving her face for a second. 'Maybe I'll get a chance to look at the table on my next round.'

Laila rolled her eyes and glanced at Maahi, disgruntled to find that she was beaming excitedly at JD. 'Just take a look at the damn table!' Laila said.

'*Tere chehre se nazar nahin hatti, nazaare hum kya dekhein,*' JD sang softly, walking backwards, away from the counter, his eyes still on Laila.

'God, stop,' Laila groaned, just as she heard Maahi giggle next to her.

'What? It was playing at RH all day! Not everything is about you, you know?' JD called, and with that and a wink, he turned around and disappeared.

10

FANCY AFTER-PARTY

'Yes, ma'am. We use organic ingredients only,' Laila said, smiling much wider than a normal person should. 'Gluten-free.'

'I'm actually lactose intolerant ...' said the woman in a bottle-green gown, which made the bottom half of her body look like a mermaid's tail.

'Not a problem—we have dairy-free options too. Here, let me show you,' Laila said and pointed to the dairy-free section. The lady picked one and Laila placed it on a napkin and transferred it to one of the expensive-looking plates they'd been provided. Laila handed the lady a fork and said, 'Enjoy!'

'The eggs we use are a hundred per cent free range,' Maahi was informing a guest. 'We do have low-fat options too. These ones here were made using fat-free milk and cream.'

Once Maahi was done with her guest, she sat down, clearly exhausted.

'I feel you,' Laila said. 'People are more concerned about

what's not in the food than what's actually in it—gluten-free, fat-free, dairy-free, nut-free!'

'And then they don't even eat it. They just nibble.'

'I guess one doesn't fit into those fancy clothes and eat at the same time!'

'Then just eat! Why come to the party that has every single one of New Delhi's finest baked goods on offer only to not eat?' Maahi said. 'Ugh, I'm so annoyed.'

'I can see that,' Laila said. 'But take a step back and look around you, man. This is so freaking beautiful.'

And it was. As the sun had begun to set, all the lamps surrounding the lawns had turned on. To begin with, their side of the lawn, the one that offered all the dessert and sweet treats, wasn't in demand. The other side had all the appetizers and alcohol. Slowly, people had begun filing in and spreading out and the more they ate and drank, the more they leaned towards dessert. It was already close to midnight, and after the hours they spent serving the guests and constantly replenishing their stock, exhaustion was a given. Laila didn't know about Maahi, but she personally felt more exhilarated than exhausted.

'And that's the last of it,' Aparna said, bringing four large boxes of cupcakes, closely followed by Javed carrying the cookies. They set them down behind the counter and began filling up the empty spots on the table, while Maahi got busy with another guest. Ram returned with the tray.

As Laila helped him load it up again, she said, 'You guys are definitely getting a bonus.'

'*And* a raise,' Javed declared.

'Well, that depends—if we get this account. But a bonus I can promise,' Laila said.

'And a treat. We have to celebrate!' Maahi added, once her guest had left with a cookie on a fancy plate.

'Zaroor,' Laila said. She had a good feeling about this. She'd tried all night to keep her nerves in check, not look towards other stalls, and not overthink things when Aparna came back with all sorts of local news. The continuous activity on social media was both exciting and slightly scary. Maahi was doing a great job of documenting the highlights of the night on their social media, but so were the others. The response on their social had been phenomenal. There was a buzz of enthusiasm all around, which Laila found thrilling.

When she looked around at the end of the night, she felt satisfied. It had been an immensely fulfilling experience.

'You guys should go home now. It's midnight,' Laila said to Javed, Ram and Aparna.

'You sure?' Javed asked.

'Yeah, everything's out of the freezer, right? We can handle the counter. The crowd's thinning anyway,' Laila said, examining the crowd. 'I'd say we're at less than fifty per cent capacity.'

'Can one of you make sure Aparna gets home first? It's late,' Maahi said.

'We can take her,' Javed said, looking at Ram, who nodded his agreement.

'Perfect, thanks again, you guys. Go team!' Laila cheered as they began to leave.

'How are they going? We all came in one car,' Maahi said.

'Wait!' Laila called out. When Javed turned, she gave him her keys. 'Take my car. We'll order a cab. You have to go all the way to Gurgaon, but we only have to go to Chanakyapuri.'

'Are you sure?' Javed asked again.

'Haan, haan. You go!'

After they'd left, the party also began to thin out. Over the next hour, the guests had more or less cleared out. Apart from the full display on the counter, they had two boxes of cookies and one of cupcakes left, which they stashed under the table and took turns to clear out the trays, empty boxes and extra cutlery. Laila stacked the chairs one on top of the other and took them to the back of the house. When she returned, Maahi wasn't alone. She was leaning against the edge of their counter, chatting happily with JD, who had got rid of his stupid bowtie and looked far less funny with his collar button undone and his coat open.

'Inspected the counter yet?' Laila asked as she approached them.

'I did, in fact,' JD said, once again looking at Laila as if she was the only person that existed in the world.

'Well, it's of no use now, isn't it? We could've done with your criticism *before* the party,' Laila said.

'Good thing I didn't have anything to criticize then.'

'Right. What did your boss think?'

'Too drunk to remember,' JD said, looking at the big, round man in a pearly white suit, which matched his hair perfectly. He laughed loudly at something one of his guests said and took a long swig from his glass. 'We got the votes though, so we're good.'

'Votes, as in with a ballot box and all?' Maahi asked.

'Nothing that extreme,' JD laughed. 'A group of RH employees and I sort of … *mingled* with the guests and casually asked their opinion on the dessert and noted down the names. All in here.' He tapped his phone.

'So you know?' Laila asked.

'Not yet. We'll all have to sit down and gather and analyse the data.'

'When will that be?'

'Since it's the weekend, we'll probably regroup on Monday—'

'So we'll know by Monday?'

'Cannot promise that. After we have all the data, and final numbers, we'll obviously have a meeting after to discuss every highly rated bakery and then decide which ones to choose,' JD said. He chuckled. 'Damn, you girls are all about business, aren't you?'

'Our relationship *is* professional, after all,' Laila said haughtily.

'Come on, yaar,' Maahi said. 'He gave you his orange.'

JD's eyes immediately darted to Laila. 'I see you've been talking about me.'

'It means nothing,' Laila said quickly. 'I tell her everything.'

'She does.' Maahi nodded.

'Did you girls wake up today aiming to completely destroy my ego?' JD frowned at Laila.

'Nah, we woke up aiming to kill it at the fancy party—which looks like it's over now, by the way,' Laila said, scanning the almost empty lawn. All of the stalls were still there, but only a few guests remained.

'Right. The fancy CEO wants the stalls to wrap up only once all of the guests have left. It's rude to start wrapping up while the guests are still here,' JD said. Glancing at Laila and Maahi's expressions, he hastily added, 'Which is stupid, if you ask me. In my opinion, the guests who are still here are very rude to keep the host and all of the staff waiting on them.'

Maahi giggled. 'Wow, Laila, you keep a tight leash.'

'Shut up,' Laila muttered.

'Looks like the last of them is leaving,' JD pointed at the three men who had been chatting with the CEO and were now shaking his hand.

Laila, Maahi and JD watched the small group intently, making sure they were actually leaving, and once they did, they cheered.

JD exclaimed, 'Finally!'

Maahi sighed with relief. 'I'm packing up!'

Laila bent down, pulled empty boxes from under the counter and set them on top. She began stuffing one of them with whatever was left on display. Maahi was doing the same.

'We should take these back for the kids,' Laila said.

'Yea—'

'You have kids?' JD asked.

'You're still here?' Laila looked up.

'Ouch. I think I'm trying to see how many more insults I can take before I reach my limit,' JD said. 'You didn't answer my question.'

'Not our kids. We're both single and straight,' Maahi said.

'I see—'

'I meant the kids in our neighbourhood. We don't throw away perfectly good food. And they've come to expect it from us,' Laila said.

'If we are carrying this home with us, I should first order a cab,' Maahi said.

'You guys are taking a cab?'

'Yeah, we gave Laila's car to our team,' Maahi said, fidgeting with a taxi app. 'What's the exact address of this place?'

'I can drop you. Where are you guys going?' JD asked, looking from Maahi to Laila.

'Dude, you've got to draw the line somewhere. You don't need to offer to drive us home just for a chance to flirt,' Laila said. She filled her box and set it aside. She opened another one and began piling cookies in it. 'Especially at, like, two in the morning.'

'Exactly. It's 2 a.m., please let me drop you home,' JD said, looking part-worried, part-hopeful. 'And the chance to flirt is just a perk—an enticing one though.'

Maahi looked at Laila.

'All right, fine,' Laila said.

'Awesome. I'll meet you over by the front in fifteen minutes?' JD said and departed at high speed, without waiting for their response.

When Laila and Maahi were done wrapping up their table, it took two trips to bring everything to the front of the bungalow. They set the boxes down and waited for JD, watching everyone else clearing away their stalls. The night was beautiful in the light of the dull lamps, a cool breeze playing with their hair. Laila took a deep breath.

'Mission accomplished,' Maahi said.

'We did our part,' Laila said. 'Which is all we can do.'

'I really hope we get the account.'

Laila nodded. She had a good feeling about it, but didn't want to say it aloud for fear of jinxing it.

'So …' Maahi said in a small voice, 'JD's pretty awesome.'

Laila grunted in response.

'Funny, and *so* cute, with the hair and all—'

Just then JD and his car appeared where Jasmeet had the day before. JD got out and helped them with loading everything in the trunk. When he rounded to get back into the driver's seat, Laila muttered to Maahi, 'I'm sitting in the back.'

'Wha—?' Maahi looked confused for a second, and then walked up to the passenger side. 'I guess I'm riding shotgun,' she said, sitting next to JD.

JD glanced at Laila and said, 'Stone cold.'

'I never said I'll sit with you,' Laila smirked.

'I like Maahi better anyway. She's funny, and not to mention, much nicer. So, Maahi? Tell me about yourself!'

'Umm, I like *Game of Thrones*?'

'Ah, great taste in TV—slightly gory and porny but great. What else do you like?'

'Cricket, Bollywood, big fan of Arijit Singh and Priyanka Chopra is love. Of the Brontë sisters, I love Emily the most, even though *Jane Eyre* is my favourite Brontë book. Also, I love cupcakes, which I guess you must've figured out by now,' Maahi said. She glanced back at Laila and added, 'I love cookies too.'

'Of course, of course.' JD nodded.

'God, seriously! You guys act like I'm Hitler!' Laila scowled.

'You're not Hitler. You're just … disproving of certain things,' JD said.

'A lot of things,' Maahi added.

'Fun things,' JD said.

'Fine, exchange biodatas if that's your idea of fun. Just leave me out of it.' Laila sat back and decided to ignore them for the rest of the drive home. At least she pretended to ignore them at first, but it was hard to do so in such a confined space. Once JD began playing R.D. Burman and he and Maahi started singing along to '*Sar Jo Tera Chakraye*' there was no turning back. After the first few minutes, Laila reluctantly joined them, sticking her head between their seats and being the third vocalist.

Suddenly, they were pulling over outside her house in Chanakyapuri. They tried to be as quick as possible, carrying the boxes inside through the main gate, which creaked again, and Laila made a mental note to oil it again. They piled all the boxes by the front door and came back for a final scan of the trunk.

'I guess we got everything,' Maahi got the last of the napkins and said, pushing the trunk shut. She looked from JD to Laila, and said, 'I'm going to … not be here. Thanks, JD!'

'Anytime. Good night,' JD beamed.

Laila was slightly annoyed at how much energy this dude had at 3 a.m., after such a long day at work.

'My phone …' she muttered, peeking into the back seat through the window. When she couldn't find it, she got inside and bent to check under the seat. 'Give me some light, please?'

'Of course,' JD said and got in too. He switched on the torch on his phone. The open door on his side caused a cool breeze to waft in, causing goose bumps on Laila's exposed stomach. As the light from JD's phone hit her, she saw JD glance at her stomach. Catching her eye, he quickly looked away. For all his flirtatious ways, he could actually be very shy on occasion. Warm in the face, Laila swore never to wear a sari again, but at the same time, she wanted to wear one every day.

'Found it!' Laila said, rescuing her cell phone from between the seat cushions. As she turned to open the door, JD stopped her.

'Wait!' he said, his hand on hers. 'Just … sit with me for one second.'

'Why?'

'Because. I'm trying to get to know you, but you're hell-bent on making it impossible!'

Laila turned back towards him with a dramatic, 'Fine.' She adjusted the stupid sari with as much poise as possible in the limited space and sat back.

JD closed his side of the door and sat down facing her. In the faint light coming from the streetlamps, his face was partly visible—curly hair falling playfully over his forehead, lopsided grin in place, eyes that refused to leave Laila's.

'Very cute,' Laila said, narrowing her eyes suspiciously.

'What?'

'This whole act.' Laila motioned in his general direction. 'The happy boy thing you've got going.'

'Not an act—it's just me.'

'Oh yeah?'

'A hundred per cent. Fine, I'm not always the happy boy, but I'm very happy right now, especially in my present company,' JD said, smirking at her. 'So tell me, who's *your* favourite Brontë sister?'

'I don't have a favourite Brontë sister. I have a favourite Brontë book.'

'Yes?'

'*Wuthering Heights*.'

'Ah, a romantic!'

Laila snorted. 'I used to be, I guess. I haven't read it in ages.'

'Maybe it's time to re-read it now.'

'Maybe. Who's your favourite writer?'

'R. K. Narayan,' JD said, his face splitting into another childish grin. '*Malgudi Days*, *Swami and Friends* … I grew up on his books.'

'You're very rooted in Indian culture,' Laila observed.

'I guess so. I'm not old-fashioned or anything, but along with adapting to the new that's coming from the West, I like to keep the old, which is sometimes the Indian, alive.'

'Good point. There's a lot of great stuff to find right here.'

'Exactly. Like this,' JD said and leaned forward to turn the music back on. As Lata Mangeshkar began singing '*Lag Ja Gale*' he said, 'Ah, classic!' and started singing along.

'God, you're so cheesy,' Laila grinned.

'…*jee bhar ke dekh leejiye, humko kareeb se…*'

'Stop!'

'…*phir aapke naseeb mein, ye raat ho na ho…*'

'Seriously, stop!'

'…*shayad is janam mein, mulaakaat ho na ho…*' JD continued singing devotedly, his teeth displayed in a wide smile as he moved with the music.

At that point, Laila gave up and sat back, letting him do his thing.

When he reached the chorus, he finished with a flourish and said, 'Have you fallen in love with me yet?'

'Not yet, no.'

'Not *yet*, but soon?'

Laila pushed him away and laughed. 'Dude, you're good at normal conversation. Just stick with that, you were doing well. Why do you have to go be weird every few seconds?'

JD paused and studied her. 'If you want the truth…'

'There's a truth?' Laila raised her eyebrow. 'I thought this is just who you are!'

'It is, but ... I become weirder than usual sometimes because you scare me. A little. Sometimes. And I buckle under the pressure and start singing cheesy, old Bollywood songs, which are great by the way—no offense, Lataji,' he said, looking up.

'Lata Mangeshkar isn't dead,' Laila pointed out.

'I know. I'm imagining myself at her feet, hence the looking up.'

'Ah, of course.'

They laughed, which ended in an awkward silence, broken by the song changing to '*Gulaabi Aankhein*' which JD promptly started singing along with.

'All right, can I go now?' Laila asked, shaking her head at his silliness. She reached for the door handle, but a part of her wanted to stay just a little longer.

JD stopped singing immediately and held Laila's elbow to stop her. 'I don't get a good night?' he asked, his face falling.

Laila turned back towards him, 'Good night,' she said, hiding a smile, her hand still on the handle.

'Ugh, you're killing me. Literally the least romantic person in the whole world.'

'Deal with it.'

'I guess I'll have to.'

They looked at each other, JD with his eyes wide and hopeful, Laila smirking.

'Go home, kid,' she said.

'You *didn't*! I'm a grown-ass man of twenty-six!'

'Age is just a number. Still a kid.'

'I'm actually almost twenty-seven!'

'I'm twenty-eight. So, still younger than me.'

'Age is just a number,' JD said and added seriously. 'I'm a person and you're a person, and we like each other—that is all that matters!'

'You've decided that I like you?'

'You're here, aren't you?'

'I'm going to have to go now, however,' Laila said, smiling. JD stayed where he was, still holding her elbow.

Laila was very aware of the touch of his fingers on her bare skin. Her heartbeat quickened as she looked at those dark eyes, shining under the streetlamps, refusing to leave her eyes. In that moment, locked inside that car filled with his scent, their breaths mingled with each other's in the still darkness, and Laila couldn't think of one reason why not. In that moment, every cell in her body wanted to taste his lips. Laila suddenly began to resent whatever little distance there was between them. She placed her fingers lightly on his cheek and leaned towards him. She watched his eyes widen slightly as he realized that it was really happening. In a split second, his expression changed from shock to joy, and he met her halfway, grinning as wide as ever.

Laila touched his lips with hers, and JD's grin disappeared. His mouth closed around hers, her fingers still resting on his cheek. Feeling his warm breath on her face, Laila tilted her head to the right. She held his eyes for a second, her heartbeat pacing even more. JD closed his eyes and Laila followed suit. As they kissed, her fingers slipped softly from his face to his neck and she struggled for air. She trailed his jaw with her thumb, as a shiver ran all the way down to her toes. JD groaned and pulled her closer to him by her elbow and—

Laila suddenly gasped and pulled back. She jerked away from him, breathing heavily, trying to catch her breath. She felt as if she had just run a mile. Her throat felt raw, her eyes dry. *All he did was pull me towards him, that's all*, she told herself. *It's okay, it's okay, it's okay.*

'Is everything okay?' JD asked uncertainly. His face was scrunched up in confusion as he studied her. 'I mean, did I do someth—'

'No!' Laila breathed hastily. 'No. You were fine.'

'Then what—?'

'Nothing,' Laila said, plastering a forced smile on her face that she hoped would fool JD. She looked up at him briefly and nodded, as if that would assure him that all was well. 'I've got to go now. Thanks for … bringing us home.'

'Yeah,' JD whispered, frowning. 'Laila…'

Before he said any more, Laila got out of the car and crossed the street to her house. She opened the gate slowly, trying to minimize the screeching, and once inside, she turned back and waved JD bye, still pretending that all was well. He waved back unsurely, looking at her in confusion. When he didn't drive away, Laila turned her back to him and walked away. However, she didn't actually enter her house just yet. She knelt on the small patch of grass outside, trying to compose herself. A few minutes later, she heard JD's car pull away. After he was gone, Laila put her face in her palms and closed her eyes.

Will this never end?

11
LOSERS

'How the fuck are you asleep?' Laila said as she walked in through the front door and threw her keys on the drawer against the wall. 'This could potentially have been our biggest milestone so far for Cookies + Cupcakes. Bring out the tequila.'

'I'm tired,' Maahi mumbled, her face hidden in the sofa.

'Get up!' Laila went over and sat on top of Maahi, who was lying face down.

'What are you doing?' Maahi groaned.

'I'll just sit on you till you get up.'

'I don't mind. You're not heavy and I'm getting a free back massage. Could you give me a shoulder massage too?'

'Fine. Three minutes of sitting on your back and a shoulder massage. But then you have to get up and make me that disgusting ice cream cocktail thing from the other night,' Laila said, squeezing Maahi's shoulder. 'Deal?'

'Deal.'

Laila massaged Maahi's shoulder, squeezing it extra hard to annoy her, but Maahi seemed to like it. They were quiet for three minutes, sitting in the light of a lone lamp by the dining room door, which made the room look a sickly green. Laila tried to focus on the moment and not let her thoughts drift back to what happened with JD just moments ago. She needed Maahi's help to distract herself from it, but she couldn't actually tell Maahi anything, or else it would become a whole thing.

Three minutes later, Laila ceased squeezing and began pounding Maahi's back lightly. 'Get up, get up, get up,' she sang.

'Fine,' Maahi moaned. 'Fine!'

Laila got off Maahi and they both went to the kitchen. While Laila brought out the tequila, Maahi flipped two glasses on the counter and started scooping ice cream into them. 'Do you think we're going to get it?' she asked, yawning.

'The account with Roast House?'

'Hmm.'

'I hope so,' Laila said, thinking back to the last few days of preparation and then the party that night. The appreciation and encouragement they'd got from the guests still ringing in her ears. Their phones were constantly buzzing with all the likes and comments their posts had received. 'I feel good about it, but even if we don't, we gave it our all. So I'm still satisfied.'

'Me too. Everyone else was really good too though, so anything can happen. Pour the tequila over these,' Maahi said, holding out the glasses. 'It's going to be hard work for whoever decides.'

'That's why they have a whole team. At least that's what JD

said.' Laila poured tequila into the glasses, filling up the spaces around the ice cream.

'He said we won't know for a while. They'll meet to tally on Monday. Who knows how long it'll take them to reach a final decision. Just discussing each of the twenty-seven bakeries that participated is going to take so much time.'

'Dude, lighten up! This is not ideal 3 a.m. conversation. Especially not with these,' Laila pointed to the drinks Maahi was stirring on the counter.

'Right.' Maahi sighed. She finished mixing the drinks and handed one to Laila.

They walked back to the living room and sat down on the carpeted floor, across from each other with the centre table separating them, their backs resting against the sofas. Laila looked at Maahi apprehensively. It was strange to see her so subdued and quiet, even considering that it was the middle of the night. Maahi had never been very good at masking her emotions. It was just as easy to spot her sorrow as it was her joy or excitement. Laila decided it was best to let her friend be—at least for the moment. If something was bothering her, Maahi usually told Laila herself anyway.

But the vibe only got weirder from there. Laila didn't want to think about JD, so she needed to be talking, or listening— be actively involved in a conversation in one way or another. Maahi looked exhausted as she sipped her drink slowly. Her eyes were unfocused and she kept sighing. When she didn't speak at all for the next few minutes, Laila couldn't take it anymore.

'What's going on with you?' she finally asked.

Maahi looked up from her glass. 'I miss Siddhant,' she said shortly, taking another sip of the disgusting cocktail.

Laila nodded slowly. She was unsure how to handle this, of what to say. They usually talked about boys flippantly, without paying them too much attention or taking them too seriously. This, however, seemed serious. Unable to find a way to redirect the conversation, she said, 'I'm listening.'

Maahi drained the last of her cocktail and said, 'Let me make another one,' before going into the kitchen and returning with the bottle of tequila, two tubs of ice cream and a large spoon. She sat back down and began mixing her drink wordlessly, if not a little furiously. It was as if she hadn't even heard what Laila had said.

Laila was getting genuinely concerned. It wasn't like Maahi to keep things bottled up; that was Laila's defence mechanism. Maahi talked things through—that's how she dealt with her problems. 'Maahi,' Laila said.

'Yes.' Maahi stopped stirring abruptly and sat back. Her face contorted and she began speaking very fast, in short sentences. 'I don't know what to tell you. There's nothing to say. You were there. You saw what happened. What I did.'

'Do you think you would do things differently if you could go back?' Laila asked evenly, unaffected by Maahi's tone.

'I can't go back—that's not how it works!'

'Humour me.'

'Yes. Yes, of course, I would've done things differently, especially with Kishan. I wouldn't have let him back in … after everything …' Maahi shook her head repeatedly. 'I'm so stupid, stupid, stupid.'

'Not with Kishan—he doesn't matter. I'm talking about Sid. Would you have done things differently with Sid?'

'I ...' Maahi paused, as if suddenly losing all energy. She shut her eyes as her face screwed up. She threw her head back, chin in the air. Eyes still closed, she muttered, 'I don't know. Yes. No. I don't know. I don't know! It got so messy towards the end with so much going on, I didn't know what to do, about anything. There was Kishan and Siddhant and Cookies + Cupcakes. I felt so suffocated. I just needed to get out of it. End it. Breathe.'

'Which you did.'

'Laila!'

'Hey, I don't mean it in a bad way,' said Laila. She remembered vividly how miserable Maahi had been after ending things with Sid, and the weeks and months leading up to the break up. They had been struggling to set up their first Cookies + Cupcakes shop and Maahi had also been facing a lot of pressure from her family, who then weren't entirely supportive of her decision to open a bakery. To add to that, her relationship with Sid had become increasingly strained because despite being so much in love with each other, they were both setting up their careers and simply hadn't made enough time for each other. Sid had just finished medical school and was interning at AIIMS, which was all-consuming, and Maahi had started college and was also working tirelessly to set up a start-up. It simply wasn't the best time for a new relationship to develop.

No matter how hard they tried, there were more and more disappointments and letdowns. The final nail in the coffin was the return of Maahi's ex-boyfriend, Kishan, the only other man she had ever truly loved. When she was eighteen, Maahi had moved to Bangalore and enrolled in an engineering college to be close to him, and when he had left her, it had destroyed her. She hadn't seen it coming, and was completely blindsided. She had returned to Delhi and built back her life from the ground up. And then he had reappeared, a few years later, and disrupted everything.

'Listen, I was there and I saw what was happening,' Laila said. 'You hated the power that Kishan had over you, but you got sucked into it all over again. I don't blame you for it; love is complicated that way. But think about it—if we remove Kishan from the equation altogether, do you think staying with Sid would've been a good idea with things going the way they were?'

'You mean, did Siddhant and I still have a chance if I hadn't cheated on him by kissing that asshole Kishan?' Maahi said angrily.

'You didn't cheat on Sid. You didn't kiss Kishan. Stop beating yourself up for it. That dude messed you up. He did it once before, years ago, and he did it again last year. He confused you and took advantage of the way you felt about him. Right from the beginning—you were a teenager when you first met, he was five years older than you. He manipulated you!'

'It's not quite *that* black and white. He didn't do anything against my will. I was an adult and I was in love with him, I was actively involved in everything—all the bad decisions I made, all the dumb things I did—everything. He never made me do anything.'

'I'm sure that's the way you see it,' Laila said. 'Maybe he sees it that way too. But the truth is that he was selfish and unkind and he always put himself first. You were never a priority to him, which is really sucky. You should be a priority to a person who claims to be in love with you. You did all of that because you were in love with him, but what did he do for you? You moved away from your family, moved all the way from Ghaziabad to Bangalore when you were eighteen, joined a college you didn't actually want to for a course you weren't actually interested in, just so you could be closer to him when he moved to Bangalore for work. And what did he do? He didn't stop you. He knew you didn't want to be an engineer, but he was selfish. And once he settled down in his new job, met new people, made new friends, how long did it take him to get rid of you?'

'Laila!'

'I don't mean to sound like a bitch. I'm just telling it like it is. He left you, and didn't care about what it did to you. It took you years to recover. And when you finally had things back on track and you were finally starting to be happy, that pathetic loser, he returned and fucked everything up for you all over again. He knew you were engaged to Sid; he knew you needed to concentrate on the bakery you worked your ass off to build; he knew things were stressed in your family, he knew you were vulnerable and defenceless, but he didn't care about any of that because he never cared about you. He only cared about himself, and what he wanted. And that shameless piece of shit, that manipulative, devious lowlife, he went ahead and ruined your life once again.'

'He didn't mean to … He apologized and he told me he still loved me,' Maahi said softly, her expression pained, her voice lacking conviction.

'Stop fucking defending him! You see what he does to you? You're stupid when it comes to him. You, the wonderful, smart, talented human being who never loses hope in the toughest of times and is always vibrant and kind and caring—he turns you into this anxious, obsessive mess and you don't even realize it. Damn Kishan with his mind games and arrogance. He constantly put you down, never appreciated anything you did, made fun of …' Laila shook her head in frustration. 'See, this thing—us still talking about him after he's been out of our lives for so long, I hate it. I hate him.'

'You're biased.'

'Well, yeah. Maybe I hate him more than he deserves to be hated, because I'm on your side. Because I love you, and so I hate him. But you have to agree that most of this hatred is justified.'

Maahi nodded slowly. She'd finally finished mixing the drink, the ice cream completely melted. She passed one across the table to Laila. 'I hate him too. And never again—he's toxic, he clouds my judgement, he plays with me, he makes me dumb, I hate myself when I'm with him and I don't even know it till it's too late.'

'Stop talking about him in present tense,' Laila said, gulping down the warm cocktail that was now more disgusting than ever.

'Right. He's dead to me.'

'Better. Anyway, what I was asking you is—even without Kishan's rude, unwanted interference in your life, do you think you and Sid were working?'

Maahi swallowed and looked straight at Laila. 'I love him. I love him, Laila—present tense. Letting Kishan kiss me and then ending things with Siddhant … doesn't seem like a good decision to me right about now.'

'You can only look back and judge it clearly now because

you're out of it. When you were in the middle of that mess, it was the only thing to do. Kishan coming back shook the foundation of your relationship with Sid. You couldn't just get over it in a second. Sid certainly wouldn't have been able to. Sid and you both needed time apart, with yourselves, to decide how you felt,' Laila said. She and Maahi hadn't discussed Kishan or Sid very often since the mess last year, certainly not at this length, but Laila had thought about it a lot and she knew that Maahi had too. 'I think it was the right decision.'

'To end things with Siddhant?' Maahi looked surprised.

'Yes. It gave you both a possible future. If Kishan could disrupt everything so quickly, both you and Sid knew you clearly weren't over Kishan for whatever crazy reason. Or maybe you were over him, but not over what he did to you and how it made you feel. In any case, you needed time to sort it out. And again, even taking Kishan completely out of the equation, you guys weren't working. It was as if Kishan's return sort of exposed the weaknesses in your relationship with Sid. I'm not saying you weren't in love, or that it wasn't real, but we … we often think that it's in our hand, love. That we can decide what we want and ensure the way it's going to be. We forget how powerful timing is. It wasn't the right time for you. If you'd stayed with Sid, it would've got worse and worse till you reached a point of no return. You wouldn't have been able to come back from that. You would've started hating each other—resentment, grudges, failed expectations … In a way, Kishan's return didn't break the relationship, it just exposed it. It showed you and Sid that both of you weren't ready just yet.'

'I think I know that. We wanted to be together, but we were frustrated because we never were around each other enough, and it just wasn't working ... and we wanted it to work so desperately, but neither of us had the time to actually make it work.'

'It's like a writer with a beautiful story in his head, sitting in front of a laptop with an empty document. He has thoughts and ideas, his laptop is charged, his pencils are sharpened, his notebook is open, his brain is caffeinated, his stomach is full ... but he simply isn't writing. There's nothing stopping him, nothing in his way, except fear. Everything's in place but unless he actually writes, it's all useless. You guys had all the raw material for a perfect relationship—except time. Neither of you had any. You were both driven people who loved each other, understood each other and wanted a future together, but neither of you had any time. You barely had a chance to talk, let alone meet. The story was never written.'

Maahi was quiet for a long time after that. Laila could almost see her rehashing everything she had just said in her head. Finally, Maahi sighed and said, 'You're a very smart person.'

Laila snorted. 'I'm glad that's the conclusion we reached after this long chat. Ooh, wait, I thought of a better analogy—it was like chemistry class—you guys had all the raw materials and chemicals but because there was no interaction, there was no reaction. You've got to put it all in a beaker, make them meet, heat it up and what not – that's the only way there could be magic!'

'Mmm.' Maahi made a face. 'I like the writer one better. I'm not sure that mixing science with magic works.'

They laughed. The room was steadily becoming brighter, the dull light coming through the windows indicating early dawn.

'I wish we could afford to stay closed tomorrow.'

'We can't. We're poor.'

'True.' Maahi pointed at the empty glasses on the table. 'How much did that last drink suck?'

'A lot. We're such losers—on the floor, the second week in a row with our sob stories and tequila!' Laila laughed. Then she asked Maahi evenly, 'You're in touch with Sid, right? You guys ended on decent terms, stayed almost friends?'

'Not really. It was just unbearable to accept that we'd never see each other, so we decided to stay friends. But we've only texted, like, once a month or less so far. We bumped into each other, like, six months ago, I told you. He looked good.'

'You guys don't talk now?'

'Nope. We were cordial that day, smiled, asked each other what's up, but I don't know … After that, it was just too awkward to text. He hasn't texted either.' Maahi pursed her lips.

'Maybe you can text him now? Hang out? Talk?'

'Maybe. I had to cancel my Tinder date this week because of the fancy party.'

'You were doing the whole online dating thing as a distraction anyway. You were never really into it,' Laila said. 'Talk to Sid. Maybe you could work things out—or not—but at least you'll know. It's been over a year, so you can get whatever perspective or closure you need—depending on how it goes. You kids would be good together.'

'Don't. I can't dream.'

Laila rolled her eyes. 'Drama queen. Enough serious conversation for tonight. So jaa ab. We only have a few hours till we have to be at the bakery.'

They got up and cleared the table. Once they were done, they left everything by the sink and Laila said good night and went to her room.

'Wait,' Maahi called out from the door of her room. 'How did it go with JD tonight? You know? After I left?'

Laila turned around and leaned her back against her door frame. 'Fine. I'm going to give him a chance.'

'Really?' Maahi seemed shocked, and quickly covered her expression and added, 'I mean it's great! It's awesome!'

Laila collected her thoughts for a second and said softly, 'Yeah. I don't feel fully ready, but I might never be. He seems like a good, genuine person. I'm going to give him a chance.' She turned around and walked to her bed, wondering if JD would still be interested in her after she freaked out and bolted just because he pulled her closer to him. She was a grown woman, not a nervous teenager. She didn't want to think about why she had acted the way she did. Instead, she focused her energies on wondering what JD must make of it.

12

THE WAIT

The next few days went by very slowly while they waited to hear from Roast House, much to Laila's frustration. She wasn't as anxious as Maahi, who was saying every scary thought that popped into her head out loud, making Laila anxious too. 'Did you see that one table with everything made from Rice Krispies? I'm sure they'll get chosen!' she would say. Immediately, Laila would find herself looking up the Rice Krispies bakery on the Internet, pulling up all information she could find.

Aparna had done a good job as a spy and had gathered business cards from all the counters at the party, making stalking them online much easier. Laila wasn't sure it was helping. It was good to know what they were up against, but finding out just how talented these other bakers were only added to their insecurities. They had given it their all for the party—stretched their budget as far as they could, baked their best stuff, concentrated on presentation, customer service, brand recall and everything else they could think of. There was nothing more to do now but worry.

Laila spent Saturday morning at One, baking with Maahi. They were both operating in the strange zone between drunk and hungover. They also hadn't got nearly enough sleep, so they worked slowly and silently. The previous night's conversation was still fresh in Laila's head, but she was hesitant to say anything to Maahi, who she could tell was going through everything they'd talked about in her head too. By noon, when their team arrived, they had baked enough to fill up the counter display.

Ram took over baking for One, while Laila, Javed and Aparna took the other half to Two. Later that evening, after the team was gone, Maahi came over to Two, and waited with Laila for the kids to come claim their sweets. Sure enough, they arrived jumping up and down with excitement. Laila sat them down inside in the now-closed bakery, and offered them platters of dessert from the party. The pig was a big hit among the kids, who not only got to eat as much as they liked, but also took home boxes for their families. In return, they assured Laila and Maahi that they were the best at the fancy party and they were going to win the competition for sure.

On Sunday, they didn't have enough baking to hide behind. This would've made Laila anxious anyway, but especially now when she needed to keep busy, it was even more painful. Javed, who was in a bad mood because his parents hadn't kept their word and criticized his girlfriend's parents openly when they met, wanted to be left alone. He muttered something about stupid honour being more important than one's own children's happiness as he exited Two, and a few seconds later, they heard the angry roar of his motorcycle as he rode away.

Maahi arrived with Ram shortly after, almost scared of Javed's volatile temperament. With four anxious bakers in the bakery and no baking to do, they took to cleaning any surface they could find. They gave the kitchen a deep cleansing, moving everything out of its place and scrubbing over and under. Once they were done, they cleaned the office and bathroom. The only place still remaining was the shop section, which Laila cleaned with Maahi once Ram and Aparna had left after closing. They reached home, carrying bags of takeout— starving, exhausted and too tense to talk. Laila didn't sleep well at all that night, her thoughts oscillating between Roast House and JD. She wondered what was going on in his head, and if he was thinking about her at all.

Monday came and went without a word from JD. Since both Cookies + Cupcakes shops were open seven days a week, each person took a day of their choice off every week after coordinating with the others. Javed, who usually had Mondays off, showed up to work promptly, looking from Laila to Maahi questioningly.

'What? It's 8 a.m.! They probably haven't even had the meeting yet!' said Maahi, who was clearly stressed out. She reacted the same way when Aparna arrived a few minutes later. When Ram entered a few minutes after that, Javed and Aparna warned him against engaging with Maahi. They ended up having another tense day with everyone on the edge, staying out of each other's way. Laila saw that they were all being more productive than usual, channelling all their energies towards work. Nobody was seen scrolling through their Instagram. Aparna didn't post a single selfie with some silly filter on Snapchat.

By Tuesday, the team had reached a whole new level of anxiety. If the meeting happened on Monday as scheduled, they were definitely going to hear about the results by Tuesday. Only, they didn't. At closing time, when they still hadn't heard from Roast House, Maahi and Ram came over to Two, and together with Javed and Aparna, forced Laila to enquire about the status.

'We have to know what's up,' Aparna cried.

'It's only 7 p.m.—just call that tall guy and ask,' Javed said.

'I'm with them,' Maahi said, looking expectantly at Laila.

'Me too,' Ram added.

They all stood side by side, facing Laila, as if ready to put up a physical fight if she said no or decided to escape without giving them what they wanted. 'Let's all take a seat,' she said finally. 'There's no need for a revolution or whatever the hell it is you guys are planning. I'll ask him. An email would be more professional.'

'Who knows when he'll see it!' Ram revolted.

'It's easy to ignore emails. You have to put him on the spot. Call him,' Javed said, throwing his hands up in obvious frustration.

'If I put him on the spot, you think he'll give us the account? Even if his company decidesd otherwise?' Laila raised an eyebrow.

'Why would they decide otherwise?' Aparna asked, biting her fingernails.

'I said *if*. Calling won't change their decision, but it might annoy him and impact the decision if they haven't yet made it.'

'You're thinking way too much,' Maahi said and slumped down on the chair next to Laila. 'But yes, let's just email him. This is 2016. I'm pretty sure he has push notifications on.'

'Exactly. Email's the new text message. No one calls anyone anymore,' Laila said and pulled out her laptop to compose the email. She wasn't going to be the first one to call after the first (attempted and good until interrupted) kiss. JD hadn't texted her at all since Friday night, which she was trying not to think about. She made sure her mail sounded strictly professional in case he thought she was using business as an excuse to talk to him.

From: laila@cookiespluscupcakes.com
Cc: maahi@cookiespluscupcakes.com
Date: Tue, Sept 8, 2016 at 7:18 pm
To: diwakar.jayesh@roasthouse.in

Subject: Follow-up

Hi JD,
It was great to be a part of Roast House's party. We were honoured to have been offered the opportunity to showcase our products to the team and guests.
    We were wondering if RH has reached a decision about the collaboration account yet. When can we expect to know?

Thanks,
Laila
--
Laila Kapoor
Co-founder
Cookies + Cupcakes

'There,' Laila said as she hit 'Send'. The team huddled behind her, peering into her inbox as if to make sure she had actually sent it. Laila frowned. 'God, have some faith. It's not as if I don't want to know what's going on!'

'You didn't seem too keen on finding out,' Maahi pointed out.

'I just ... don't want to seem too desperate—or whatever. Shut up!'

Maahi threw her hands up in surrender.

Javed and Ram analysed the email, standing behind Laila, who was about to ask them to stop crowding her, when she was distracted by a scream in her ear.

'New mail from Jayesh Diwakar! New mail from Jayesh Diwakar!' Aparna cried suddenly, pointing at the bottom right of the laptop screen.

'Open it!' they yelled in unison.

'I am!' Laila said, her fingers trembling slightly as she clicked on the new mail.

From: diwakar.jayesh@roasthouse.in
Cc: maahi@cookiespluscupcakes.com
Date: Tue, Sept 8, 2016 at 7:24 pm
To: laila@cookiespluscupcakes.com

Subject: Re: Follow-up

Hi Laila,
It was great to have you be a part of Roast House's party. We were honoured to have you showcase your delicious products to our team and guests.

The team at RH hasn't reached a decision about the
collaboration account yet. You can expect to know
by tomorrow.

Best,
JD
--
Jayesh Diwakar
Head of Marketing
Roast House

'Is this a joke?' Maahi muttered, inspecting the email closely.
'It reads like a joke.'

'Except it isn't funny, is it?' Laila asked. JD's mail read like
it was mocking Laila's. 'At all.'

The team dispersed immediately and began collecting
their bags, preparing to go home. Laila looked at Maahi,
who shrugged, sitting back motionless in her chair, her eyes
wandering, watching the team pack up.

'Aw, come on. Big day tomorrow!' Laila tried to cheer them
up, but they muttered their gloomy goodbyes and left.

After another sleepless night, Laila arrived at Two, having
dropped Maahi at One. She kept telling herself that she was
calm, that she had to be, for the team, but it simply wasn't
working. Her agitation rubbed off on Javed and Aparna. They
were way past the working-in-silence phase and had launched
into an analysing and over-analysing one. Laila kept out of the
discussion while Javed and Aparna worried themselves sick,
going over the what-ifs.

Maahi and Ram kept texting them throughout the day, checking for updates. When Maahi called the fifteenth time, Laila lost her cool. 'How many times do I have to tell you: you're copied on the email. You'll know when I know—we'll both know at the same time. And if they call me, don't you think I'll call you the very next second?'

'I can't. I can't do this,' Maahi said. 'I'm coming over.'

Before she hung up, Laila heard Ram complain in the background about being left alone at One. Fifteen minutes later, Maahi arrived with Ram, shrugging helplessly.

'Well, closing early is hardly good for business,' Laila observed.

'We put up a sign saying our HKV shop is open. Also, they can order online. Also, I don't care,' Maahi said.

'Winning attitude.'

Maahi sat down at the corner table by the glass window, looking out, squinting in the bright afternoon sunlight. Ram sat down with her, which prompted Aparna and Javed to join them too. Maahi put her phone on the table and kept glancing at it every few seconds.

'O…kay,' Laila said, frowning. 'I guess I'm handling the counter then.' Her whole team was falling apart. The longer they waited to hear from Roast House, the bigger deal getting the account had become. Laila watched the sunlight get dimmer and dimmer without a word from Roast House.

'Maybe they forgot about us,' Aparna said.

'Maybe they're only getting back to the bakeries they selected. Maybe they'll send out rejection emails tomorrow—or later,' Ram said.

Javed looked from Aparna to Ram as if they were stupid. 'Don't you get it? They won't bother telling the rejects at all! Roast House is a giant. They can't be bothered with rejects.'

'We're not rejects!' Maahi cried. 'Stop calling us rejects!'

They continued arguing, and Laila adamantly stayed out of it. Nothing good ever came out of getting involved in the melodrama. She also, however, placed her phone on the counter and kept pressing the power button every other minute to check for notifications. Once again, it was closing time, and they still hadn't heard from JD.

'Forget it, we're not getting a raise,' Ram groaned. 'I'm giving up.'

'A raise?' Maahi asked.

'Getting the Roast House account means C+C takes off, which means more work for us, which means a raise, right?' Javed looked from Maahi to Laila.

'Right?' Ram pressed.

Maahi looked at Laila for help, prompting all eyes to turn to her.

'Look, we haven't discussed it yet. We've been trying not to count our chickens before they hatch,' Laila said evenly. Before the team began to protest, she added, 'But we can discuss it for sure.'

'Now?' Javed asked.

'It's time to close and we're all waiting anyway,' Aparna said.

'Okay,' Laila allowed. 'What do you want to know?'

'Are we hiring more people?' Javed asked.

'*If* we get the account, there will certainly be some more money. Roast House will give us the capital to expand our productions and other resources to help us, including mentors, experts and what not. Also, there's always RH's marketing team that can guide us. We might not be big enough to take care of production in-house. We'll most probably have to outsource it,' Laila explained.

'So … you won't need us anymore? We're losing our jobs?' Ram asked, panicked.

'NO! No one's losing any jobs. If we take our production for Roast House to a bigger factory, Maahi and I will oversee it for the first few months. Meanwhile, Javed and you will train the new bakers we'll hire for the shops, one each, probably. Also meanwhile, Maahi and I can train Javed and you at the factory too. So, in a few months, ideally, we'll have a fully trained set of bakers for the shops and Javed and you will know all there is to know about the shops and also the collab with RH. Think of it as a promotion.'

'With a raise,' Javed added.

Laila laughed. 'With a raise.'

'Awesome.' Ram grinned.

'What about me?' Aparna asked. 'I stay where I am? Do I get a raise?'

Maahi chipped in, 'Irrespective of what happens today, Laila and I have been thinking about hiring two new people for the counters. You will get to train them and oversee their work.'

'Kind of like a supervisor?'

'Exactly like a supervisor. Of course, you'll also be given additional administrative responsibilities—you'll be in charge of sheets and inventories and deliveries,' Maahi said. She looked at Laila and added, 'If we do get the Roast House account, you'll have even more work.'

'Yep,' Laila agreed.

'I can do it,' Aparna said excitedly and then repeated it in quick succession, 'I can do it. I can do it for sure!'

'Three more times and we'll believe you,' Javed teased.

Some of the tension lifted after this conversation. But as they waited for news, it seemed to build up all over again, and now it was even higher—if that were possible. Now the team knew what was at stake, and was hoping more desperately than before for good news. After closing, Laila joined them at the table briefly before getting up and pacing around. Sitting motionlessly was proving to be hard.

'Call him,' Maahi said, suddenly getting up, as if unable to sit any longer.

'Yes, call him,' Javed said.

'He said we'll find out today, so we'll find out today. There are five more hours in today,' Laila said firmly, silently cursing JD for not having called yet.

She thought they'd dropped the matter when Maahi sat back down and everyone resumed their silence, but five minutes later, Maahi spoke again, this time demanding Laila send another email at least.

'You're copied in the email. You send it,' Laila said.

'Fine.' Maahi picked up her phone and began typing. A minute later, Laila received the email.

From: maahi@cookiespluscupcakes.com
Cc: laila@cookiespluscupcakes.com
Date: Wed, Sept 9, 2016 at 7:44 pm
To: diwakar.jayesh@roasthouse.in

Subject: Re: Re: Follow-up

Hey JD—haven't heard about your decision yet—
dying here. Let us know soon please?
xx

--
Maahi Kothari
Co-founder
Cookies + Cupcakes

'Dying here?' Laila raised an eyebrow. 'Very professional, that.'

'My present state of mind does not permit me to fake professionalism.'

'Ironic.'

They didn't have to wait long for a response.

From: diwakar.jayesh@roasthouse.in
Cc: laila@cookiespluscupcakes.com
Date: Wed, Sept 9, 2016 at 7:47 pm
To: maahi@cookiespluscupcakes.com

Subject: Re: Re: Re: follow-up

LOOK OUTSIDE :)))))

JD
--
Jayesh Diwakar
Head of Marketing
Roast House

Laila and Maahi looked up from their phones and out the glass windows at the same time, to see JD, tall and happy, striding towards the shop.

13

BARGAIN

'Does that mean yes?' Maahi exclaimed as soon as JD entered the shop. 'You're here, when we were supposed to be hearing from you. You're here, and you're smiling—so is that a yes?'

'He's always smiling,' Laila pointed out.

'Did she just talk about me in third person, right in front of me?' JD looked from Maahi to Laila.

'You did the same just now,' Maahi said.

'I know. Funny, right?'

Maahi did not look amused. Laila's eyes were cold as she stared fixedly at JD. The rest of the team followed suit.

'Tough crowd,' JD muttered. 'Okay, down to business. I have a condition—'

'What?'

'Is this a joke—'

'Relax, people! Have a sense of humour,' JD said quickly and turned to Laila. 'My condition is that I'll tell you Roast House's decision if your boss lets me take her out on a date after.'

'Done,' Javed said.

'Traitor.' Laila glared at Javed, before turning to JD. 'That's just stupid—I'll have to go out with you even if you say no?'

'Fair. So you'll go out with me if RH says yes?'

'Has RH said yes?' Maahi asked excitedly.

'If I say yes to the date, will you tell us RH said yes even if they said no?' Laila asked. 'If so, will you then go back to RH and convince them to say yes, or just lie to us now and then tell us "Sorry, no" later?'

'Wow,' JD said shortly.

'I don't ... What?' Maahi looked confused.

Laila and JD looked at each other—and neither of them looked away. After a few seconds, Laila took it upon herself to not be the first one to look away, so she continued glaring at him.

'Guys, you're killing me,' Maahi said, looking from Laila to JD and back at Laila. This Laila knew because she could see Maahi from the corner of her eyes, while her eyes remained locked with JD's.

'Say yes,' JD said softly, his eyes not leaving Laila's. Laila felt a strange weight in her stomach as she looked at him and remembered the last time she was with him. He was behaving completely normally, as if nothing strange had happened that night.

'Are they serious?' Aparna whispered.

'Say yes,' JD repeated.

'You say yes,' Laila said.

'Yes,' JD said instantly.

'What?' Laila was taken aback enough to break eye contact. Her team shouted together, 'WHAT!'

'Yes,' JD repeated.

'Oh my God! Oh my God! Oh my God,' Maahi jumped up and down briefly, before throwing herself on Laila. 'We're in, Laila, we're in!' she chanted happily.

The rest of the team hugged each other, and then joined Laila and Maahi, making it a big bear hug, which JD joined without invitation, grinningly widely.

'We did it,' he breathed, and Laila frowned at him over Maahi's shoulder. After a moment of celebration, JD said, 'There's a ... um, more to it though.'

'What?' Maahi narrowed her eyes. Everyone looked at JD as if he was a criminal.

'Can we sit down?' JD asked, looking around himself at the suddenly hostile group of people looking at him. He ushered everyone back to the table they'd been occupying for the past several hours and sat them down. He pulled up a chair and joined them, keeping a safe distance. 'We met on Monday to tally the votes, and then again on Tuesday to discuss the top ten bakeries individually. Today, we met once again to put the longlist to a vote. Every member voted for three bakeries, and that's how we now have a shortlist of six bakeries, including Cookies + Cupcakes.'

'How many will you pick from the shortlist?' Laila asked.

'Two.'

'Two out of six?' Maahi asked, her forehead frowning. 'Are those odds better or worse?'

'Worse,' Laila said.

'Wait, how?' Aparna asked. 'Aren't we one step closer?'

'Yes. But 10 out of 27 to make the longlist meant 1 out of every 2.7 bakeries. But for the shortlist, 6 out of 10 meant 1 out of every 1.6 bakeries, which were much better odds. And now, 2 out of 6 means 1 out of every 3 bakeries.'

'So, from 1 out of every 2.7, we went to 1.6 and now we're at 3.0, which are the worst odds of all?' Aparna recounted dramatically.

Javed spoke, scowling at the calculator on his phone. 'We had a 37 per cent chance to make the longlist, then a 62 per cent chance to make the shortlist and now only a 33 per cent chance to, like, win?'

'It's like you guys are running a maths club over here,' JD observed.

'Shh.' Laila turned to the team. 'These odds are based strictly on the number of bakeries participating. That's all. There are so many other, more important factors that come into play— taste, quality, saleability, ease of transport, perishability.'

'Right,' Maahi added. She looked at JD and said sincerely, 'There wasn't a single crushed cookie or smashed cupcake when we transported them to the party last Friday.'

'Good to know,' JD said. 'But, to be honest, we considered most of those things in the initial stages. I'm now inviting representatives from each of the shortlisted bakeries for private meetings with the team at RH. Over the next week, we plan to meet with each of you and hear about your plans to scale up. So, you know, figure out details like packaging, which will depend on the target demographic, both for RH and C+C, in this case. Then there is the setting up of the team. Of course, we can help set you up at the Roast House factory—we have a budget, but you'll have to hire and train the team, and come up with a solid plan of how you'll scale up from pilot size to factory. Adjusting recipes, buying raw materials—'

'Ingredients,' Laila corrected.

'Ingredients, yes—that sort of thing. They want to see if your establishment is sturdy enough to handle such a big change in scale of production and distribution. And marketing—because we'd like each bakery we collaborate with to have a good story behind how it happened, when it happened, what the founders and the team are like—basically your core vision and mission,' JD finished.

Laila thought over it for a minute. Everyone else was quiet, thinking, occasionally glancing at her. Laila smiled at last. 'Sounds wonderful.'

'It does?' Maahi asked.

'It totally does.'

'Perfect,' JD said and stood up. He stuck his hand out to Laila. 'Pleasure doing business with you!'

Laila took his hand and got up, disappointed at his impending departure. 'You're leaving?'

'You don't want me to go?' JD continued holding her hand.

'You can go if you want. Or, you could join us. We promised everyone a treat if we were selected,' Laila said, looking at Maahi. 'And even if we don't make it in the end, the rest of the team has already done their part and they deserve to celebrate!'

'Yes, come with us!' Maahi said, getting up excitedly.

'It's Wednesday—ladies' night at most clubs,' Aparna said. 'Let's go clubbing!'

'Who am I to say no to three beautiful women?' JD grinned and turned to the boys, 'What do you say?'

'Sure,' Javed said.

'Absolutely!' Ram added.

'All right then. We'll worry about work tomorrow. Tonight,

we party!' Laila chimed in. 'Now, if only you would let go of my hand…'

'Right.' JD chuckled and let her go.

As the team began filing out of Cookies + Cupcakes, Laila, who held back to close the shop, said to JD, 'You suck at bargaining, by the way.'

'Yeah?' JD raised an eyebrow.

'I would've gone out with you anyway. Even if you'd said no.'

'I would've said yes anyway. Even if you'd refused to go out with me.'

Laila laughed. 'I figured. Guess we both suck at bargaining then.'

'Or we both want the same things.'

'Or that.'

Maahi rounded through the shop, turning off all the lights and making sure nothing was plugged in, and came out front. 'Ready?'

'Yep,' Laila said. They closed the shop and walked together to the parking lot and caught up with the rest of the team. It didn't take them long to decide. Aparna swore by a club in Chanakyapuri, where Wednesday ladies' nights were apparently lit AF. Laila and Maahi went with it because Chanakyapuri was really close to home. Laila drove with Maahi and Aparna, while JD followed in his car, and Javed and Ram came on Javed's loud motorcycle. On the way, Laila was hounded by both Maahi and Aparna with questions about what was going on between JD and her. She refused to say anything, but couldn't contain her smiles at the mention of his name, which attracted a lot of 'Oohs' and speculation about possible romantic scenarios that might arise between them in the future.

They met outside the hotel where the club was located, and Aparna said something about being glad she was wearing heels to work because apparently the bouncers didn't allow you in unless you were hot enough. She dragged Laila and Maahi to the ladies' room and insisted they put make-up on. Thankfully, both Laila and Maahi were wearing outfits that were club-appropriate. Laila was in tight, distressed high-waist jeans and a spaghetti-strap crop top and ankle boots—all in black, and Maahi was wearing a dull pink flare dress that ended above her knees, teamed with a denim jacket and wedges. Aparna, who took dressing up for her job very seriously, was very pleased with herself for wearing a successful work-to-party outfit, including four-inch pumps.

As they painted their faces in the restroom, Aparna texted the boys to go ahead without them. Maahi, who wasn't as interested in make-up as she was about music and dancing, grew more and more annoyed with every stroke of Aparna's mascara. Laila was getting impatient too, but she hid it, lest Maahi realize that she was eager to join JD inside. So instead, she stood by the door with Maahi, watching Aparna outline her lips carefully with a shocking red pencil.

'Can we please go now?' Maahi moaned, practically on her toes, her ears cocked towards the thumping of music inside the club every time the doors opened.

'Okay, done,' Aparna finally said, shoving everything back into her bag and following Laila and Maahi out of the restroom.

They walked across the foyer and the bouncer checked their

IDs and stamped a pink panda on the inside of their wrists, after which they promptly rushed in through the doors. Aparna hadn't been kidding—the club seemed to be very popular, especially with it being ladies' night, which meant free drinks. For a club, they were there quite early, but the place was already at capacity. The dance floor was pulsing with people dancing to Nicki Minaj.

Once they got their drinks, Laila spotted JD over several popping heads, and made a beeline towards him. Laila smiled at JD, feeling a rush of relief and excitement. After five agonizing days of being unsure if she would ever even hear from him, it felt amazing to have him around again. Also, he smelled amazing and Laila had to force herself to look away from his mouth.

Javed and Ram decided it was a good idea to chug down their drinks and head straight to the dance floor. A minute later, they were all dancing happily in a loose circle, with strangers popping in and out every once in a while. The song changed to a Disclosure number, and Javed brought out his best moves.

Laila danced with JD and Maahi on either side of her, and even though she wasn't the average club-going type, right at that moment, she couldn't think of anywhere else she'd rather be. For all his goofiness, JD had some fancy moves. They kept stealing glances at each other, smiling as if they held a secret between them. Every time he smiled at her, Laila felt warm inside. There was something between them—a fire, an undeniable, thrilling energy.

While they danced in a circle with the others, Laila and JD formed an invisible bubble of their own, and the group was clearly having a good time too. They danced for hours, pausing occasionally to cool down with another drink and getting right back on the floor. Several times unknown men circled their group and tried to dance with one of the girls, only to be blocked by Javed and Ram, who had taken up the roles of body guards. Laila found it hilarious how protective they were being and was also grateful, because neither Maahi nor Aparna seemed to be in a mood to engage with strangers at the moment. And Laila was already dancing with the one person she wanted to engage with. They were all very self-sufficient in their group.

Laila leaned in towards Maahi and spoke into her ear, 'No more boys?'

Maahi smiled and said, 'Only Siddhant!'

Laila smiled back, glad that at least her friend knew what (or who, in this case) she wanted. Beaming, Maahi held her hand and dragged her to the bathroom, where they waited in line for several minutes.

'How's it going with JD?' Maahi yelled.

'Girl, way too loud.' Laila frowned, narrowing her eyes against the light above. They were in the back of the club, the corner with the most light and least music.

'Sorry. How's it going though?' Maahi giggled.

'You're drunk.'

'And I'm going to keep asking!'

'It's going okay,' Laila said finally. 'I mean you're there, you're seeing it too.'

'You should go take a walk with him outside. They always do that in the movies—going out to get some air.'

'Dude, go pee.' Laila rolled her eyes and pushed Maahi softly towards a stall that had just emptied.

When they got back to the dance floor, the music had mellowed. Javed and Aparna said they wanted another drink, and Ram said he would go with them too. Maahi nudged Laila pointedly, and followed the group to the bar.

'What was that?' JD leaned towards Laila and yelled.

'She wants you and me to go outside to get some air or something,' Laila confessed.

'Cool. Let's go outside and get some air or something,' JD said and marched towards the door. Laila stared at his back as he walked away, then at the bar where the group was, and back at him. He kept walking, and so she followed.

'Having fun?' he asked, once they were outside the doors and in the foyer, brightly lit in the sort of beige light that immediately looked expensive.

In her boots, Laila reached JD's shoulders, and had to look up to speak to him now that they were walking so close to each other. 'Yes,' she said. 'Javed is on fire!'

'That dude can dance!'

'You're not so bad yourself,' Laila said, and JD laughed.

'I have six moves total. I keep looping the same six over and over.'

'Which is what anyone who dances not-professionally does. We don't need to follow a choreographed routine to have fun!'

'True. But Javed, that guy can bring the house down,' JD pointed out. 'Let's get out from under these cruel lights.'

They walked out of the building, after making sure the bouncer would let them back in once they showed their pink panda stamps. They remained within the premises, strolling by the side of the hotel building where the lights were much less harsh.

'Does this count as a date?' Laila asked, looking straight ahead as they walked.

'This walk?' JD asked, and Laila felt his eyes on her, but she continued looking ahead.

'Yeah, why not? I hear quiet walks at night are super romantic and all.'

'Well, let's see. You're not walking barefoot on the grass, slinging your shoes in your hand, with your other hand holding mine. There's no moon—at least I can't see it from here. The breeze is quite nice, I'll give you that. And of course, the great pleasure of your company—I think this could be a great date!'

'Also, there's that fountain,' Laila pointed out, spotting a round three-tier concrete overflow fountain straight ahead. It wasn't very big, but the pool that encircled it was lit from within, which made it look beautiful so late at night.

'Definitely adds to the romance of it all,' JD agreed.

They walked towards it and sat down on the concrete edge. A few droplets of cold water splashed on them every now and then as they sat facing each other, the fountain on their side.

'I would like to take you on a real date, but if that's not going to happen, I guess I'll take this,' JD said seriously, looking up at the fountain, and then at Laila, his face lit on one side by the light reflected from the water.

The grin was still there, but Laila could read the question he was hiding underneath. 'You think it's not going to happen?'

'It didn't seem very promising the last time we did something date-ish.'

Laila laughed. 'Just ask.'

'Fine.' JD sighed exaggeratedly, making light of things for Laila's sake. 'Why did you freak out after we kissed?'

'*During* the kiss, actually. If we're getting technical here—'

'We're not.'

'I'm just saying, *if* we are—'

'Seriously, woman, you infuriate me!' JD groaned. 'Just tell me what's up.'

Laila smiled at his agonized expression. 'You really like me, don't you?'

'Not right now, I don't! You're torturing me.'

'You do though. Fine, I'll tell you.'

'Sometime tonight?' JD asked, his annoyance evident.

'I didn't freak out. Or … I guess I did. But it wasn't anything you did or said. I don't know how to explain this without telling you my whole life story, and I'd really prefer not going there right now,' Laila said, studying JD's face. She realized that she was nervous about his reaction. She didn't like talking about her past, and hoped he wouldn't prod further.

JD nodded slowly, as if trying to make sense of her non-explanation. Then he said quietly, 'Okay. I don't need to know your whole life story right now for sure. But … are you good? Just tell me that you're okay and we're okay and you're still interested.'

'Who said I was ever interested to begin with?'

'Lailaaa,' JD groaned. 'Meet me halfway here.'

Laila laughed and instinctively placed her hand on his. 'Yes. Yes, I'm good and we're good and I'm still *interested* or whatever.'

JD looked down at their hands and clutched hers tighter. 'And look at that—there's hand-holding and everything. We're legit.'

'Yep. We don't play around.'

They laughed, the tension that existed between them ever since their first kiss finally dissipating. They sat by the fountain a little longer, holding hands, talking occasionally but were mostly quietly. They got up and walked back to the club when Laila got a text from Maahi asking where she was.

'Question,' JD said, as they retraced their steps.

'Mmm?'

'Are we counting this as a real date? If yes, may I kiss you now? If no, I shall wait until the real date.'

'You will wait until the real date.' Laila grinned as they went back into the club and joined the others, JD's hand resting lightly on her lower back.

14

THE PLAYERS

The rest of the week went by at breakneck speed, with both Laila and Maahi delegating their baking responsibilities fully to Javed and Ram, while they tried to learn everything there was to learn about scaling up the production without compromising quality—and fast. JD had scheduled their meeting with Roast House for Friday, which meant they had to be one of the last bakeries presenting their scaling-up plan, assuming the rest of the meetings were happening through the week. This was good, since it gave Cookies + Cupcakes a few extra days to prepare, and they needed all the time they could get.

Laila closed her laptop, stepped out of her tiny office and into the dark bakery, which Aparna had closed before leaving an hour ago. She left the lights off, preferring the occasional beams from the street flowing in through the shop windows. The day had been cloudy, slowing down everything they were doing. Even though everyone on the team had their own mountain of work to do, they'd gone about it in a relaxed manner, as if there was no rush.

Laila sat on the windowsill and rubbed her face with both her palms. They needed Roast House to choose them. And for that to happen, they needed to be good enough to leave Roast House with no other choice. She was doing everything she could think of, and so was Maahi, but every time she paused to do other things, she started worrying about the meeting and had to go right back to preparing for it. Knowing that she was doing everything she could, preparing, over-preparing—it was the only thing that kept her calm.

Maahi had decided to spend the weekend with her parents in Vaishali, so Laila was going to have the house to herself. She hadn't spent any time there alone ever since her mother had gone to Patna, and she wasn't looking forward to the prospect. The sun had set and the clouds finally broke out into rain as Laila watched. She felt restless, as if there was a void—she was missing something, or someone. She didn't want to be alone. She called her mother, watching the rain through the windows.

Maa picked up the phone after eight long rings and said hello much louder than necessary in a sing-song voice.

'Pranaam maate. Kaisi hain aap?' Laila said, her lips curling into a smile.

Maa laughed at Laila's old-fashioned, formal address. 'Khush raho, beta. I had left the phone in the kitchen and was sure the call would disconnect by the time I got there.'

'Oh, is that why it took you so long to pick up? I thought you just didn't want to talk to me.'

'Woh bhi hai.' Maa laughed again before asking, 'What's going on?'

Laila sighed. 'Nothing much. We have that big meeting coming up next week, so we're preparing furiously.'

'Accha, haan. How's that going?'

'Good, good. I think we know everything we need to know in theory, but we need to go out and meet people who have factories and see it in practice now.'

'I'm sure it'll all go well,' Maa said. Not that she had any way to actually be sure of that, but her confidence in her daughter made Laila smile.

'Ji, maate,' Laila said. 'How's everything in Patna?'

'Your nana refuses to stop eating fatty food,' Maa said, and Laila could hear her grandfather in the background, defending himself. Her mother went on to tell Laila about how he went on a walk religiously every morning as a way of taking care of his health, but ended up having samosas and jalebis with his friends after the healthy walk. She put the call on speaker and Laila advised Nana that if he had to do things he wasn't allowed to, he should at least do a better job at hiding it, at which point Maa and Nani exploded at Laila, accusing her of enabling her grandpa's bad behaviour. They argued good-naturedly about that, and then Maa told them about one of her students who skipped school without permission but was caught because of his several posts on Instagram documenting his day out.

Laila felt nostalgic about her family. Being on the phone with all of them together, laughing about small things made her want to be with them physically. She had been thinking about visiting them sometime soon—maybe after the meeting—if everything went well. In fact, if things didn't go well, it'd make even more sense for her to take a break and go to Patna for a while. She hoped it wouldn't be raining there as she looked out of the window, now splattered with tiny raindrops.

She had mixed feelings about rain. It definitely made her feel lazy, and her days ended up being less productive, but it wasn't just that. It also made her feel … less than whole. Like there was something missing in her life. The wet mud, the jammed roads and the filth in general annoyed her, but what made her feel even more agitated was the emptiness she felt deep within herself when she smelled the fresh smell of the earth after the rain. When it stopped raining and the world became quiet, the still trees and clean leaves bothered her. Rain tended to put her on the edge and made her gloomy, and she didn't know why.

'JD … ?' Laila muttered, spotting him outside. He was with a few other people, who Laila figured were his friends. As she watched the group walk away, JD suddenly stopped, as if realizing or remembering something. He turned around and looked straight at Laila, who now stood by the door, her foot holding it open. She waved.

JD grinned widely, like a child just given some chocolate, and said something to his friends, who departed promptly, but not before casting a glance towards Laila. JD walked to her, his long legs covering the distance between them in five steps.

'Laila!' he exclaimed cheerfully when he reached her, pulling her into a bear hug as if it was the most obvious thing to do.

'Hi,' Laila said in a more normal tone. She spoke into the phone, 'Maa, I'll call you later, okay?'

'Who is it?' Maa asked curiously, dropping the conversation about social media's impact on the new generation.

'It's just … someone I know from work,' Laila said. She didn't miss JD's raised eyebrow. 'Bye now.'

'Bye, beta,' Maa said and hung up.

'Just someone from work?' JD questioned as soon as Laila was off the phone.

'Did I hurt your feelings?'

'Badly.' JD rested his hands on top of each other over his supposedly aching heart. 'I might need surgery.'

'Yeah, yeah,' Laila said. 'I broke your heart. Get used to it.'

'Get used to it? Are you implying that you're going to be doing this repeatedly, which would then imply that you intend to remain a part of my life for an extended period of time?'

'No, I just meant get over it.'

'Argh,' JD said, his hands flying back to his chest. 'You did it again!'

Laila laughed. How was he so upbeat and dramatic all the time? How did he even have the energy to be so happy? Especially after this stupid rain! Everything around them was all clean and beautiful and annoying. But somehow, Laila noticed the fresh air didn't bother her as much as usual as she breathed it in, standing outside Cookies + Cupcakes with JD. 'What are you up to?' she asked.

'Friend's birthday, another friend visiting for the weekend, Friday night—the usual,' JD said. He looked behind her at the dark bakery suspiciously and asked, 'What are *you* up to?'

'Going over plans for the meeting.'

'Alone?'

'Yep.'

'Where's Maahi?'

'She's staying with her family for the weekend so she had to leave early. Her parents live all the way in Vaishali,' Laila said.

'And so you decided to sit in the dark all by yourself?'

'I'm not sitting in the dark. I was working in the office on my laptop, which has a screen and a keyboard, both of which have backlights. And there's a lamp on. I came out to the bakery to call my mom and now I'm here talking to you. Stop being so dramatic!'

'Okay, okay!'

Laila smirked, tilting her head. She liked that he was so tall. It was a big part of his personality—the tall, lanky dude with the unruly curly hair and constant grin. That grin. Did it ever disappear? Did he grin professionally, all day, all night long? Laila realized that she had been staring and quickly looked away. 'Go back to your friend's thing.' She waved a hand in the general direction of where his friends had gone.

'Why, you don't want me to join you in your dark place?'

'It's not a …' Laila began heatedly, then abruptly let it go. She said, in a much calmer tone, 'You know what? Come. Please sit with me in my dark place.' She moved the foot that had been keeping the glass door open and stepped back inside the bakery.

JD followed her quickly before the door shut singing, 'Sweet.'

'Don't even think about it,' Laila said.

'I don't know what you mean. I'm not thinking about anything.'

'Really? You and I, in the dark, alone—and you're not thinking anything?'

'That's right.'

Laila snorted. 'Would you like something to eat? Maahi baked these fancy cupcakes for tomorrow with beer and almonds in them. They taste kind of funny.'

'Wow.' JD seemed very interested as he peered at the counter in the dark. 'You guys do such crazy things. Very innovative and unusual.'

'That's kind of our USP, which you should know since you're planning to buy from us,' Laila said, and then added, 'hopefully, if things go well.'

'That is correct. If that happens, I think it'd make sense for Roast House to pick out a few of your wacky flavours for their menu. I mean, as opposed to the classics.'

Laila frowned, thinking about it. 'Not that it matters right now, for the next stage. You said the meeting is about scale up, more than anything else, right?'

'Yep. But you could talk about putting beer and what not in your food at the end, to wrap up. Beer's always a good selling point,' JD said. He finished examining the counter display and turned to Laila. The lights outside in Hauz Khas Village were brighter now that the rain had stopped and Friday night crowd had begun pouring in, and Laila could see JD's inquisitive eyes clearly.

'Noted,' she said. JD had stopped looking around the bakery curiously and was now looking singularly at Laila, who suddenly felt nervous, though in a good way. She cleared her throat and waved towards the chairs to divert his attention. 'Want to sit? I'll get you some cupcakes.'

JD sat down at the table by the window, which Laila thought was everyone's favourite table, since it was the first one to be occupied every morning and was barely ever empty. 'Just to be clear—this is still not a date?'

'That is correct,' Laila said, bending to pick out cupcakes from behind the counter. She placed them on a plate and walked back to the table. 'Still not a date.'

'And I need still save my kiss for the date?'

'That is correct too.'

'Damn it.' JD looked like a kid denied sweets, which was ironic, since at that very moment, he bent forward and picked up a cupcake. He bit into it and spoke with his mouth full, 'So, do you sit in the dark often?'

Laila sat next to him so they were both facing the bustling street. She pointed to the young crowd of people outside and said, 'Yeah, I'm that weirdo that sits in the dark and people-watches.'

'Do you also serial kill?'

'Not yet. But maybe someday, you know? Why limit yourself?'

'You speak the truth,' JD nodded intelligently. Shoving the rest of the cupcake in his mouth, he said, 'Also, this cupcake is really good. I can taste the beer but it kind of tastes like … you know when you leave a half-empty bottle of beer outside and fall asleep and then wake up in the morning and it's all warm and bitter and disgusting but you drink it anyway and love it regardless?'

'That's what it tastes like?'

'Almost exactly.' JD seemed proud of himself for having nailed down the exact experience required to achieve that particular flavour.

'God. That hardly sounds like a compliment!' Laila laughed.

'But I'll pass it along. Maahi loves disgusting things, so she might appreciate it.'

'Do you also love disgusting things?'

'I've come to love this one disgusting cocktail thing that Maahi makes. But it has tequila in it, and it's hard to hate anything with tequila in it.'

'Yeah? I wouldn't know. You'll have to show me sometime. I mostly stick to beer since my friend is still trying to fatten me up. Also, I'm kind of a lightweight, so hard liquor's not a good idea for me,' JD confessed sheepishly.

'You'll be fine. Always remember—quality over quantity.'

'Where quality is usually disgusting?'

'Exactly. I love all things disgusting,' Laila said.

'All right, ma'am. I look forward to tasting this disgusting cocktail!' JD chuckled. He pushed his chair at an angle so that he was looking at the street and Laila at the same time. He then sat back quietly and just looked at her.

'Weirdo,' Laila muttered. She grew strangely warm under his gaze and decided to ignore him and look out at the street instead, very much aware that his eyes were darting towards her every few seconds. As much as she had unresolved issues with the rain, she had to admit that it had left Delhi more beautiful. Everything was cleaner—the buildings, the trees, the roads—and fitted right in with the excited people who had clearly dressed up for the night. There were bright colours everywhere, from clothes to string lights to walls. Sitting next to JD and watching the after-effects of the rain, Laila didn't feel so restless and hollow anymore. She suddenly didn't mind the rain at all.

'So, what's your story?' JD asked.

She turned towards him to find him looking out and watching people too. She turned back to resume her people-watching. 'What's yours?'

'Unfair! I asked you first.'

Laila glanced at him again, but he continued facing the window. She could tell that he knew she was looking at him, but he didn't give any such indication. He was looking away, but still, somehow, Laila knew that she had his undivided attention. And in that moment, something changed.

It was as if a switch had been flipped. Laila could feel the change physically, in every atom of her body. JD had stopped grinning for the first time since Laila had known him, and she realized that he was then thinking about that interrupted kiss, about their walk by the fountain, about her sitting alone in the dark. It was evident that even though he was constantly happy and chatty and upbeat, he didn't miss the undercurrents.

And that revelation had an unexpected reaction within Laila. It broke down the fences around her heart. It was as if she opened the door, let him in and now they were on the same team. He no longer felt like a stranger, an enemy. She could pull the fences down, let him in. And in that moment, Laila, who had never talked to anyone about Abhishek since his death, not even her mother—those two minutes with Maahi being the only exception—began telling JD about him.

She followed his gaze outside the window and watched a girl with a high ponytail and shy smile as she spoke slowly, clearly. 'I don't play. I mean, I do play, all the time—I take everything lightly on the surface and make fun of things—but I don't play when it comes to relationships. I take them seriously. I fell in love on my first day of college. It wasn't stupid to me. On the contrary, it felt very meant-to-be. My parents were divorced when I was three and Maa brought me to Delhi. I pretty much never had a father, and I held that against the parent I did have. So I sort of blamed her for not trying harder to make the marriage work—for my sake.' She glanced at JD quickly to find that he hadn't moved an inch before resuming. 'And so, when I met Abhishek and fell in love with him, it was as if my lifelong belief that love exists and it works and is the only thing that matters, was validated. We were crazy about each other. All through college, we were inseparable. We were that annoying couple everyone referred to as a single entity. It was always Laila and Abhi or Abhi and Laila. Our names were always said together.'

Laila's face stretched in a small smile, as she thought back to her college days and remembered her carefree self—madly in love, ready for everything. 'As soon as we graduated and got jobs, we told our parents about our relationship and got married. Maa thought it was too early for me, I was only twenty-one. But I told her that when it's right, it's right and that she shouldn't worry about me making a hasty decision because I was sure and was going to do anything to make it work—I would never get a divorce.' Laila laughed a dry laugh, full of self-loathing. 'I think I was proving a point of some kind, when in truth, I didn't know anything about why my parents' marriage ended. I thought it was easier just to hate my mother for denying me my father. But anyway, I digress from the point. Abhishek and I were in love and we figured there was no reason to not be married. So we got married. Eight months later, he died in a car accident.'

JD's head jerked towards her. 'Shit,' he muttered and then stammered, 'I mean … I'm sorry—so sorry to hear that…'

Laila nodded, unable to look at him. The girl with the high ponytail and shy smile walked away with two other girls. Laila shifted her gaze to a boy in a T-shirt two sizes small for him. She had half a mind to keep going, but JD began speaking and she lost her courage.

'I'm sorry I asked,' JD said, 'such an idiot.'

'It's okay.' Laila forced a laugh and looked at him. Her voice was unusually high when she spoke again, 'You didn't know. Also, that answers your question in a way, I guess. I hesitated during our kiss because there hasn't been anyone since Abhishek.'

JD nodded, still clearly apologetic for having initiated this conversation in any way. He said in conclusion, 'You don't play.'

'I don't play.'

After that, they fell quiet. At first, JD continued to seem apologetic, followed by nervous, and fidgety, as he kept stealing glances at her. But eventually, they fell into a comfortable silence, sitting side by side, looking at the street and sometimes at each other. It was only when Laila told JD that he should go hang out with his friends for whatever was left of the night that he got up, although still looking unsure about leaving.

'I find it hard to trust a man who ditches his friends, especially one that's come from out of town just for one weekend,' Laila said, looking up and smiling at him.

'I should really go, shouldn't I?' JD said in a defeated tone.

'You should.'

He sighed loudly, dramatically, almost back to his usual

form. 'Still saving the kiss for the real date,' he said, pulling Laila casually into a hug.

'Good thinking,' Laila said, wrapping her arms around his back and placing her cheek next to his on tip-toe. What started as a friendly hug felt a little more intimate, a little more real, as the seconds passed. It felt almost too real, which shook Laila for moment, her heart tightening in her chest. She laughed dryly. 'Do you feel sorry for the young bride who became a poor widow too soon?'

JD broke the hug but did not release her. Holding both her elbows, he pulled back to look at her, his brows knitted in anger, 'Don't say that. Don't ever … Do you think that's funny? 'Cause it's not.'

'Okay, okay.' Laila continued laughing, trying to break the tension.

'Laila, I'm serious.'

They looked at each other, and despite Laila's efforts to let it go and go back to the way things were before she'd told him, it couldn't be reversed. She'd never seen him angry or this serious before. She finally muttered, 'I don't like talking about it.'

'I get that. That's understandable and totally justified. But you told me, and I'm glad you did because it means you trust me, at least a little bit, to have shared something so personal with me. I feel honoured. But don't say shit like you're a poor widow or whatever. You're a poor nothing. You're one of the most capable, admirable, talented and hard-working people I know,' JD said. 'Never undermine or underestimate that.'

'It was a joke.'

'Well, then it's not funny. Your jokes need work.'

'Noted. I will work on my jokes and get back to you with better ones,' Laila said sincerely. Too sincerely really, which made her laugh and she could tell that JD tried to fight it, but he joined in too.

They said goodbye and JD hugged her again before turning to leave. As he walked away, Laila stepped back into her office to get her stuff and go home. She had stayed out longer than planned and since she was driving back alone, she decided it was best if she did the rest of her work for the meeting from home. Just as she had finished collecting her stuff and was about to leave, JD appeared at her door again. He pulled it open and stuck his head in, although Laila could see all of him through the glass door.

'You scared me!' she exclaimed, walking towards him. 'Did you forget something?'

'Yes, to tell you something. Just so you know—I don't play either.'

Laila stopped in her tracks.

'I don't play either,' JD repeated. 'And ready or not, here it comes—I'm falling in love with you. And it's not because of your poor-widowness or whatever. I've been falling in love with you since the first time I saw you, and gave you my orange. The beautiful woman whom I annoyed by invading her space, claiming her seat, chatting to when she was clearly trying to work. The woman who moved mountains for my fancy CEO's fancy party. The woman whose eyes tell a completely different story from the rest of her, no matter how many fronts she puts up. The woman I will one day finally take on a date and hopefully get to kiss. That's the woman I'm falling in love with.'

Laila stared at him, speechless. She opened her mouth to speak, maybe make fun of his drama, but couldn't form words. Her vision got blurry. She gulped.

'Just thought you should know.' JD shrugged casually, turned around and left, leaving Laila following him with her eyes till he disappeared out of sight. She readjusted the bag on her shoulder and walked out as normally as she could, even with her heart beating rapidly in her chest and the blood pumping in her ears. She locked the shop and made her way to the parking lot, not minding the freshly wet earth at all, and knowing that there was no way she was going to get any more work done that night.

15

FAMILY

In Maahi's absence, Laila had the house to herself for the weekend. The team at Cookies + Cupcakes was working smoothly and Laila trusted them to handle the shops for a few days while she stayed at home and used that time to do as much work as she could before the meeting.

This, however, wasn't going as well as she had hoped. She found herself getting easily distracted, one thought leading to another till she lost track of what she had been doing in the first place. Maahi wasn't there to provide some sort of structure to Laila's weekend either, so she stayed in bed for hours after waking up, reading up on her laptop. When she got hungry, she got up and threw some eggs together in a pan and scrambled them for lunch. After all day of having been fixed to the laptop screen, she found herself flat on her back on the living room carpet, Backstreet Boys playing unnecessarily loudly in the background. Uncountable times during the day, she caught herself smiling, her thoughts wandering to JD and his stupid grin. And his stupid hair. And his stupid everything. It made her feel stupid too, for behaving like a teenager in love. So she forced herself to act like an adult, stop the '90s boy band music and read articles about scaling up production, sitting in her towel because she'd been too lazy to put on clothes after showering and 'What's the point of clothes' anyway.

After an entire weekend of this chaos, on Monday morning, Laila decided it was time to go to work, be around fellow humans, and remind herself what existing in a community felt like. She first dropped by One, only to find it packed with customers. They didn't have enough space for a sit-down area, which left more room for customers to stand. Since most orders at One were takeout, people didn't stick around for too long, but even so, when Laila arrived, the place was full to the brim.

'Need help?' Laila said to Ram, who was handling both the register and the orders.

'Yes, please. Maahi's at Two,' Ram said.

Laila put on an apron and took over the orders. Together, they serviced the line in ten minutes, and even though the bakery remained packed all morning, there wasn't a long line at any point. Working behind the counter relieved a lot of the stress Laila had been carrying around with her about the meeting with Roast House. No matter what happened, they'd always have their bakeries, which was what mattered more than anything else. She covered for Ram while he took his lunch break, and when he returned, she decided to go check on Two quickly before heading home and resuming her work for the meeting.

JD. She stopped in her tracks, spotting him leaning against the counter inside Two, chatting happily with Maahi and

Aparna. Laila gave herself a cursory glance in the window to
see how she was looking and adjusted her hair before walking
in. 'Why are you always here?'

They all turned to look at Laila.

'Hello to you too!' JD said, all tall and smiley.

'You're here!' Maahi said. 'JD came to see you.'

'But I wasn't here. Why didn't you just text me?'

'I was in the neighbourhood for a meeting and thought I'd
drop by and say hi,' JD said. 'Hi.'

'Hi.' Laila pretended that she wasn't happy to see him, and
diverted their attention to a customer who'd just walked up to
the counter. 'Aparna, could you help her? Let's give them some
space, guys.' Laila pulled Maahi and JD away towards the door.

'Are you kicking me out?' JD asked.

Laila laughed. 'You can stay if you want, but I must tell you
how unprofessional this is, dropping by unannounced.'

'Oh, I don't mind,' Maahi chirped in.

'Good thing nobody asked you,' Laila snapped.

'How mean!'

'Don't you have work to do?'

'Fine. And by the way—hello, friend. It's nice to see you.
I missed you. I feel like I haven't seen you in forever,' Maahi
said, growling at Laila before turning to JD and adding more
sincerely, 'It was nice to see you, JD. I'm going to let Laila bully
me into working.'

'Always a pleasure, Maahi,' JD said.

After she went to the kitchen, Laila turned to JD. 'I haven't
told her yet!'

'What?' JD looked confused. Even when confused, he looked
half happy. He was always at least half happy, irrespective of

whatever other emotion he might also be experiencing at the moment.

Laila held his wrist and pulled him outside the shop. He looked quite handsome in his maroon and black plaid shirt, but Laila didn't let that distract her.

'Why are you throwing me out?' JD asked.

'Because I haven't told Maahi anything about you, or us, yet. And she's a pain—she reads too much into everything. Trust me, you don't want that overenthusiastic child jumping up and down while we are only just getting to know each other.'

'Getting to know each other?' JD frowned. 'Laila, I told you I'm falling in love with—'

'Shhh!' Laila said loudly, looking around to make sure no one heard him. 'I'm telling you, don't encourage her. Once she starts, she doesn't stop. We aren't even a thing … or anything. Can we please keep this private?'

'Wow.'

'Oh, come on! Don't give me that hurt puppy look. I'm just thinking practically.' Laila tried to dismiss the conversation, but JD's genuinely bothered expression made her heart sink.

'How romantic,' JD said, his eyebrow raised as he watched her.

Laila opened her mouth to counter that but closed it again. For some reason, all that went down between them in the darkness of that night felt distant and almost unreal in the light of the day—like a dream. Now, thinking about it, she was surprised that she had opened up to him about something so personal in the first place. She barely even knew him. But at the same time, she also felt that she knew him on a whole different level—as if they understood each other. Even though

they weren't yet caught up on everything that had happened
in the other person's life so far, it hadn't stopped them from
forming this deeper connection with each other. After a pause,
she shrugged. 'I'm sorry—I'm not a very romantic person.'

'Ah, that's all right. I'm romantic enough for the both of
us. Do you fancy another Kishore Kumar song? Perhaps some
Mohammed Rafi?'

'Thanks, but spare me, please!'

'Are you sure? I sing "*Dil Kya Kare*" beautifully. I can even
play that one on the guitar. Girls used to go crazy over that in
college,' JD said, his chest proudly thrust out.

'Quite a rock star, haan?' Laila punched his arm playfully.

'Yes, ma'am. Listen,' JD lowered his voice and said, 'if
I can be completely honest with you, now that Aparna or
Maahi can't hear us, I didn't just come here because I was in
the neighbourhood and it was convenient. I mean, I was in
the neighbourhood and it was convenient, but I came here
because I missed you. And if you have a few minutes, let's
walk or something?'

Laila looked from him to Two, where Aparna was busy
with a customer and Maahi couldn't be seen from outside. She
looked back at JD, his words playing repeatedly in her head. *I
missed you. I missed you. I missed you.* 'Let's walk,' she finally
said, 'or something.'

Thankfully, the sun wasn't too hot and the buildings lining
the twisty road kept them in the shade as they walked.

'I guess we're walking towards the fort,' JD observed.

'I guess so too.'

'Lovely. There's a lake there. Very romantic.'

'It's a nightmare,' Laila said. 'Kids skipping school to

make out in nooks and corners of the fort. Be prepared to be grossed out.'

'Or we could be one of those people grossing others out,' JD said. He immediately took it back and said, 'But clearly, we're not going to do that because we're not into PDA much.'

'Also, you will still save the kiss for our real date.'

'I will, yes, sadly. Or maybe we could renegotiate and find a way to change that ...' JD came up with several innovative ideas to expedite the pending kiss, and Laila shot them down one after the other. They reached the fort in no time and Laila looked for a spot with a good view, while JD racked his brain for more ideas to get her to kiss him. The fort was relatively deserted, and Laila made her way to the edge of a stone structure and sat down with her legs dangling, the afternoon sun hidden behind a tree. JD joined her, sighing in disappointment. 'For real though, that real date needs to happen soon,' he said.

Laila laughed, shaking her head at his silliness and enthusiasm. 'I'll be caught up in work this whole week, thinking of ways to dazzle Roast House.'

'True. Maybe after the meeting on Friday then? I could take you out to dinner or whatever you think counts as a real date.'

'Maybe.'

JD smiled at her and when she smiled back, he quickly looked away, making Laila suspicious. 'What's going on?' she asked.

'Nothing.'

'JD.'

He looked conflicted. 'I don't know whether I should tell you or not. I don't know if you'd want to know. It's related to Roast House.'

'Well, is it, like, legal for you to tell me? Would you be breaking any laws, or something less dramatic, like rules?' Laila asked curiously.

'It's legal and everything. I know something and I guess it could help if you knew too, but I'm afraid you'd yell at me and say you don't need my help to succeed, and you're capable of doing it on your own and all.'

Laila laughed loudly. 'Are you serious? I am confident about my work but at the same time, I'm not too proud to accept help from you. I'm not insecure enough to think that accepting your help would mean I'm incapable of succeeding on my own or I'm using our private chemistry for professional gain. That's absurd!'

'Yeah, but who knows how you might react!'

'Are you scared of me, JD?'

'Of course not!' JD snorted. 'Now *that's* absurd.'

'Admit it. You're scared of me.' Laila stared at him fixedly until he gave in.

'Fine. A little. But not too scared to tell you that ...' JD's demeanour shifted to a professional one, like it had the first time they'd met—as soon as he'd realized that they were on a business meeting, he'd changed gears completely. 'Okay, so, as you know, we have six bakeries on our shortlist, out of which we're going to select two finalists. Now, what I didn't tell you was that when we voted for the longlist, we did it based on a point system, according to which Cookies + Cupcakes was at sixth.'

'We got the least points out of all shortlisted bakeries?' Laila asked slowly.

JD nodded and said quickly, 'That might not mean anything

at all, since the shortlist was based on the products and people have different tastes, which are unquantifiable and subjective. And in the final round, they want to see your business scaling strategies more than anything else, so it's a completely different set of parameters. But I just thought that since I knew that C+C was at the last place, I should tell you, if it helps at all.'

'It helps us get panicked a little bit!'

JD looked nervous as he said, 'Which would hopefully make you guys work harder for the meeting? I mean, of course, not that you're not working hard enough already or there's anything lacking whatsoever.'

'God, JD,' Laila chuckled. 'Relax! What are you so afraid of? I'm not going to hate you for telling me this!'

'Thank you.'

Laila held his hand and squeezed it, but when she pulled back, he wouldn't release it. She smirked at him and said, 'I'm not a hand-holding kind of person.'

'I know. But I am.'

Laila let him have it. It did feel kind of nice. JD brought her hand to his lips and kissed it briefly before returning it to his lap. Laila's heart quickened. She felt like a teenager with a secret—as if that was just hers, that no one else knew about, something that made her glow from the inside, all over.

'I brought you this,' JD said, plucking a tiny yellow flower from the weed growing by their feet and offering it to Laila.

'You literally just pulled it off the ground right now—in front of me.'

'I still brought it, though, from over there.'

'How sweet.' Laila snorted and accepted the little flower. JD was still holding her hand, and sitting there with him, she realized that she could easily lose track of time. She thought about all the work she had left to do for the meeting, and it made her nervous, now more than ever.

'Don't go yet,' JD said, as if reading her mind.

'JD…'

'Five more minutes.'

'Okay.' Laila gave in. She allowed him to take her on a walk, hold her hand, give her a flower, and make her stay just a little longer. What was happening to her? Her mind was buzzing with how quickly she'd come to accept him in her life and how excited just being around him made her feel. It felt good but also a little scary. She looked at him, while he was busy watching his thumb tracing her fingernails. 'Listen, JD, I just want you to know that this is not going to be easy.'

'Hmm?' JD looked up.

'Whatever this is—you and I. It's all new and exciting and silly now, but the one thing I'm certain it's going to be is complicated.'

'Because I'm guessing everything is complicated with you?'

Laila smiled sadly. 'You have no idea.'

'It's okay. I'll get an idea soon enough, and you'll hopefully get the idea that I can handle it. I can take complicated and with you especially, I'd take super-mega-absurdly-complicated too. Anything. Because like I said, I'm falling in love with you and I'm rarely ever practical about that stuff. Simple's no fun anyway.'

Laila came very close to tearing up. Even though he spoke nonchalantly, as if he were talking about the weather, Laila felt a shiver down her spine as she realized that he meant every word of it. It was evident how much he cared about her and just how selflessly.

'Okay,' she said softly. He was falling in love with her and there was nothing she could do about it other than let him. She knew it was a bad idea, and most likely wouldn't end well, but she couldn't stop herself from falling in love with him either. She could feel it happening, feel his charm seep right under her skin, slowly but surely.

A second later, he suddenly began singing loudly, startling Laila and a few passers-by. '*Dil kya kare jab kisi se, kisi ko pyar ho jaaye, Jaane kahan kab kisi ko, kisi se pyar ho jaaye…*'

Laila tried to stop him by covering his mouth with her palm, but it only made him sing louder and attract even more attention. Finally, she let him sing. He always did whatever he wanted anyway—the same way he had entered her life one day, out of the blue, and made it his home.

16

FIRST DATE

Laila felt Maahi's grip on her hand tighten under the table, and she squeezed back reassuringly. She, however, wasn't very reassured herself. The meeting had gone as well as they could've hoped, but now that they had finished presenting their plan and were sitting in front of the seven intimidating corporate employees sitting on the other side of the long oval conference table, the momentary silence in the room made her anxious.

Maahi released Laila's hand and glanced at JD, who was sitting in the very corner, opposite Maahi. Laila caught the kind smile he offered Maahi before winking surreptitiously at Laila. She hastily looked away from JD and at the other important, but less playful looking members of the Roast House team. The CEO smiled at them, but Laila could tell that behind that smile was his best poker face, giving absolutely nothing away.

'Thank you for coming in,' said the CEO, rising from his chair and extending his hand towards Laila. 'We'll get in touch with you soon.'

'Thank you,' Laila and Maahi said as they got up and shook his hand. They smiled at the rest of the team, and Laila tried not to look in JD's direction as they left the conference room and made their way wordlessly to the elevator.

'Fancy office,' Maahi whispered under her breath, looking around at the brightly lit corridors. 'Everything's so, like, sharp and clean. And shiny—definitely shiny.'

'Fancy CEO's fancy office,' Laila said as they got into the elevator.

They discussed the meeting as Laila drove them to Cookies + Cupcakes. They'd done their very best, and were aware that it still might not be good enough for Roast House, a concern elevated by JD's revelation that they were the last on the shortlist. However, they were what they were and they'd gone out of their way to prepare for the meeting—not being limited to just research and planning but also physically going out to meet with and talk to people who had been successful doing similar things, visiting factories, talking to their advisors and mentors and everything else they could think of. Maahi had even involved their customers online, conducting mini surveys with them on social media to get a better picture of their wants and expectations from Cookies + Cupcakes in order to discover what they were doing right.

'We played to our strengths,' Maahi said, her head resting against the closed car window. 'People like us for our innovative, strange recipes and if RH doesn't want that then I guess we don't want to sell basic chocolate chip cookies and red velvet cupcakes either. That's not who we are.'

'There's nothing wrong with the basics, but it's definitely not our USP. If they only want a couple of basic ones, we're not what they're looking for.' Laila frowned, thinking about it. It was easy to get carried away with the instant scaling up and the increase in their reach, popularity and money that it would bring with it. But when she looked at the big picture, that was not what they built Cookies + Cupcakes for. They built it to experiment with new ideas, bake fun, innovative recipes and make a living out of doing something they loved. 'We don't want the basic recipes representing us in all these cities and states RH would be distributing to. We want our original, creative ones that people love us for to symbolize our brand! Like the cupcake you bake with lemon zest and Italian meringue frosting, or the other one with dark chocolate and bourbon vanilla buttercream.'

'But definitely not the cookie you make with carrots and apricots.'

'Carrots and walnuts,' Laila corrected, laughing. 'But yeah, maybe not that one. How about the glazed apple crisp or a deep dish one filled with potato chips or something?'

Maahi nodded thoughtfully, looking out the window again. 'I hope they want us, and we want what they offer us, but there's so much that could go wrong.'

'Hey, if they don't want us, or they want us for something we don't want, it means that this wasn't for us. We'll still have what we have, and that's pretty damn awesome.'

Even though Maahi agreed, Laila could tell that she really wanted this collaboration with Roast House to work out. Laila, however, was tired of thinking about it, and looked forward to a day of baking and normalcy at Two. After being only a businesswoman for a week, she needed to put her baker's hat on and relax—and that is exactly what she did.

Customers came in a steady flow throughout the day, but Laila remained in the kitchen, leaving Aparna and Javed to handle the counter. She baked a variation of a new recipe she'd come across on Pinterest, making thick, round logs of dough containing cream cheese and pecans, and then slicing them into thin cookies. She placed the rounds on a baking sheet and after they were baked, she topped them with jam in the centre. Javed said they almost tasted like raspberry cheesecakes, but crispy.

After the long day of work, Laila found herself happier and more satisfied than she had been in a long time. As much as she loved running a business and was successful at it, the pleasure she derived from baking brought her a whole other kind of joy. She noticed a similar joy in Maahi when they drove home together.

'We should really hire more people as soon as we can afford to so that we could rotate shifts and all get a couple of days of break. This seven-days-a-week thing is killing me,' Maahi said, unbuckling her seat belt as Laila parked outside the house. 'The rest of the team at least gets one day off every week!'

'The price of being the boss,' Laila patted Maahi on the back.

The gate creaked again when Laila pulled it open. She groaned and reminded herself to oil it soon. As they circled around the small patch of grass in front of the house and reached the steps leading up to the main door, Laila came to an abrupt halt, pulling Maahi back with her. There was a man sitting on the topmost step in the dark.

'JD!' she exclaimed. 'You creep! You scared the shit out of me!'

'Why are you sitting alone in the dark?' Maahi asked curiously.

'I thought that wasn't creepy at all,' JD told Maahi and grinned at Laila. 'Right, Laila? You, of all people, shouldn't find sitting alone in the dark creepy.'

'What's he talking about?' Maahi looked from JD to Laila.

'He's just being dumb. Who sits outside other people's houses, so quietly, in the dark?'

'He does, clearly.'

'Like a thief.'

'I feel very left out and attacked by this conversation,' JD pointed out. 'You girls should perhaps involve me more and consider being less mean.'

Laila laughed.

Maahi was still looking from JD to Laila suspiciously, as if trying to figure out what was going on between them but missing a piece of the puzzle. She tilted her head towards JD. 'What are you doing here though?'

'Picking up Laila for our date,' JD said simply.

All eyes turned to Laila, who felt stupid. Of course JD was going to hold her to the date. What the hell else had she expected? 'Right,' she muttered. 'But just so we're clear, I remember saying *maybe*, which is not a *yes*.'

'It's also not a *no*, so I took my chances. You coming or not?' JD asked.

Laila studied him. She knew she was going to say yes—what else could you do when the only person you've been able to think about all day, all week was sitting outside your home, waiting to take you out on a date?—but she wanted him to suffer for just a few more seconds before agreeing.

'Maan jao, yaar,' Maahi said, sitting next to JD on the topmost step in the dark. 'I'll keep him company while you get changed. You're not going in that,' she gestured to Laila's outfit with her face scrunched.

'What's wrong with this?' Laila challenged, looking down at the power suit she'd worn for the fancy meeting with the RH CEO and team.

'You're not going to a romantic date with my boy over here dressed like Batwoman,' Maahi said with an air of finality. Laila opened her mouth to argue but Maahi said, 'Or Catwoman or Batgirl, or any other kind of superhero dressed menacingly to kill.'

'Whatever, dude,' Laila said, walking up to the door and unlocking it. She left the two of them outside and closed the door, catching JD saying something along the lines of, 'I actually find the whole menacing superhero outfits thing hot, to be honest…'

Laila shook her head and rushed to her room. She was going out on a date. A date. With a person she actually liked. For the first time in so long. Her throat tightened when an image of her and Abhishek lying on the living room couch of their tiny apartment flashed into her mind—noise from the TV in the background, half-empty pizza boxes and a Pepsi bottle on the table, her head resting easy on his shoulder—vivid as if it had happened yesterday. She shook her head and pulled open her cupboard.

Five minutes later, she was pulling on a pair of pumps and rushing outside, wondering what Maahi and JD had been talking about. Hopefully not about her, she thought as she pulled the door open and stepped out.

'Much better,' Maahi nodded her approval at Laila's dress and got up. 'I'm going to let you guys go now. Have fun!'

'Bye,' JD said, getting up too, his eyes fixed on Laila. After Maahi disappeared, they walked out of the creaking gate and to JD's car. JD still wouldn't look away from Laila.

'Stop.' Laila grit her teeth to stop herself from blushing.

He looked as if he'd just won the lottery. 'You're so beautiful,' JD muttered, finally looking away as he got into the car.

They didn't drive too far. In under twenty minutes, JD was pulling up outside the restaurant he'd chosen, one that he told Laila had the best seekh kebabs in Delhi. His excitement as he handed over his keys to the valet and stepped inside the gate, pulling her hand, seeped into Laila too. They walked on the gravel path, which curved around the restaurant building and to the back, where painted wrought iron tables were set on the grass, surrounded by pure white tapestries and lamps that dimly lit the garden, creating a relaxed, charming atmosphere. They were led to a table by a tall potted plant, where some sort of welcome sherbet was waiting for them. They thanked the server and sat down rather awkwardly, not speaking. They hadn't spoken much on their drive over either. This real date thing always tended to become quite awkward.

Laila smiled at JD but when he smiled back, she couldn't hold eye contact and looked away at her beautiful surroundings instead. 'This is lovely,' she said, gesturing nervously.

'Lovely?' JD raised an eyebrow.

Laila let out a laugh. 'I guess that's what people say on dates?'

'Lovely seems to be a date-appropriate word, yes. A word I personally choose never to use under normal circumstances, unless sarcastically.'

Laila smiled at that but soon, a silence fell between them once again. This was hard. Everyone was always talking about how hard dating was, and Laila herself was well aware of the many pains that accompanied it, but she'd hoped it would've been easier because it was with JD. Everything was easier with JD. They had met several times before, talked easily about most things under the sun, and even though they never called it a real date, their relationship with each other hadn't started off in a platonic setting. It had been romantic from the very beginning. It bothered Laila that they were silent now, glancing at each other occasionally, smiling warily, just because this time they'd labelled it a *real* date.

'Umm,' JD said, and Laila looked up from her menu. He looked nervous, but he was fighting it. He said casually, 'What now? Date-appropriate conversation? Small talk?'

'Just as long as you don't ask me my hobbies!' Laila said, and told him about her date with Ronny. JD, in exchange, told her about a girl he went out with, who insisted on wearing five-inch-heels everywhere, all the time, but could barely walk straight without clutching his arm and leaving nail marks all over. Talking about previous unsuccessful dates seemed to break the ice, and they found themselves laughing comfortably after that.

'We're horrible people—making fun of other people when they're not here to defend themselves,' Laila said.

'We just convert personal disasters into funny anecdotes. That hardly makes us horrible,' JD countered. 'Hard to believe that you've ever done anything truly horrible anyway.'

'You'd be surprised.'

'Yeah? Tell me then. What's the most horrible thing you've ever done to another person?'

'Well, okay.' Laila thought about it for a minute. The response she had in mind was truly too deep for their light-hearted conversation, but then again, this was JD. And he did say he could handle complicated. Laila chewed the inside of her cheek for a second, before deciding to go for it. She spoke swiftly, 'Not exactly something I *did*, but *felt*. When Abhishek, my husband, when he got hit by that car, I was there. He was follo—I mean, he was behind me. I heard the crash. I turned around and saw him lying there in the middle of the road in a pool of blood, and the first emotion I felt was relief. It passed in a second, and I felt all levels of shock and sadness and grief for a very long time, but the first thing—relief.'

'Wow. Shit just got real.'

'You asked.'

'Were you unhappy in the marriage?' JD asked. He looked up as the waiter arrived and they ordered their food. Once they were alone again, JD looked at Laila expectantly. 'You don't have to answer that if you don't want—'

'No, it's okay, I don't mind,' Laila said. 'And no, it wasn't an unhappy marriage. Minus a couple incidents, things were as perfect as they got.'

'Some incidents they must have been.'

Laila shifted the focus on him. 'What about you? What's the most horrible thing you've ever done?'

'Me?' JD rubbed his chin. 'I didn't know we were playing this game.'

'Seems like date-appropriate conversation.'

'Very. Hmm, let's see. The most horrible thing I've ever done … that would be not going to my best friend's funeral. And not because I was too devastated by the loss, which I was, but because after months and months of battling the tumour in his brain that made him an asshole to everyone around him, including and especially to me, because I was the only person apart from his parents who stuck around, when he finally died, I felt free. I had an obligation, as his friend, to be with him and support him for as long as he lived, but when he took his last breath ... I guess I felt relieved too. He was dead anyway—what did he care if I made it to his funeral or not?' JD laughed dryly.

Laila could tell that he was trying very hard to sound nonchalant and not actually feel the words coming out of his mouth, so she decided to help him with distraction. She sat back in her chair and tilted her head to the side. 'I'm so winning this.'

'What?'

'Mine was way more horrible than yours. I saw my husband die in front of me and felt relieved. You only stuck with your best friend and supported him as long as he lived and didn't show up to his funeral. Funerals are designed for the living anyway; the dead don't give a fuck about them. So, that wasn't exactly horrible, was it?'

'I didn't know we were competing,' JD said. He pulled back when the waiter arrived with their dinner and spread it on the table. When he'd left, JD said, 'But okay, let's do another round. Your turn.'

Laila picked up her fork and pierced a piece of kebab, which smelled delicious. She put it in her mouth and nodded her approval. 'This is really good, just as you promised. Anyway, the second most horrible thing I've ever done is make someone fall in love with me, literally, without returning his feelings.

This was way back in school though. Everyone had a boyfriend, and life was easier if you had one too. I knew this guy from my class had a huge crush on me, so I encouraged it. And we did the whole boyfriend-girlfriend thing kids do in class eleven, you know, behaving as if we're grown-ups, falling in love, committing to a lifetime of togetherness. But we finished school, and I did love him, but not enough to spend the rest of my life with him. I'd known it all along, but I still didn't stop him from falling in love with me, because I was selfish and I liked being his girlfriend in that pretend world.'

JD's jaw was hanging open in utter shock, but a small smile hung around the corners of his mouth. 'Dude, that's messed up. Brutal.'

'Yep. I don't think I'll ever forgive myself for it. I found him on Facebook years later, and convinced myself that in what I could see of his profile, he looked happy. He didn't accept my friend request though.'

'Ha! So he had the last laugh.'

'I'm glad he did, truly. Good for him. And again, selfishly, it makes me feel better that I didn't scar him for life.' Laila shook her head, remembering how mean she had been as a teenager. 'Your turn.'

JD told her about the time he threw a stone at a stray dog when he was nine and his friends dared him to. They spent the rest of their date sharing horrible stories about themselves and determining who the worse person was. Laila watched JD as he talked animatedly about the horrible things he'd done in his life, and all she could think about was how perfect it would be if she could just sit with him and tell him everything about herself. She wanted to know everything there was to know about him. She wanted to spend the rest of her life in conversation with this man.

They could catch up on each other's lives, find out everything that ever happened up until they met and once they were all caught up, they could build a life together. She wanted to share her life with him—past, present and future. Her feelings towards him overwhelmed her. She felt a wave rise within her, but she was more excited than afraid.

By the time they got dessert, they knew more about each other than the people they'd probably known for years. Most of these were terrible secrets, but sharing their imperfect actions only helped them remove the façade of perfection and reveal themselves as human. Soon after, they walked back outside slowly, JD's hand around her, resting lightly on her elbow. Laila didn't want the night to end; she was enjoying being with JD too much and she could feel that he felt the same way in how he held her close to him as they walked outside. Just as they were about to reach the gate, he stopped and turned to her.

'Is this where I collect my first kiss?' he asked, grinning widely at her.

Laila blushed and looked away like a silly teenager. Then she came back to her senses and met his eyes. 'I still think you have no idea what you're getting into,' she whispered.

'Come on, what are you talking about? I know all of your deep dark secrets now!'

'Not all of them.'

'Aw, you'll tell me when you'll tell me. What's the rush, right? From what I do know about you, I think you're exactly the person I need in my life. And this isn't just the romantic in me who thinks you're perfect and is in love with you and

wants to spend the rest of his life with you. I'm saying that even
thinking like you do—from a practical point of view—I think
that you're perfect for me. There's a song for it too—"*kabhi
kabhi mere dil me, khayaal aata hai* ..." but it's not right for the
occasion, because I'm about to say something very important
to you, which you know but refuse to see.' His smiled faded a
little and JD hooked his finger under her chin and pulled it up.
He studied her face and said, more seriously than he'd been
all night, 'I think if you stop denying how you feel, you might
just realize that I'm perfect for you too.'

'Is that so?' Laila raised her eyebrow.

'Yes, ma'am.'

'I'll give it a thought, if you're that confident.'

The words had barely left Laila's mouth when she found
JD's face inches away from hers. She felt his breath on her
mouth, but only for a second, before his lips touched hers
and his arms circled around her back and pulled her closer to
him. She stood on the tip of her toes and kissed him back. She
watched him for a second and smiled briefly, thinking about
this kiss that had been planned for so long and how impatient
he'd been. Then she closed her eyes and gave him the best first
kiss she had promised him. Her hand reached around him and
gently played with the curls at the nape of his neck as her lips
played with his. Everything about him pulled her to him. She
was wrapped against his chest, his warmth running through
her body, all the way to her toes. When they pulled back for
air, just for a second, she breathed in his smell and reached
for his lips again.

It was only when things began to get too heated that they
pulled apart. JD bent forward and rested his forehead against

hers as he breathed in and out rapidly. Laila had to catch her breath too. JD's arms were still wrapped around her back, keeping her close to him. After a moment, they caught each other's eyes and smiled in a part-shy, part-gleeful sort of way. The kiss felt like another secret they'd shared.

Laila looped her arm around JD's and they walked out of the gate without another word to each other. Outside, JD told the valet to get his car and they waited by the side of the road, trees covering them from direct light from the street. This time, their silence was far from awkward. It didn't feel uncomfortable; Laila didn't feel as if there was a need to fill it with words. They'd had enough words for the night, and so they stood there, side by side, occasionally stealing glances at each other, smiling about the many, many secrets they'd shared.

17

UNDERWATER

Laila stood next to JD, perfectly happy, looking around at the road that wasn't too busy, the middle-aged, kind looking watchman by the main gate and the small group of men a little to their left laughing loudly every once in a while. She looked up at JD, who caught her glance and began singing '*Kabhi Kabhi*' under his breath.

'Dude, shut up.' Laila suppressed a chuckle and looked away.

The valet brought JD's car through the gate and stopped it right in front of them. JD walked around the car to tip him, which prompted the watchman to stand up too. As JD walked back toward the gate to tip the valet, Laila heard the group of men behind her call out to her. She paused on her way to the car but didn't turn around. The valet came to open the passenger door, when they heard someone else call out. JD and the watchman, who were at a distance, couldn't hear it.

'Kahan jaa rahi hain, madam?' one of the men sang in an exaggerated tone. He appeared to be in his mid-twenties, skinny in his loose shirt that had the first few buttons undone.

Laila met the valet's eyes and they both turned around to find the three men even closer to them than before. She ignored them and was about to get into the car when another one of them cried out, 'Bahut jaldi mein ho?'

'Arre, bata to de kahan jaa rahi hai?' the first man asked again, louder this time, walking even closer to her.

Against her better judgement, Laila spun around and spat, 'Usse aapko kya karna hai?'

'Ma'am, ignore karo, please,' the valet said nervously, still holding the door open for her.

'These people think they can say or do whatever to any woman on the street and get away with it,' Laila muttered as she turned towards the car again.

'Nothing will come out of talking to these people. Please, ma'am, sit.'

'Talk to us also, naa! What's wrong with us?' the third man called.

'What's happening here?' JD asked. He had returned to the car and was frowning suspiciously at the goons.

'Nothing. Let's go,' Laila said firmly.

JD looked at Laila for a second and nodded. He held the door open as she got in.

'Abey, usko dekh. That's who she's with!' called a loud voice from behind them.

JD paused and looked back at the men, his hand still on the half-closed door.

'Come with us also some night, naa. We'll show you a good time,' another voice said.

'What did you just say?' JD thundered.

'JD, stop. Let it go!' Laila stepped out of the car quickly and held his arm to stop him, just as JD took an angry step in the direction of the three men, who were clearly drunk and not worth their time or energy.

'Ooh, look how angry he's getting!'

There was a loud sarcastic laugh. 'Ha! Jaise kuch kar lega!'

JD took another step towards them, but Laila pulled him back forcefully. They were now at only an arm's distance from the goons, who had been walking towards them the entire time.

'You need to leave right now,' JD said through gritted teeth, glaring at them.

'Accha? Or else?'

'Come on,' Laila muttered to JD and pulled him back. This time she succeeded in bringing him a couple steps closer to the car, and was beginning to feel relieved about the situation having diffused before it got ugly, when the goons spoke again, making JD spin around again.

'Haan, haan, le jaa,' one man yelled loudly.

'We don't even want a whore like you,' the skinny man shouted, his face scrunched up in disgust as he spat in Laila's direction. As Laila jerked back to avoid it, she felt JD yank himself out of her grasp and launch himself at the goons.

'HOW DARE YOU!' JD barked, pulling his arm back and punching the skinny man right on his nose. He pulled his arm back only to punch him again, and again, and again.

But Laila, who was pushed backwards against the car when JD forcefully jerked out of her grip, remained there, frozen to the spot. Her eyes were open, but could only see the kicks and punches in a vague blur. It was as if she was underwater. There was absolute silence. Her ears had tuned out the outside world completely. All she could hear was her own ragged breaths as she slipped down to the ground and tried to push away the vivid memories that raided her mind.

She gasped for air as his grip tightened on her jaw.

'No, stop. Please, don't!'

'Did you think I would never find out?'

'Please, Abhi, it's nothing like that. You have to believe me.'

'Do you think I'm stupid?'

Her head hit the wall with the force of his slap across her cheek. She felt her face heat up with sharp pain and she clutched her head in one hand and her cheek in the other.

He pulled her towards him by her shirt collar.

'Please, stop! She tripped over the coffee table and fell to her knees.'

'He grabbed a handful of her hair and dragged her across the room.'

'Abhi, stop it, Abhi! What are you doing?'

He held her down on the floor with one hand holding both of hers over her head.

'I SAID STOP.' She jerked her hand away and pushed him lividly.

He slapped her across the face again and this time, held her down by the tight grip of his fingers on her neck. His other hand ripped off her clothes angrily.

Her eyes widened in horror as she realized what was coming next. Her words got stuck in her throat, squeezed shut by his fingers.

Laila's breath came fast and sharp as she sat on her knees against the car. She blinked rapidly to remove the images from her past from her head. The blurs in front of her slowly sharpened and the world came back into focus. And finally, she could hear more than the sharp ringing in her ears. It was as if she'd come up for air after being plunged underwater for hours, almost drowning in her past.

'Sir, sir—jaane do,' she heard the valet plead desperately.

The watchman had arrived too and was in the middle of JD and the goon, trying to break them apart. Even though it seemed as if she'd spent a long time underwater, it had only been a few seconds. She shot to her feet and rushed to JD.

'STOP IT!' she screamed.

JD, who was busy throwing a punch at the goon, didn't seem to hear her.

She pushed back the second man who reached for her and held JD tightly around his midriff. 'JD, STOP THIS RIGHT NOW!' she cried. The valet and the watchman were yelling at the goons who were hurling abuses at her and JD, but she had managed to pull JD off the man he was fighting. When they were a few steps away and the watchman and valet were successfully holding the goons back, Laila released JD and stood squarely in front of him, her hand on his chest. She was standing between him and the goons, separating them.

'JD, look at me,' she said firmly. 'LOOK AT ME.'

JD finally broke his angry glare and looked down at Laila, his expression pained. He was seething, his heart beating frantically under her palm.

'Walk away,' Laila said, pushing him back with both her hands on his chest. 'Walk away, JD.'

There was a crowd assembling around them, passers-by stopping to watch. More restaurant staff had appeared and were driving away the goons, who were moving backwards, still hurling abuses. The valet rushed to Laila and apologized profusely.

'Get in the car,' Laila muttered to JD, her face burning. She walked around the car and got into the driver's seat. As soon as JD got in, she turned the key and zoomed away at high speed. Her hands shook as she clutched the steering wheel with all her might. JD was taking deep, rough breaths next to her. She drove fast, the tension in the car rising with every tortured breath they took, as if radiating from their skin and collecting in a thick cloud above their heads.

'Those assholes—' JD began angrily.

'SHUT UP,' Laila snapped.

'What—?'

'JUST—' Laila exhaled loudly, then spoke deliberately. 'Shut. Up.'

When she stopped the car outside her house, she immediately grabbed her bag from the backseat and turned to leave.

'Wait, Laila, are you all right—' JD reached out and held her hand as she was about to get out of the car.

Laila noticed the blood on his knuckles and asked, 'Are you okay to drive yourself home?'

'What?'

'Your hand? Is it hurt badly?'

'I'm fine,' JD said quickly. He looked confused as he studied Laila's face anxiously. 'But are you okay? I don't know what you're thinking right now.'

Laila pulled her hand out of his and got out of the car, without looking back at him. JD caught up with her just as she reached her gate. He put a hand on her shoulder and said, 'Laila, talk to me—'

Laila jerked away forcefully. 'Don't touch me!'

'Laila—'

'Leave me the fuck alone!' she cried and rushed away. The stupid gate creaked again but she ignored it as she ran past the small lawn, up the stairs and to the front door. Her fingers shook violently, and she struggled to put the key in the lock. Once she got it in, she swung open the door, stepped inside, shut it behind her and suddenly, as if losing every last bit of energy, she collapsed to the floor with her head inside her hands, sobbing uncontrollably.

She was drowning all over again. It was unbearable. Over the years, the waves had come over her repeatedly, pulling her back with them. But she had learned to face them. She liked to believe that she was getting better, forgetting, maybe even forgiving the past, but then something triggered the memories and took her all the way back to where she'd started. Who was she fooling? This was never going to end. There *was* no end to it. She would always live in that dark place he left her in when he died, leaving her with questions she tried to find the answers to every single day, and conflicts that took place within her constantly.

Laila wished she had been the one that died that day; death was merciful. Only the living were punished and God knows if one of them deserved punishment, it was Abhishek. She hated him. She loved him, of course, she would always love him, but in that moment, she hated him more than she loved him. Why did he get to die and leave her battling all these impossible emotions and questions?

She suddenly remembered JD's face when he had launched himself furiously at the goon, pushing her away. She felt the hard, cool surface of the car on her back. She was deep underwater again. Her insides shuddered and she held herself together by wrapping her arms tightly over her knees, pulling them closer to her chest, as wave after wave came over her and left her shivering.

There was a muffled noise coming from the dining room and in the next moment, Maahi appeared at the door. Her voice was uncertain as she called out, 'Laila, is that you?'

And Laila resurfaced again, the air finally reaching her lungs.

18

THE DARK

'Laila, is that you?' Maahi repeated, louder this time, taking another step towards her. She flipped on a switch, spilling light over the cowering form on the floor by the door. 'LAILA! What happened?' Maahi rushed to her and dropped to her knees.

Laila sobbed harder than before when she saw the concern and panic on Maahi's face. She wiped her face and sat up straight.

'Laila! Tell me what happened. Was it JD? Did he say something? Laila, did JD do something to you?' Maahi held Laila by both her arms and frantically looked for answers in her tear-clouded eyes.

'Nothing, it's nothing,' Laila spoke in a voice she didn't recognize as her own.

'No,' Maahi said forcefully, shaking her head repeatedly. 'There's no way you're doing this again. I'm not going to let you this time. You can't keep shutting me out forever! There's clearly something wrong and I mean—look at you. Laila, you *have* to tell me. I can't see you like this. No, you HAVE to tell me, *right now.*'

At that, Laila's hands shot to her face to hide the misery she was sure it reflected. She had never talked about it before to anyone. No one knew about it, not even her mother, or her closest friends at the time. The friends she had, she'd grown distant from and eventually cut all ties with after Abhishek died, because she couldn't keep this secret from them and still be reasonably normal around them.

It was between her and her husband, and she had to keep his secret. He was dead, and what good could come out of tainting his memory? No, she couldn't tell anyone about it. He had left his secret with her when he died, and now she had to keep it with her till she died. But right then, broken down on the floor, Laila felt as if the secret might kill her. And then she was overcome by another strong bout of hatred and rage, pushing her over the edge, towards insanity.

'Okay, you want to know what happened? Fine, I'll tell you what happened?' Laila said savagely. 'Remember that night I told you about my husband, the love of my life, the only man I've ever loved? How he died just months into our marriage?'

Maahi, who was crouched before her, nodded rapidly, her eyes wide with fear.

'What did you think when I told you he died? What was the first thing that it made you feel?'

Maahi looked uneasy and fearful as she said, 'I—I felt bad for you. And sad ... because you had to go through that when you were so young...'

'Exactly. That's how everyone in my life felt for me. Pity. Like I was broken and would never recover, and that my life was over and I was just a shell of the person I used to be, because I'd lost my soulmate and would never be the same again. But you know what? You don't know shit. You have no idea how I felt when my husband died!'

Maahi didn't say anything. She simply sat down more comfortably on the floor and held Laila's hands, waiting.

Laila sniffed and pushed away the hair from her face. 'I was glad. He died right in front of me, and I looked down at him, covered in blood that kept increasing every second, and I felt glad that my husband was dying. Because the moment before that—before he was hit by that car—he had been chasing me, and when he caught up with me, he was going to rape me—for the second time.'

Maahi gasped. And when Laila saw her lower lip begin to tremble, she looked away, and continued speaking, violently, years of pent-up rage flowing through her veins and out of her mouth like venom. 'We were happy. We were so in love and so, so happy! I had known him for years, loved him for years and I had let him know me better than anyone else. He knew everything about me, every last thing. He was everything to me, I literally gave him everything I had. He was the one person that I put before myself and, trust me, if I had to take a bullet for him, I would've done it without second thought. I know it sounds cheesy and clichéd, but it's true.'

Laila shook her head, her lip curling in disgust. 'And after all that, everything we felt and shared ... I'm not a bad judge of character, you know? In fact, I think I'm quite good at gauging people. He wasn't a bad person, he wasn't a liar or a cheater, and it wasn't a loveless marriage—we weren't lying to ourselves. It was real. It was all so real, and for both of us. I was so sure of it. Until one day, he got into his head that there was another man in my life, a co-worker, and he got obsessed with it. I didn't realize it at first, I just thought he was jealous. And I thought it was okay, even sweet in a way. But then one night, we got into an argument about it, and I was annoyed, and honestly, I felt a little betrayed that he would even think that I had feelings for another man. Abhi and I—we were such a tight circle. There wasn't any room for anyone else. And I expected him to know that, because I knew that there wasn't any room in his heart for another person either. But he wouldn't let it go—he kept asking me to say it, say the words, to swear on him that there was nothing going on between me and that man. And I wouldn't say it. I told him that if he didn't trust me enough to not need to ask that question, what was the point of our whole relationship? That maybe I'd misjudged the place we held in each other's lives. So, there we were, both furious, both feeling betrayed by the other. And then, it happened for the first time.'

Laila felt physically revolted as the memory of that night came back to her. It was the beginning of the end of their love. Even though it hadn't felt that way back then—they had no way of knowing what was going to follow. But that night, when he hit her the first time, it changed the way she looked at their entire time together.

'Laila ...' Maahi looked too terrified to speak.

'He slapped me,' Laila said calmly, even though her body was shaking again. 'One moment, we were standing on the opposite ends of our bed, screaming our lungs out at each other, the next minute, he was hitting me across my face to physically shut me up. Oh, don't look at me like that. I wasn't some poor girl he was going to overpower and supress. He hurt me emotionally more than physically. All I felt at that moment was blind fury. I was so pissed off with him. I pushed him away and stormed out of the apartment. He didn't follow me, or attempt to stop me, because he knew it wasn't going to do him any good. He had never seen me that angry before—I don't think I'd ever been that angry before. So he let me go. I stayed with Maa that night, which was the last thing I wanted to do, because I had spent my whole life trying to prove to her that true love exists and that even though she failed at it, I was going to be successful. Yeah, I know. I was a selfish, arrogant bitch, and I cared more about proving my mother wrong than the reality of my relationship with Abhishek.'

Tears were flowing down Maahi's cheeks, but again, she didn't speak and Laila continued. Now that she had started, she didn't want to stop.

She released a long, shaky breath and said, 'Abhishek was there the first thing next morning. We didn't even speak to each other. I just got up in the middle of breakfast and went home with him. He must've apologized a thousand times. He took full responsibility, begged for forgiveness, pleaded temporary insanity, swore it would never happen again, and I accepted it. I was too in love with him to let one mistake in the heat of the moment ruin our lives. And things almost went back to the way they were, but I guess I just wanted to believe that illusion. Now, I think that things were never the same.

'Anyway. So that was the first time, and then there was a second time. Just a month after the first. And this time, it was no heat-of-the-moment thing. If it was, that was the longest fucking moment of anyone's life. It was ... I don't know what it was. Abhishek didn't feel like a person I even knew. It was as if he was possessed by something. We were fighting about the same damn thing, and this time, he thought he had some kind of proof that I was cheating on him and he didn't just hit me once—it wasn't a spontaneous, accidental thing—he beat me repeatedly. And he forced himself on me, while I begged and pleaded for him to stop. When I realized that he wasn't himself, that he wasn't even listening, I fought him; I hit him back, but that only made him angrier and he beat me harder and raped me.'

Laila let out a dry, tortured laugh and said, 'The funny thing is that he couldn't even go through with the rape. He suddenly collapsed on me and began sobbing, muttering things like a madman, apologizing. I was nearly passed out, but I came to my senses, and pushed him off of me. And I ran. I didn't think he would follow me, but he knew he had gone too far this time, and he couldn't let me escape. So he chased me. I was bleeding all over, my clothes were ripped, my legs could barely support me, but I ran faster than I ever had. And that's when I crossed the street and he followed, and he died.'

'Laila …' Maahi moaned and wrapped her arms around her. Tears were flowing unchecked down her cheeks, and she was shivering harder than Laila.

'I later told people that we both tripped in front of the car to explain the bruises all over my body. I was so sad, so depressed after my husband's death that no one questioned my lie. Not even Maa, but I knew that she knew something was wrong. I guess she never said anything because she didn't want to embarrass me and my attempt at proving the existence of true love. And he was dead anyway, so how did it matter?'

'How could it not matter?' Maahi cried. Her eyebrows knotted in anger as she spoke. 'He was a horrible, abusive person and you're letting people believe that he was this great … angel, the perfect husband … just because he's dead? Death doesn't change what kind of person he was!'

'Yes, but I never did find out what kind of a person he was, did I? Never got the chance. Because he's dead, and he was my husband, I have to give him the benefit of the doubt.'

'What do you mean? He raised his hand on you—he raped you, Laila! I don't understand why you're defending him!'

Laila brought both her hands to her face and rubbed her forehead, trying to clear her head. 'I have to defend him because I loved him for weeks and months and years, and I hated him only for a couple hours. I don't know what happened that night—maybe he actually was mentally ill, maybe it really was temporary insanity and he had no control over what he was doing—I cannot ever know!'

'NO! It didn't just happen once. He might have accidentally hit you once, but he beat you and raped you the second time, and that's not forgivable. There's no way you can give that the benefit of the doubt, no matter how you look at it,' Maahi said fiercely. She had stopped crying, but her cheeks were still wet, and her eyes were red, though that was more out of anger than sadness.

'You think I haven't thought about that?' Laila pushed back and dragged herself across the floor. She closed her eyes and leaned against the back of the sofa behind her. 'What were my options? He was either a horrible person throughout, which makes our whole relationship, the love we shared, a lie. Or, it was all real, but he made big, terrible mistakes at the end. And no matter what the reality was, it didn't change the fact that he was dead. And I was left battling myself, because I loved him and hated him in equal measure, and I was equally sad and happy about him dying. I would feel guilty for feeling happy, and then I would feel awful. When that passed, I would try to forget him altogether, and I would succeed for a few days and then again, I would feel guilty, because if I didn't remember him, who would? His memory would be lost, and my husband deserved better than that.' Laila let out a snort. 'And then that would make me feel guilty again, because being a woman, how could I love and protect a husband who was abusive? As a human being, how could I condone him hitting another person?'

'Because … you couldn't … it wasn't your fault…'

'There are no simple answers, Maahi. Trust me, I have tried. You could go around in circles, till you're dizzy, but still find no answers.'

'But you're saying—' Maahi began, paused, and spoke again, as if struggling to make sense of everything. 'You keep saying that no matter what conclusion you try to draw, you feel guilty, right? When you feel glad about him dying, you feel guilty. When you feel terrible about him dying, you feel guilty for feeling that way about an abusive person and protecting him. And when you try to forget him altogether, you still feel guilty. Right?'

'Basically.' Laila opened her eyes and met Maahi's.

'Okay. So what I'm saying is that that's one thing you shouldn't be feeling. No matter what happened, none of this is your fault. You shouldn't take the blame, or feel guilt about any of it. We might not have answers to a lot of questions, but that's one thing that's completely clear to me.'

Maahi spoke with so much conviction that Laila's heart felt a tug. A tear escaped the corner of Laila's eyes as Maahi continued speaking.

'Also, another thing that's very clear to me is that hitting another person is never right or acceptable.'

Laila pursed her lips, trying hard to hold back tears. She swallowed the lump in her throat and smiled weakly. 'See, that's one thing I can agree on too. Which is why I'm never seeing JD again.'

'JD? What—oh, fuck, Laila, did he hit you? What the fuck happened tonight?' Maahi's eyes were wide again and she crawled to the back of the sofa to sit next to Laila.

'JD got into a fight tonight,' Laila said, showing Maahi her palm, which was stained with blood from JD's knuckles. Watching Maahi's expression, Laila added quickly, 'No, this isn't my blood. He didn't hurt me, at least not intentionally. He was just so full of rage that he pushed me into his car without even realizing what he'd done. I guess he gets points for that— the spur of the moment insanity and blindness. Doesn't make him an abusive person, right?'

'I ... I don't know what to say,' Maahi said helplessly, looking at Laila, whose face was stretched in a hard smile. 'What happened, exactly? Who did he get into a fight with?'

'Just some random drunk men who were catcalling me outside the restaurant—'

'Oh, that's different then!'

'How is that different? They were just hurling abuses and were clearly drunk. There was no need to get physical—'

'But he was protecting you! Which is the opposite of what Abhishek did!' Maahi said wildly, looking at Laila as if she was being stupid understanding such a simple thing.

'No,' Laila said sharply. 'What JD did was exactly the same. Both the incidents were driven by the same principle. And trust me, you don't want to argue with me on this. I have thought about abuse for years, and all forms of abuse originate from the same root—the belief that you have power over another person's body and have the right to hurt them. It's the thought that you have the right to decide how another human being should behave, and when they don't, you have the right to punish them. That is what Abhishek did both those nights and exactly what JD did tonight.'

Maahi was shaking her head, but Laila could tell that she was mulling over what Laila had said.

'And anyway, it doesn't matter. Thankfully, there's a simple solution to this—I never see JD again.'

'Simple solution?' Maahi looked taken aback. 'You're in love with him. You know that, right? How is this going to be simple?'

'Not simple, but far simpler in comparison for sure,' Laila said bitterly. She knew Maahi wasn't convinced, so she added, 'Listen, Maahi, after Abhishek's death, I was depressed for months, even years. The first couple of years were torturous. It's a cold, dark, terrifying place. I can't go back. If I'm ever pushed back there, I don't think I'll be able to come out again.'

Maahi's face was dry now, and so were her eyes. They looked too bright under the light, surrounded by her tired face. When she spoke, her voice was barely a whisper. 'This is not the same thing.'

'Maybe not,' Laila agreed. 'Perhaps JD is completely different from Abhishek, if we're looking at Abhishek as the villain. But even then, I don't think I have it in me to find out. I never found out about Abhishek and I don't want to find out about JD.'

'Laila…'

'Maahi, you have to understand. I'm not broken, or damaged, or scared … Well, maybe I am all of those things, but I don't let those things rule my life. When I first met JD, it was the first time I felt something for a man ever since Abhishek, and it wasn't because I was still mourning the loss of my husband, or I was too terrified to try again. It was because I simply hadn't met anyone that I felt that way about.'

Laila paused for a moment, collected her thoughts. 'I think about myself when I was with Abhishek, missing possible red flags, making mistakes, being so naïve and unconcerned, and I want to run to that girl and protect her. I feel like that girl will be ruined forever, and I have to save her, but then I remember that it has happened—that girl is already ruined and has become a person who can take it. You know what I mean? The person I've become can take whatever happens to her because it can't get any worse. So trust me, I'm not ending it with JD because I'm scared to try again—it's because I simply don't have the energy to.'

Maahi nodded slowly, and slipped her head onto Laila's shoulder. Laila tilted her head on her friend's, and they sat there for a long time. Maahi eventually fell asleep like that while Laila stayed up, going over everything that had happened that night, not thinking about Abhishek at all. She wondered what

JD was doing, if he was hurt badly, if he'd fallen asleep yet. She hadn't checked her phone since she ran away from him. Had he called or texted? Was he angry with her?

Laila released a short laugh. How did it matter anyway? He'd done the one thing that ensured she would never talk to him again, the one thing she detested the most and couldn't condone in anyone. Whether he realized it or not, he was the one who had essentially ended their relationship with the first punch he threw at that man and the push he gave her. She shuddered as the memory came back to her vividly. The horror that she had felt in the split second it had taken her to realize that JD had thrown her off himself and right onto the car. The man she was in love with. The man she had to forget.

19

ESCAPE

Even though they got too little sleep, when the sun came up, they pretended as if nothing had happened the previous night and followed their usual routine. Maahi looked at Laila nervously from time to time, but Laila went about her morning drill without hesitation, and Maahi followed suit. Laila ignored the multiple missed calls and messages JD had left on her phone when she plugged it in to charge. She took a quick shower, afraid that spending too much time without company would result in her breaking down, and rushed to get dressed and join Maahi in the kitchen for breakfast.

They read the news as usual, went over the plan for Cookies + Cupcakes for the day, and cursed the gate when it creaked on their way out. Maahi insisted that she join Laila at Two, at which Laila had to look her friend in the eye and assure her that she was absolutely fine and didn't need a babysitter. Maahi looked unconvinced at first, but buckled under Laila's steady gaze.

A few hours into the day, Laila had almost fooled herself into believing that the day was fine, she was fine, everything was fine, when she heard his voice. She was in the kitchen, finishing up a batch of cookies with Javed, and the second she heard his voice, her first instinct was to hide.

But Javed looked up at her, having heard JD too, and asked, 'Is JD here? Are we hearing about the decision already?'

'It's been less than a day,' Laila said calmly.

'Right.' Javed went back to work immediately.

Aparna popped her head into the kitchen and murmured excitedly, 'Someone's here to see you!'

Laila offered her a tight smile and dropped the tray she was holding on the counter. She had no choice but to go out and see him, unless she wanted to create a scene in front of her team. Her heart thumped loudly in her chest as she walked out of the kitchen, racking her mind for something to say to him. And then she saw him, over the heads of their Saturday morning customers.

JD was clearly distressed. He stood away from the customers, near the door, shifting his weight from one leg to the other, fidgeting nervously with his phone. He looked up towards the kitchen door and their eyes met. His mouth opened as if on its own accord as soon as he spotted her. He paused, became completely still, except for his brows which came together as he studied her, his eyes holding a million questions.

Laila was frozen by the kitchen door. She couldn't do this, not right now. She didn't have the energy to. She could barely stay upright without holding on to the wall behind her for support. Her entire body grew warm as the events from the previous night replayed in her mind. She was so angry with him. Why did he have to go ahead and ruin everything just when she had begun to fall in love with him? And now she had to tell him that it was over when she didn't even want to talk to him, something he should've known when she didn't return his phone calls and messages.

They kept looking at each other from across the bakery, never breaking their gaze, while customers moved around. Unable to take it anymore, Laila looked pointedly at JD and stomped to her office. He followed her wordlessly. Once inside, Laila turned around immediately, just as JD entered and closed the door behind him. They stood very close to each other in the cramped office, both breathing heavily. Laila's face distorted as she bit down on her lower lip hard to keep it from trembling. She tried to contain all her emotions and her entire body shook with the effort. She was feeling so many things at the same time that she was at a loss for words to express anything at all. And in the end, nothing came out, so she simply stood there, glaring at JD, breathing desperately through her mouth.

JD seemed to be having trouble finding words too. He stepped back and rested his body against the door he'd just closed, his hand still behind him on the doorknob. His chin slowly rose as he leaned his head back on the door, looking down at Laila. His nostrils flared with every breath he took. His fist was clenched by his side, his entire body stiff and unmoving as he stared at Laila.

She could feel the anger emanate from his body and heat up the room. Under all of that anger, Laila could tell that there was hurt and confusion and distress, but she wasn't doing so well herself. She tried to pace around in the tiny office desperately, two steps to the right and then back. She looked at the floor, then at him, out the window, then at him again. She caught sight of his bruised knuckle and her heart felt heavy in her chest. Then she remembered him swerving to avoid a fist and pull back to punch that man from last night, and her face grew hot.

In the end, she stopped pacing and stood in front of him. They were inches away from each other, so close that Laila could feel JD's troubled breath on her face. He pulled his head away from the door and bent forward, towards her. His forehead was almost touching hers, a hair's breadth between them. But neither of them moved to close that distance. They stayed fixed where they were, looking at each other.

When it became too painful for Laila, she closed her eyes. Suddenly, one second she felt him close to her and the next, he melted away. She felt the loud slam of the door reverberate through her more than she heard it, leaving her alone in a gust of air. A few tears escaped the corners of her closed eyes and she took a moment to embrace the pain that tore her heart apart.

They hadn't had to say anything. It was over—and they both knew it.

Now that he was gone, she craved to hear his voice. The last time he'd spoken to her properly, giving her his full attention, was the night before, when they were outside the restaurant and he'd sung 'Kabhi Kabhi' to her. Laila felt a lump in her throat when she remembered that.

In the next moment, she had wiped all traces of the tears off her face and was back in the kitchen, doing what she did best— pretend to be okay. It was fine, she was fine, and everything was fine. But this time, she couldn't fool herself, not even for a minute. The next thing she knew, she had grabbed her bag and walked out of the bakery without a word to anyone. She drove home, but once she got there, she couldn't get out of the car and go inside that empty house. She couldn't go back to work because she didn't trust herself to be able to hide her pain. She couldn't go to Maahi because she knew her friend would freak out more than her. She really, desperately wanted to go to JD, but they'd just established that that was permanently out of question. So there was only one place left to go.

Laila got out of the car, walked up to the house, cursed the creaking gate and ran up the front steps. It took her less than ten minutes to pack a suitcase of clothes and essentials. She couldn't text or call Maahi, who would know something was wrong and would try to stop her. So Laila called herself a cab and left her car keys on the dining table for Maahi, along with a one-word note: *Maa.*

Five hours later, she was in Patna, knocking on her grandparents' door. When her nani saw her, her face lit up with joy, which immediately brought tears to Laila's eyes. She hugged her grandma warmly, and let everything else go. She was with family now, and nothing else seemed important.

Apparently, her grandpa had taken her mother to meet one of his old colleagues, no doubt to show her off to his friends, so Laila had time to sit with her nani and not talk about anything she usually talked about. Work didn't matter, her life in Delhi, her friends, her now ex-boyfriend, her career … it all seemed so far away as she listened to Nani's stories about their distant relatives who were getting married, sending children abroad to study, having babies and every other good thing that was happening in the family. Maa arrived home with Nana a couple of hours later, surprised but overjoyed to find Laila there.

'Arre, Laila!' Nana exclaimed exuberantly. 'Tum kab aayi? What a pleasant surprise!'

'She didn't even tell me!' Maa said, pulling her daughter into a hug, which almost reduced Laila to tears again, but she held herself together. She might have been able to fool Nani into thinking they were just tears of happiness, but she wasn't going to fool her mother. So as her eyes brimmed with tears, Laila blinked rapidly to make them disappear and held Maa a moment longer to buy more time. Maa pulled back and studied her face. 'How long had you been planning this?'

'Not very long,' Laila said shortly, her throat tight.

'Should I make some of your favourite pyaz pakoras?' Nani asked animatedly. 'You always liked those!'

Before Laila had a chance to respond, Nana said, 'I have a better idea! Why doesn't Laila bake us some of her world-famous cookies?'

'Why don't we do both?' Laila laughed.

'That's best!' Nana agreed.

Laila's time with her family kept her from falling apart, but if she thought she was successfully pretending that everything was okay with her, she was mistaken. Over the next week, every time she laughed or even smiled, her eyes threatened to fill up. She couldn't sit in one place and have a conversation with anyone for an extended period of time; she had to keep taking moments to herself to calm down, push back the emotions that were always at the brim, continuously rising. She couldn't be happy without feeling sad. Surrounded by so much unconditional love, she couldn't appreciate her blessings without feeling the sting of her loss.

It was on Sunday, a week after she'd arrived in Patna that her mother brought up the subject of her unexpected visit. And inexplicably, as soon as Maa mentioned it, all of Laila's anger and frustration shifted on to her mother. She was suddenly furious with her.

'Why did you leave Papa? Why did you end it?' she blurted out heatedly.

They were in the balcony at the back of the house, where Laila had been sitting on an ancient swing and Maa had come out to dry clothes. Maa's hands froze mid-air, and after a moment, retreated to her side. She dropped the kurti she was holding back into the bucket and returned Laila's gaze. 'I was wondering when you'd ask about that,' she said simply.

'What's that supposed to mean?'

'It means that as a child, you asked me that question repeatedly, and the only answer I ever gave you was that it was in all of our best interests and that you would understand it one day when you grew up. But when you grew up, you never asked me about your father again,' Maa said calmly.

'So tell me now!'

Maa walked over to her slowly and sat down next to her on the swing. She turned and looked at Laila squarely.

'What?' Laila said. She spoke bitterly, directing all of her pent-up feelings at her mother. 'Tell me what was so bad about the marriage that you couldn't give him another chance? You denied me a father my whole life, because of what? What did he do that was so bad, so unforgivable? Did he cheat on you, is that it? Had an affair? Lied to you? And you left him for one mistake without considering forgiving him for the sake of your family, your daughter? Did you not even care enough to—'

'Stop,' Maa said quietly. 'You're looking for someone to blame, and you're deliberately saying hurtful things to me and it's not going to make you feel better. But the truth isn't going to make you feel any better either.'

'But I deserve to know it!'

'Yes. Yes, you do.'

Laila waited as she saw Maa hesitate. Her mother looked at the back door, and everywhere around her, before meeting Laila's eye and saying gently but very clearly, 'Your father was an alcoholic and when he was drunk, he was abusive.'

There was a stunned silence that followed her mother's declaration. Laila looked away, unable to bear meeting her mother's gaze. All these years, she had blamed Maa for everything that had ever gone wrong in her life—it all boiled down to her mother deciding to leave her father and separating the family. Over the years, Laila had also wondered if there was a possibility that her father had been abusive, along with a hundred different excuses she had thought of to justify the divorce. But somehow, it had always been easier to blame Maa than find out the truth.

Laila stared into her lap, where her hands lay clutched together tightly. She felt furious at her father, she felt terrible for her mother, but more than anything else, she felt ashamed of herself.

Maa continued evenly, 'It wasn't always like that. I was married off when I was only nineteen and I had your father's family's support, which was good enough for me in the beginning. I lived in their joint family, where they supported me through my BA, which was very liberal of them at that time, considering the kind of community we were living in.

Your father worked in a town a few hours away, so he only came home once a week. But then I became pregnant with you, and he decided we needed to live together. I had to drop out of college and move to another town. It was a hard adjustment for me in the in the beginning, living away from my own family, but then you came along, and I suddenly had everything I needed. A few years later, your father lost his job and no matter how hard he tried, he couldn't find another one. I suggested we go back to his family, but he was too proud to consider it. And then, he began drinking and venting his anger on me.'

'Maa…'

'It's okay, beta. It doesn't hurt to talk about it anymore. There was nothing more to it. I thought about going to his family. They were good people, but I wasn't sure they would accept a daughter-in-law and a granddaughter over their son. I couldn't go back to my own parents because back in those days, a married daughter returning to her maternal home with a child …' Maa shook her head. 'So you and I, we started over.'

Laila found it hard to speak, and she knew an apology just wasn't enough, but she had to say it. 'I'm so sorry. I've always … I've been so mean, so cruel to you…'

But Maa simply laughed. 'Ah, I've never paid attention to any of that nonsense. I knew you never meant a word of it, and I couldn't blame you even if you did, because I was the reason you didn't know the truth. I was happy to be your punching bag, at least as long as it made you happy!'

'Maa, please. Don't say that! I feel horrible about behaving like that…'

'Okay, I won't say that, if you tell me what you were trying to blame me for this time,' Maa said simply. She was inspecting Laila closely, a warm smile on her face. 'You think I don't know what's going on? Every time something goes wrong, you turn to me to put the blame on instead of dealing with it. And this … you coming here, it's exactly like that night with Abhishek.'

Laila's sucked in air. She defended him automatically. 'That was nothing.'

'It wasn't nothing. Something was wrong, otherwise you wouldn't have come to me that late at night just to sleep over. And left the next morning with him before I even had a chance to ask you anything.'

Laila looked at her mother with a pained expression on her face. There was no point telling her. It might make Laila feel better to get it off her chest, but the amount of pain it would cause her mother … No, she thought firmly. She wasn't going to burden Maa with her past too.

'It's okay—you don't have to tell me,' Maa said. She was still watching Laila closely. 'But just as long as you're not making the same mistake again…'

'What do you mean?' Laila asked.

'With Abhishek—now I'm not saying you didn't love him, but apart from that—you also had a point to prove. You wanted to prove to me that love existed and you could do a better job at it than me. And perhaps to prove that point, somewhere along the way, you overlooked some signs that were right in front of you. I'm only saying that don't do that again. Whatever you came here to blame me for, I'm happy to take the blame, but don't live your life in the fear of failure. I didn't know what was happening that night you came over, but I certainly knew after *he* got into an accident and there were bruises all over *your* body, bruises that didn't look like ones caused by a car. Maybe I'm completely wrong here in saying this—and forgive me if I am—but I think that you excused some of his behaviour, some warning signs, because of how badly you needed the marriage to work in your own head.'

And now, maybe she was punishing JD and herself for something that Abhishek did all those years ago. Now the point that she had to prove was to herself—that no sort of physical abuse was justifiable, under any circumstances, ever. No matter how deeply depressed she had been, or what her state of mind had been like, but over time, that's the one thing she had believed in. Maybe she was wrong. Maybe there were exceptions. Laila gulped. 'I don't blame you for anything, Maa.'

'It's okay even if you do. I know that over the years, you've hated me several times. But every time that happened, I just reminded myself how much more you would hate me if I'd stayed with your father. It wasn't uncommon in that time for husbands to be abusive, and I wasn't always brave. I was weak and terrified, but I stayed with him as he continued to get drunk, pick fights and emotionally and physically …' Maa shook her head in indignation. 'But the first time he raised a hand on my three-year-old child, I knew that was the last he was seeing of us.'

Laila didn't have any words left. She couldn't apologize. It would be weightless, useless, of no consequence. She fell sideways into her mother's lap and clutched her around the knees. Maa pushed back hair from Laila's face and patted her head nonchalantly, as if Laila was being overdramatic, and they hadn't just shared the deepest heart to heart.

Maa's voice was choked as she said, 'What happened with Abhishek … it destroyed you. But he's dead and you're alive. I just want you never to lose hope or live in fear.'

Laila nodded in her lap.

'You're my daughter,' Maa stroked her hair and said. 'Hopeful and fearless.'

20

TOO LATE

❦

Laila waved a final goodbye as she walked in through the airport doors in Patna. She turned around once more to find Maa, Nana and Nani all still standing there, waving at her. She motioned them to leave, turned around and walked inside with a heaviness in her stomach. Their goodbyes had lasted forever—first at home and then at the airport. Her bag was filled with the sweets Nani had made for her, thinking about which tightened Laila's throat, along with the thought of what was waiting for her in Delhi.

If her life were a romantic comedy, Laila would've jumped on the next plane, landed in front of JD's door, accepted that she'd been stupid and begged him to take her back. But real life didn't work that way. She had real, serious emotional issues she was struggling with and would probably always struggle with. She had burned all bridges with JD, not given him a chance or presented her side of the story. He was furious with her and no one got over something like that just by showing up at the other person's door. Besides, she didn't even know where JD lived, or what his door even looked like.

Laila knew it wasn't JD's fault. Deep down, she had always known what he had done wasn't the same as Abhishek. However, she also couldn't be a hundred per cent sure that this wasn't a red flag, or an indicator of some kind, hinting at possible abusive behaviour. Hopeful and fearless—that's what her mother wished for her, but all Laila could wonder was why couldn't JD just walk away without punishing those men physically? Or in his moment of rage, how could he not have realized that he had hurt her too?

While it was unfair to compare his behaviour to Abhishek's, she still wondered what Abhishek's behaviour had meant in the first place. The first time he had hit her, he had been so sad immediately afterward. He'd looked at what he had done, panicked, confused, furious with himself, terrified that Laila would leave him. He'd fallen to his knees and begged and pleaded her to forgive him. It was easy to take one incident and hold it against another person for the rest of their lives, to let it define the way you saw them and hate them for it. But this was Abhishek, the person who she had known more closely that anyone else, and that one action went against everything she had ever known about him. In a matter of seconds, she'd questioned everything she thought she knew. And if she could somehow erase those few seconds, pretend it never happened, things would be so much simpler.

Or so she had thought when she'd forgiven him and they'd put the incident behind them. And then it had happened again, so much worse than the first time. It just wasn't forgivable. Hitting someone once was one thing, beating them repeatedly and raping them was a whole other issue. No matter what his state of mind, that action could not be justified.

Laila picked up her suitcase from the baggage carousel and set it on the floor. She pulled it behind her and walked out of the airport, thinking about what her mother had told her about her father. Maa's circumstances had been very different. She had been living in a small town with her husband, who was the sole breadwinner of the household. She wasn't a graduate, had a baby and nowhere else to go. She had taken the abuse for as long as she could, only putting an end to it when he hurt Laila. Then the house was no longer safe for her child, and she had no choice but to leave.

Laila wondered what would've happened if Abhishek hadn't died. She hated to think that they might have tried to fix things and she would've gone back to live with him, but she knew there was a very good chance that they would've done exactly that. Or maybe she would've never turned back. It wasn't like the first time; it wasn't a mistake. There was a pattern. But maybe it wasn't. Maybe he wasn't a bad person. Maybe he was a good person who'd made mistakes, done bad things—

When Laila found herself making excuses for him, defending his actions again, she froze. Now that she knew about her father and what he'd done, she felt even more repulsed by Abhishek. She put herself in her mother's shoes and tried to imagine how Maa would feel if she knew about what Abhishek had done to Laila. She would've been furious with Abhishek, and would she have been disappointed in Laila for sticking by him?

Was she doing it again with JD, when she tried to justify his actions to herself?

Her head felt dizzy as she got into a cab. She found it hard to be rational and compute the fairness or unfairness of all of these emotions roiling inside her all at the same time. It was just too much. She couldn't clear her head, which felt like it was going to explode from all of the tangled questions throbbing inside it. Laila released a long breath, feeling a violent pain in her stomach as she tried to push away all thoughts of her father, her dead husband and her ex-boyfriend off her mind.

She climbed out of the cab and pulled her suitcase behind her to the gate, which squeaked worse than ever. Cursing the stupid thing, she shut it behind her and entered her house. At first, her heart gave a violent lurch in her chest when she saw Maahi on the living room floor, bent over with her face in her knees. And then, for a wild second, she almost laughed at how they had somehow ended up at the same place repeatedly. Crying on the floor had become a norm in that house; she shouldn't even be surprised because this was apparently what they did now, on a regular basis.

And then the moment passed and she found herself leaving her bag by the open front door and kneeling down in front of her friend. A thousand horrible possibilities passed through her mind in the time it took her to hold Maahi's head up and look at her. Her face was swollen in a way that suggested that she had been crying for a long time, possibly overnight, judging by the way her lips were puffed up. Deep, dark shadows surrounded her red eyes that shone with tears.

'What is it?' Laila asked, dreading the answer.

'Siddhant …' Maahi blubbered, her eyes filling up with fresh tears as his name left her mouth. 'He has a girlfriend…'

Laila managed her expression in order to hide the relief she felt. Out of all the horrible things that could've potentially happened, a broken heart was possibly easier to fix. But even as she thought that, she knew there was more, that it wasn't just the fact that Sid was apparently dating someone. So she sat Maahi up and wiped her face. 'Talk to me,' Laila said, and sat down with her legs crossed in front of Maahi, holding both her hands in her own.

'You think this is stupid, don't you? You think I'm stupid to cry over a guy,' Maahi said hotly.

Laila didn't think that it was stupid. She knew what love felt like, she knew what loss felt like, and neither of those feelings was stupid. But her friend seemed mad at her for some reason, and Laila felt that Maahi needed her to be her punching bag, so she sat quietly, waiting for the punches.

'He has a girlfriend! He's moved on from me successfully and now I'm just a part of his past,' Maahi cried miserably. 'I know that rationally, practically, and in whatever other way we look at it, we had to break up back then. I was too messed up with everything with Kishan, Siddhant was too hurt and confused because of that stupid kiss and we just couldn't be together at the time. We couldn't, there was no way. But we always said it was the timing. And I always thought that there was a future somewhere, maybe, hopefully …' Maahi was shaking her head furiously.

Laila had no words of comfort for Maahi. What could she say that would make her feel better? There was nothing she could think of that would change the facts.

'I tried to move on. I thought I was fine and I had let go of my feelings for him and I dated random people, trying to fool myself but I was failing miserably. It just wasn't the same with anyone else. We should never have broken up in the first place! All odds were against us and whatever *but we loved each other*. We loved each other and that was the only thing that should've mattered!'

As a fresh wave of pain rocked Maahi, Laila moved closer to her and wrapped her arm around her. She rested her head against Maahi's and whispered, 'I'm so, so sorry.' Desperate to find something, anything, to make her feel better, she said, 'What do you need? Is there anything at all I could do to make you feel less shitty?'

Maahi pulled away from Laila roughly. Her nostrils flared as she said, 'Go back to JD.'

'What?' Laila was taken aback. That was the last thing she had expected.

'You have something beautiful with him,' Maahi said urgently. 'I don't know what it is, and I don't claim to understand it, but in all the time I've known you, the happiest I've seen you is when you're around JD. It's like … it's like you're okay on your own, perfectly content and even happy, but with him … I can't explain it. It's like you change in a beautiful way. Even the way you smile is different when you're with him. And you need that, Laila. You can't let that go just because … I don't know … you're afraid.'

'I told you I'm not afraid of anything,' Laila began, but Maahi was already shaking her head, this time with more anger.

'Yes, you told me that but you lied! You are scared, of course you are! Anyone would be. But JD is not that asshole husband of yours. He didn't hit you—he did the opposite of hitting you!'

'You weren't there!' Laila argued. Before Maahi could counter that, she added quickly, 'And I just found out that my dad used to beat Maa. That's why they got divorced.'

That shut Maahi up for a minute.

Laila continued. 'I can't help but look at things in this dark, twisted way because I have to. Once you see that side, you see it everywhere. You can't not see it. JD hit another person because he's the kind of person who thinks that it's his right, his prerogative to punish others for not behaving the way he expects. It's not what he did—it's how he thinks, it's who he is!'

For a moment, when they were both quiet, Laila thought she had convinced Maahi, but then Maahi pulled herself out of Laila's grasp and shot to her feet. She was shaking her head again, her lip curling furiously.

'Maahi ...' Laila got up too.

'No. There's nothing left to say,' Maahi said quietly, but her voice shook with the rage she was hiding underneath, which confused Laila.

'Why are you so mad at me?'

'You won't understand.'

'Then explain it to me!'

'Because you have everything I want and you're throwing it away!' Maahi cried. She wrapped her arms around herself and stood face-to-face with Laila. 'I'm dying here because Siddhant doesn't want me anymore and you're throwing away love that's right in front of you. You don't understand it, or value it, but trust me, when it's gone, you'll be right where I am right now. But it'll be too late. He won't wait for you forever. You don't own him. He's a person whose life doesn't revolve around you. While you're over here thinking only about yourself, he's going to move on and you'll regret all the chances you didn't take when there was still time. And you'll hate yourself for the rest of your life!'

In the seconds that followed Maahi's outburst, Laila's heart pumped loudly in her chest. She could feel it all the way in her stomach. There was a lot of truth in what Maahi had said. In all the scenarios that Laila had thought about over and over in her head, she had always assumed that JD would still be there. That it was her decision to give him another chance or not and when she made her decision, he would simply be there waiting. She couldn't believe how stupid she'd been. The thought of never seeing JD again ... or even worse, seeing him but knowing that he didn't care about her anymore. His face wouldn't light up when he saw her, his lips wouldn't expand in that grin, he'd never sing old Kishore Kumar songs for her.

Maahi wasn't done. She continued in her voice full of rage, 'Do you want to know how I found out about Siddhant's girlfriend? I met her. I saw him last night and like an idiot, I walked up to him, expecting him to be as happy to see me as I was to see him. But he looked at me as if he'd seen a ghost. And then his girlfriend introduced herself to me. She was touching him, holding his hand and smiling at me, Siddhant's old friend. Do you think you can take that? To see the man you love with the woman he loves?'

Laila tried to form words, her thoughts scattered around her mind in pieces. 'It's not that simple,' she mumbled. 'It's not that I don't love him ... but it doesn't change the fact that he did what he did—'

'OH MY GOD, STOP!' Maahi yelled. 'STOP IT. Enough of this. He spat on you—that goon, *he spat on you*. I would've punched him too. How can you even compare what JD did for you to domestic abuse? Fuck your stupid philosophy or definitions or rules or whatever. These are two very, very different things that do not operate on the same principle. It just isn't the same. Not even close.'

Laila didn't say anything.

'Ask yourself if you wouldn't have done that for me!' Maahi challenged. 'And if you say no, I'll punch you in the face right here!'

They stared at each other, their chests rising and falling in sync. And then, suddenly, the tension between them melted away and they both burst out laughing. They laughed for a long time, throwing their heads back, clutching their stomachs. When they finally slowed down, Maahi looked at Laila with such sadness in her eyes that Laila felt as if someone had physically squeezed her heart out of her body.

'It'll be okay,' Laila whispered, putting an arm around her friend.

Maahi nodded slowly. She tilted her head to the side and rested it on Laila's shoulder as they looked out the open front door. 'He's not Abhishek. And I know you have a lot of questions … but the good thing is that JD isn't dead. He can answer those questions for you.'

'What if he doesn't want to?' Laila voiced her fear.

'I think he does. He came looking for you after you'd left. He's the one that told me that one of those men spat on you! How could you leave that detail out? I swear I would've punched that guy too.'

'JD came looking for me?'

'Yes. Technically, though, he came to tell us that the deal is on. Roast House chose us!'

'WHAT!' For a second, Laila forgot every shitty thing happening in both their lives and her heart did a somersault. 'Are you serious? Roast House picked us?'

'YES!' Maahi screamed. 'We were so psyched when JD first told us—the whole team went crazy! I didn't tell you because I wanted to tell you in person … I'm sorry—this is the worst possible circumstance to break such happy news.'

'Our lives have become a sad circumstance.'

'But we have this one thing going. Got to focus on that—count our blessings.' Maahi's words lost steam towards the end.

Laila nodded. Her mind was elsewhere. She spoke evenly. 'When JD saw you … Did you tell him…?'

'About Abhishek? Of course not. When he asked me why you wouldn't talk to him, I said that only you had answers to that question.'

'Thanks.' JD deserved an explanation, and it had to come from Laila for it to mean anything. 'I'm broken, Maahi. I break everything. I almost broke him! Before I left for Patna that day, JD came to see me at Two … I've never seen him that sad. He used to be the happiest person on the planet, and I did that to him.'

'But do you love him?'

'Yes.'

'Then trust him to be able to be happy despite your presence in his life!' Maahi joked, but then spoke seriously. 'Listen, if you try, you'll find a thousand reasons not to be with him. But as long as there's love, that's the only reason you need. You can't let him go. He loves you so much. When was the last time you felt this way about someone? I get that you're scared, but get over it. Stop it before it's too late.'

Maahi's voice was a whisper, breaking slightly as she spoke, 'Do this for me. Give him the benefit of the doubt. I'm not coming from the same place that you are, and I can look at the situation objectively, rationally, and he's a good man. You can't punish him for feeling protective about you. You can't punish him for what Abhishek did to you, or what your father did to your mother.'

Laila swallowed hard. She felt much lighter, knowing what she had to do next. It was not going to be easy, but knowing what she wanted and doing something about it was far better than living in confusion. Now she knew the problem, and she knew the only way to fix it. There was no guarantee that it would work, but she would sure as hell try.

21

SUPER-MEGA-ABSURDLY-COMPLICATED

Plans don't take the unexpected into account. In Laila's plan for her life, she hadn't foreseen falling in love again. In the years since Abhishek, trying to survive, one day at a time, Laila had turned all her energies towards herself. Perhaps she'd even become a little selfish that way. When JD came into her life, she hadn't seen it coming. She wasn't prepared to be more than an individual—a part of a couple. To love another person and care for them, be responsible for their feelings. And so, in the time that she'd spent with JD, she'd only thought about how he made her feel, not how she made him feel. She'd only taken into account what the relationship had to offer her, not what it had to offer him.

Caught in all of that, she'd failed to realize that while she was looking out for herself, JD was also looking out for her and no one was looking out for him or his feelings. After that disastrous night, she'd been overwhelmed with everything she was going through. She hadn't even stopped to consider how JD was feeling. Instead, she'd come to a decision by herself and written out a sentence for JD too.

Laila had plenty of time to think about all of this, while she waited outside JD's office. Not knowing where else to find him, Laila had shown up at his office first thing the morning after she returned from Patna. When she'd asked for him at the reception, he'd had word sent out, saying he was busy. He probably thought she would leave, but she didn't. It had taken her a lot of courage to go there, and she wasn't going to return without at least trying to make it up to him. And it wasn't like she'd cared about him enough to find out where he lived while they were together. She felt another pang of guilt at the thought. If JD refused to have anything to do with her anymore, how would she live with herself knowing that she didn't do better when she had a chance?

Maahi said that one year was too late, like with her and Siddhant. Her chances should be better because ten days surely couldn't be too late? Or could it? Laila went through all the possible outcomes, sitting outside JD's office all day. Before leaving her house that morning, she'd finally taken a bottle of cooking oil to the front gate and oiled the squeaking hinges. It wasn't the right kind of oil, but it had done the job. She was determined to fix things, one at a time. But after all the preparation, when JD finally came out at the end of the day, she found that she wasn't prepared to face him at all.

JD walked out of his office carrying his bag with him, and Laila stood up immediately. Her face grew warm at the sight of him, the curly hair in place, the signature grin missing. He didn't seem angry or even sad. He just looked tired. He didn't even look at Laila as he said goodnight to the receptionist and left the building. Laila followed him outside, jogging to catch up.

'JD!' she called out, just a few steps behind him.

He froze at the sound of her voice.

Laila stopped in her tracks as well, nervous about what she would say to him, where she would even start. There was so much to say and she tried to gather courage to say it.

But JD never turned around. He stayed frozen to the spot for a few seconds and then resumed walking as if he'd never stopped.

Laila followed him and called out again, but when he continued walking, her heart dropped to her stomach and she lost all nerve. He didn't want to talk to her. He didn't even want to look at her. As that thought sunk in, Laila paused and looked around for a way to escape.

There were many people outside the building. The sun was hanging low, casting an orange light over the city, and Laila stood in the middle of all the evening rush, uncertain of what to do next. Maahi had brought her to JD's office that morning before going to work. She would bring her there again the next day—and the day after that. Every day till JD agreed to look at her again.

A sob escaped Laila's mouth. What good would that do? He didn't want to see her, and forcing him to was hardly fair to him. She would only be putting herself first, not him. And that was what she always did because she was selfish. Her thoughts jumbled up in her head again. She rubbed her forehead, which had begun to throb, and looked around, up at the sky, down at the roads, vehicles, buildings, people, trying to find answers.

The first thing she needed to do was go home. So Laila walked to the side of the road and pulled out her phone. She was trying to figure out where the nearest metro was or whether she'd find an auto or a cab, when a car stopped right in front of her. When she didn't look up from her phone, it honked.

It was JD.

Laila bent to look at him through the passenger seat window, but he continued staring ahead. Unsure whether he wanted her to get in, she reached for the door tentatively. JD remained still as a statue, while Laila climbed into the seat beside him. As soon as she shut the door, JD drove away.

'JD...'

'No.' His voice was ice cold.

Laila closed her mouth. After a few minutes, she realized that he was driving towards her house. She kept turning towards him from time to time as they drove, but he didn't look at her, not even once. His car smelled like him and it engulfed Laila. She yearned to hear his voice. She longed to be close to him. She contemplated reaching out for his hand, but if he wouldn't even speak to her or look at her, she doubted he'd appreciate her touching him. So they spent the drive in absolute silence.

When he finally pulled up in front of her house, Laila unbuckled her seatbelt and turned to him again. He'd kept the engine running, as if expecting her to get the hell out of his car and never bother him with her presence again. But he'd come for her and driven her home, so no matter how much he hated her, he did care about her at least a little. She needed to apologize to him and she had to make sure he listened.

'I'm sorry,' she blurted out. 'I know what I did was unfair to you and I'm sorry.'

'Leave.'

'JD, listen to me.'

His jaw tightened briefly. He turned off the key and looked at Laila. His voice was gruff when he said forcefully, 'If you're going to leave, just go.'

He was looking at her with so much anguish in his face that Laila could barely keep herself together. 'I'm not going to leave.'

'Oh yeah? Isn't that exactly what you did? You got up and left. Without a word to me—not a single word.'

'JD, I can explain.'

'I don't need your explanation. What I know is enough for me. From the very beginning, you haven't given a fuck about me. You didn't care if I was a part of your life or not. But I wanted you in my life, so I made sure it happened. You were never as excited to see me as I was to see you. You never cared about me as much as I cared about you. You never loved me, but I'm pretty sure I'd started falling for you from the very first time I saw you.'

Laila opened her mouth to respond, but couldn't think of anything to say. He was right. She had been selfish. She had only cared about herself and never stopped to think about him. And the guilt showed on her face now.

'You know what?' JD said bitterly. 'That night when you told me your darkest secrets, I still thought that you were the best person in the world. But who are we kidding? You never felt the same way about me. You were never in this at all!'

The fury in JD's gaze forced Laila to look away. All she could do was mumble, 'That's not true.'

'What?'

Laila slowly looked up at him again. 'You're mad at me, and you're lashing out. You're saying things that hurt you to hurt me. And that's okay. I deserve it. But you can't say I wasn't in this, because I was. And I do love you.'

It was as if JD heard the words, but didn't allow himself to actually hear them. 'No,' he said. 'You don't love me.'

'I do!'

'Don't fight me on this, Laila! I know what love feels like, and this sure as hell isn't it!' JD said angrily.

'I've done this before; I know how this works. This is exactly what happened with my friend. The only difference is that he had cancer; he was an asshole to me because of cancer. I stuck by his side while he made fun of me, said and did mean things all the time … but I stayed, because he was my friend and I loved him. You … you never loved me. I didn't mind that, and I chased you like an idiot anyway, making a fool of myself—and you let me do it, even when you never loved me. You were looking for a reason to get rid of me, and you took the first one that came your way. What's your excuse?'

'It's not like that, JD. It's not,' Laila said desperately. 'You have to believe me.'

'You left me and ran away—'

'That's not what—'

'Then what the fuck happened, Laila? What the fuck did I do to make you so mad that you had to leave the city without a word to anyone? Do you have any idea what it did to me? Do you even care?' JD shrugged, as if losing all fight within himself and said, 'All I can think of is … that night … What? Were you pissed off at me for trying to protect you?'

'No,' Laila said. 'No, it wasn't about you. None of it was about you.'

'Then what the hell *was* it about?' When Laila looked away, trying to decide where to begin, he said, 'You *have* to tell me. I deserve to know why I was punished for something that wasn't even about me.'

Laila nodded, raising her hand to make JD stop talking. She sniffed, gulped and looked up at him. She held his eyes and as if needing physical support from him, she reached for his hands. To her relief, he didn't pull away. He looked much less guarded than moments before. He was still angry, but Laila could also see concern and confusion. Holding both of his hands in hers, she spoke. 'I have panic attacks. It turns out that physical abuse is a major trigger. That night … when you hit those men, you also pushed me away pretty hard. It was an accident, I know that. But I had an attack right there.'

'Laila,' JD was squeezing her hands in his, his eyes tortured. 'I'm so sorry. I didn't realize—did I hurt you? Were you hurt? Oh, God! I didn't even—'

'No, it was nothing,' Laila said quickly. 'JD, look at me. It was nothing. You didn't hurt me. But it was scary for me … because…'

'I'm so, so sorry,' JD breathed.

Laila extracted her hand from his and held a finger against his lips. 'If we're going to do this full disclosure thing, you have to let me speak.' Her hand traced the edge of his jaw and slipped down to his shoulder. JD held it there, and Laila said, 'It was scary for me because I was abused. In my marriage. I told you about Abhishek, remember? What I didn't tell you was that the night he got hit by a car and died, he had beaten me up, raped me and was chasing me across the city when I ran to protect myself.'

So many expressions crossed JD's face at once that it became unbearable for Laila to continue looking at him. He looked tormented, his eyes wide in shock, disbelief and then finally, fury. Laila kept holding his hand in one of hers while he held her other hand to his chest. She spoke as calmly as possible, explaining what had happened with Abhishek and how it had affected her. She told him about how her heart broke the first time Abhishek hit her, and the horror of the second time. She told him about the panic attacks she'd had ever since that night. She told him about the dark place. She told him she never wanted to return there.

JD listened to her, his teeth clenched together. He maintained eye contact with her the entire time and Laila saw emotions flicker through his eyes as she spoke. She explained the conflicted emotions she felt when she thought of Abhishek, how the unanswered questions still weighed her down and pulled her back into the dark place from time to time. And finally, she told him about her father.

When she was finished, Laila said, 'I wasn't looking for a reason to end things with you. I was helpless. I can't control how I feel, or my panic attacks. Truth is, I wanted to stay. I can't tell you how much I wish that that stupid incident had never happened. I mean, first of all, it was really stupid. To hit those men, who were drunk and didn't know what the fuck they were doing. They could've hurt you badly. Did you ever stop to think about that?'

'I couldn't let them treat you like that!' JD said fiercely. 'I'll never let anyone treat you like that!'

Laila knew he meant Abhishek, and she felt a warmth spread through her belly. She had been living with this for years, she knew how to supress it or even forget it sometimes. But JD had just found out about it, and he was hurting. 'I know,' Laila said softly.

He looked so vulnerable, so tortured, when he muttered through gritted teeth, 'That asshole.'

'It's okay. It doesn't hurt anymore.'

'I swear to God, if he were alive, I would kill him right now.'

'That's not helping.' Laila laughed, but her face fell a second later.

JD looked at her, holding her face between both his hands. 'I'm not like him. I will never lay a finger on you, no matter what happens. And as for me wanting to hit someone who mistreats you and spits on you or me wanting to kill that asshole who … who raped you … No, Laila, it's not the same. It's the exact opposite.'

A tear flowed down her cheek as Laila laughed again. 'That's exactly what Maahi said. That what you did was the opposite of what Abhishek did. Also said that she would've punched those men from that night too.'

'See, I like that girl. We think alike.'

Laila laughed louder. The sun had almost set, leaving them in partial darkness inside the car. Laila was thankful for that as her lips began to quiver and she sniffed back tears. JD pulled her close, and in one swift motion, he kissed her. She felt the warm pressure of his lips as they moved around hers. She looked up at him to find his eyes closed. She reached out and placed a hand over his chest, bunching his shirt up and pulled him closer to her.

JD groaned and pulled back. He looked at her and she had barely had a chance to catch her breath when he came back in, more intensely than before. His lips felt soft, despite the pressure behind them. As the kiss grew deeper, Laila snaked both her arms around his neck and held him close to her. They were a mess—a mixture of moans and groans and gasps. When their mouths began to demand more than they could deliver right then, they finally broke away, panting.

Laila rested her head on his shoulder, her face hidden in his chest. They stayed there like that for a long time with Laila listening to his heartbeat, quick and erratic at first, and then slowly calmer.

She closed her eyes and said. 'I'm sorry you felt that I never cared about you. I know I could do a much better job expressing my feelings. I don't mean to be cold or uncaring. I just … had trouble accepting that I cared about you and showing it. You have to understand that I haven't had anyone look out for me in a long time. So I've got used to looking out for myself and no one else. I'm selfish!'

'That's not true,' JD said so softly that Laila barely heard him.

'What?'

'You look out for Maahi. You're not selfish.'

Laila pulled back and looked at JD in the dark. 'That's different. That's friendship, that's sacred. Maahi's never going to cheat on me or betray my trust or physically abuse me!'

'Those aren't the things people do in relationships.'

'Which world are you living in?'

'Fair enough,' JD said after a moment's thought. 'But those aren't things people *should* do in relationships. And they certainly aren't things I would do to you.'

'I know,' Laila said quietly and then smiled, remembering something. 'But I have to warn you—it'll still be super-mega-absurdly complicated.'

'I know.'

There was a smile on JD's face, but Laila could tell that there was still something bothering him. For a moment, it felt as if he was going to let it go, but then he spoke. 'You have to promise me that you won't bail—whatever happens. You can't just get up and leave without telling me, or even with telling me. You just can't leave.'

'Sounds a lot like you're holding me hostage.' Laila tried to laugh, but paused when she saw his face.

'I won't always have a solution. Hell, I won't always even understand what you're going through, so I definitely won't know how to solve it. I just need to know what it is. That's all. You just need to tell me what you're feeling.'

'I promise. I won't leave. I won't hide.'

'Good. I know I can't take care of you. You don't need me to either. But maybe I can help, just a little bit, by being there. And I want to be there.'

'Yes, JD,' Laila said reassuringly, her heart expanding with joy. She was happy, and she didn't want him to worry about her. She wanted him to be happy too. 'I won't push you away again. I'm in this. I love you.'

'Okay, yeah, about that,' JD said matter-of-factly. 'Just so we're clear on our definitions of love, I don't throw that term around casually.'

'Me neither.'

'Let me finish—I don't do lukewarm. I don't want anything to do with lukewarm. I want crazy-for-you-will-die-without-you. I don't want a "right now". I want a lifetime. And I want it with you. I'm all in.'

Laila's lips stretched into a wide smile as her mouth closed on JD's. She could barely kiss him because she was smiling so much. She whispered between kisses, 'All in.'

EPILOGUE

ONE MONTH LATER

'God, woman, you infuriate me!' JD threw his hands in the air, his eyes wide with exasperation.

'This is our final offer. Take it or leave it.' Laila sat back against the living room sofa, her expression smooth and unyielding, struggling to hide her grin. Maahi, sitting next to her, nodded her approval.

JD looked from Laila to Maahi and then back at Laila. There was a crack of thunder; it had been raining all day. After a moment of staring, when he realized they weren't going to budge, he picked up his disgusting tequila with coffee ice cream cocktail and drained it. 'Fine,' he muttered, wiping his mouth with the sleeve of his shirt.

As soon as he said that, Laila and Maahi burst out laughing. They'd been trying to make him put a cupcake with chilli and garlic on the RH menu. Of course, they were only joking, and couldn't believe JD actually bought their performance.

'You people are ridiculous!' he said.

'It was her idea,' Maahi immediately put the blame on Laila.

'As is everything,' Laila grumbled. Their collaboration with Roast House had been going smoothly apart from a few glitches they fixed along the way. In a few weeks, they would be ready to ship out the first batch of Cookies + Cupcakes products to sell at Roast House shops across north India. They couldn't be more excited about that.

'All right, guys, it's midnight and I don't know about you, but I need to work tomorrow,' Maahi said, getting up. 'Waise bhi, amongst us, I'm the one who does all the work.'

'Haan, zaroor,' Laila said, bowing down to Maahi. 'You're the one holding the fort down.'

'Good night,' JD called.

''Night!' Maahi said. She paused at the door and turned around to wink at Laila, who responded with narrowing her eyes at her friend. There was something going on with her, something she was keeping from Laila. Maahi had told her that Siddhant had texted her a few days ago to say he was sorry she had to find out about his girlfriend like that, and they've been texting ever since. Maahi said they were just friends, but Laila was pretty sure Maahi's feelings for Siddhant were way more than friendly. She just hoped that her friend knew what she was getting into this time.

Laila slipped down on the carpet next to JD.

He put an arm around her and pulled her to him. 'Hey,' he murmured.

His voice caused the hair at the back of her neck to rise. They had the best time together. Both of them worked really hard, but since their work was happening together at the moment, they got to spend a lot of time together at work too. He still annoyed her, sang '*Meri Pyari Bindu*' in her ear when other people were around, showed up at her house or work unannounced and did all the other small and big things that made her fall deeper in love with him.

Life had given her a fresh dream she had never considered. One day, JD had found her, and decided to keep her. He stayed, and had stuck around with her. Laila was fine before him. But it was only after she met him that she realized that she could be happy too. All the time. Just constantly happy. Even when it rained.

Especially when it rained. She no longer needed to hide from the rain; she no longer felt as if something was missing; she found everything she wanted in him.

JD's hand cradled the back of Laila's head as he leaned in to kiss her. He pulled back and grinned down at her.

'Hey,' Laila whispered back. She was ready to wake up to any new unexpected surprises life had to offer now. Hopeful and fearless.

ACKNOWLEDGEMENTS

As always, a lot of love and support from the wonderful people around me went into the making of this book. Cheesy as it may sound, I'm grateful for this opportunity to express gratitude!

My parents, who don't always understand my reasons and motivations, but support me regardless. My brother, Nishant Malay, for invariably having my back. All my cousins—Deep Bhaiya, Prishita Bhabhi, Toshi Bhaiya, Avi, Shaina, Shreela, Mohit, Sumi, Mili, Shreya and Tutu. Love, love, love you!

Shout out to those brave enough to read the first draft of this book—Alka Singh, always my first reader and self-proclaimed biggest-fan. Laura Duarte Gómez, for the much needed words of assurance and excitement! Keith Baldwin, your feedback was kind of unexpected and much appreciated! Manasi Subramaniam, for loving JD and the orange as much I did, if not more. Creep alert.

Writing this book was not easy, and while my distress was expected and acceptable, the stress that I put my friends through was perhaps avoidable. So, thank you and sorry! Nejla Asimovic, for staying up with me late at nights trying to answer my 'why do people do things?' questions. Ava Mailloux, for cursing out everything in the world with me when I was too frustrated to be productive. Ritu Srikanungo, for showing me where the best Indian food in Manhattan's at, every time I missed home. Lauren, for existing and Christopher for existing with her. Sandra and Yannick, for bringing sushi into my life (random, but of importance).

My agent, Anish Chandy, and my dream team at HarperCollins—Ananth Padmanabhan, Amrita Talwar and Prerna Gill. You guys make it look so easy!

You, for reading. (Seriously though, I hope you like the book.)

And Guruji, Sri Sri Paramhansa Yogananda, for hope....